THE VAULTS OF REGLIS

The Paladin : Part 1

The Vaults of Reglis

John W. Johnson

TATE PUBLISHING
AND ENTERPRISES, LLC

Published by Tate Publishing & Enterprises, LLC
127 E. Trade Center Terrace | Mustang, Oklahoma 73064 USA
1.888.361.9473 | www.tatepublishing.com

Tate Publishing is committed to excellence in the publishing industry. The company reflects the philosophy established by the founders, based on Psalm 68:11,
"The Lord gave the word and great was the company of those who published it."

Published in the United States of America

ISBN: 978-1-61862-678-3
1. Fiction / Fantasy / General
2. Fiction / Action & Adventure
12.02.28

TABLE OF CONENTS

PROLOGUE

Amidst the trees and light breeze of the courtyard rested an ornate coffin, its lid raised, revealing the aged face of the yard's lone occupant, a reminder that age soon catches up with all men. The man was dressed in well-polished armor bearing a family crest upon its face. A fancy blue cloak covered his shoulders and sides. His hands and fingers were tightly wrapped around a sturdy, well-polished sword. The freshly sharpened blade was partially obscured by a decorative shield resting over his midsection.

The coffin was adorned with numerous flowers, added earlier by friends and onlookers. Outside the courtyard, two dozen elvish knights stood guard, as the elf king personally saw to the body's final destination, an unpublicized location known only to the king and those most trusted servants responsible for aiding in the body's delivery. History has not recorded the dead man's name, though he was recognized as the last of the great and holy order of the Paladins. It would be almost nine centuries before the land saw the rise of a new Paladin order, years after the infamous conquests of the tyrant Lothar and the rise of his Apaethian Empire.

THE
BEGINNING

Many years after the collapse of Apaethia, the monks of a small southern monastery began returning to the ways of the Paladins. The first order of the New Age was organized in the southern town of Gant.

For years, it thrived in its tiny vestige until growth exceeded capacity. Convinced that a new location was needed, the Paladin elders appointed one of their own to investigate the lands of the distant north.

General Mayweather, an early advocate of expansion, called on his old friend Thoren Da'ad. They met outside a large tent. General Mayweather was a tall, stoic man with a well-groomed white beard and neatly combed shoulder-length hair. Da'ad was a handsome man, considerably younger, unshaven, and with shorter, unkempt hair.

The general motioned. "Shall we enter?"

Da'ad opened the tent flap and invited him, "After you."

As the two men settled into a pair of tall wooden chairs, Da'ad remarked, "There is a city in the valley near the northeast coast that might serve our needs. It's small but has a long history and operates the greatest university in all the Fairylands. I attended there myself, even taught there for a time."

His expression saddened as he remembered his late wife.

"Something the matter, Thoren?"

"I was just thinking of Sela. She was with me then."

"It's been ten years now, hasn't it?"

"Yes, almost, but there are some things we never quite get over. Funny how I'm reminded of her like this."

"It's expected that simple matters will remind us of the ones we love. Nothing to be ashamed of. I sometimes wish I'd also married, when I had the chance."

"Were you ever close?"

"No, but I could have been. That's one of the great regrets of my life."

"What happened?"

"I lacked the courage to tell her how I felt. She grew tired of waiting and married someone else."

"Did you love her?"

"I thought so but apparently not enough. I couldn't speak it."

"Always a sad time, looking back, wondering what might have been."

"It is at that," General Mayweather agreed. "There are times when I wish I could go back and try again. Sadly, I find that as an old man I have a far better understanding of the world than I ever did as a youth but less use of that knowledge now that opportunity has passed me by."

"I know what you mean. It's too bad we aren't born with the experience we leave life with."

Da'ad looked at the ground in silence.

"Perhaps we should discuss the location you were telling me about."

"Of course. The city is called Thornguard. It was settled by a team of smiths and scholars. The ruling class is made up of scholars who run the college. The second class consists of the smiths. A third class of mostly dwarves work in the quarries and mines. There is an old monastery outside the walls, which might be restored to house our order. It will need considerable renovation but should work until a more fortified structure can be built."

"What more can you tell me about this place?"

"It's one of the few northern cities that can survive without supplies from the south."

General Mayweather paused to scratch his chin. "Very well, Thoren. I'll trust your judgment. Contact your friend and see what he can do."

Da'ad stood, nudging his chair gently into the corner then exited to a chorus of crickets. He was joined outside by two soldiers, both dressed for riding. The shorter assisted him with his armor.

"We've a long way to go, so stay close," Da'ad told them.

"Godspeed, old friend," one of the soldiers remarked, as they mounted their horses.

The men rode quickly, stopping periodically to eat, sleep, and rest their horses. It took them two and a half days to get beyond the grasslands. On the third day, they reached the first settlement.

It was little more than a tiny farming community with two or three public buildings. The men took shelter in a small room, for which Da'ad paid in advance. After waking the next morning, they remained long enough to eat before returning to the road.

The shelter was the last they saw until reaching Tabor. Most nights, they spent beneath the stars.

———

While Da'ad and his companions rode for Tabor, the necromancers of Rosewood were finalizing an agreement with a mysterious woman from another land. Her face was concealed and her voice magically altered.

"Remember, you promised delivery by month's end."

"It takes time to assemble the bodies we need, but I assure you it will be ready as agreed."

"It had better be. You know where to find me. Keep this quiet."

"Our agent is in place as we speak. He knows what to do."

Nearly two weeks into their journey, with no idea of the evil they would soon encounter, Da'ad and his companions reached the edge of the Tabor Forest. Tabor was a moist place filled with moss-covered trees. The dense forest was layered in thick foliage, which completely concealed the damp soil beneath it.

The soldiers continued north for several hours then stopped suddenly.

"Why have we stopped?" the taller of Da'ad's companions asked.

"I'm looking for something. We should be close."

"Perhaps if we knew what to look for?"

"A small trail. Here it is, over this way."

Da'ad pointed to a hidden path winding deep into the forest and ordered, "Dismount. We'll be safer on foot for a while," he instructed.

"I don't recall any serious dangers in this forest," Riada, the shorter companion, remarked.

"Perhaps if you hit a tree, you may change your mind."

"Yes, I see your point."

The temperature dropped several degrees, as the men entered the trees.

After a brief stop for wild berries, they continued to a clearing, which formed a circle around a tall metal pole. The pole was approximately twelve feet high with a lantern attached at the top. A neighboring sign pointed the men deeper into the forest.

Lighting improved from there on, with lanterns spaced about every twelve feet, until they exited the trees. A great stone wall extended in all directions around the elf city.

Some distance to the east, a massive wooden gate blocked the entrance. The men could see soldiers walking along the wall above them.

Two large statues stood watch over the gate. One was of a man wearing a crown and holding a sword; the other a woman dressed in royal gowns with a spear at her side. The lack of emotion in their faces was typical of elves.

Da'ad raised a large metal knocker attached to the gate and hammered it against a steel plate until the door opened.

Several elvish soldiers watched as the men entered. "What is your purpose here?"

Da'ad was about to respond when a well-dressed woman interrupted from behind the guards. "Let them pass. I will take them to the king at once. He wishes to speak with them."

Recognizing the queen, Da'ad bowed respectfully. She acknowledged him with a nod then motioned for the men to follow.

"The king is eager to see you, Thoren Da'ad. What is it that brings you to our city?"

"Business in the north. I admit, I never expected to return to Tabor, but it is good to be back."

The woman smiled ever so slightly in a rare show of elvish emotion as she opened the palace door. She motioned for the men to enter then followed. The king was seated on a throne near the far end of the room. As he stood to greet his guests, his guards kept a keen eye on the men.

"Those are royal guardsmen. They may be the best disciplined soldiers anywhere," Da'ad whispered to the others.

He watched as several of the king's advisors made a hasty exit. One of them stopped briefly to whisper something to the king first. Archibald, the elf monarch, gave him a nod then turned back to his guests. "Welcome to Tabor. What is it that brings you here, old friend?"

"We are here on business. General Mayweather is splitting a new order from the Paladin camp in Gant. This is Lieutenant Bek."

Da'ad motioned to the taller of his two companions. "I believe you already know Sergeant Riada. We're headed to Thornguard to seek out a home for our new order."

Archibald nodded. "You may remain as long as you like. As always, Tabor welcomes you."

"There is one thing more. Can you spare us a guide to get us through the pass?"

"Someone will meet you in the morning."

"Thank you."

Da'ad bowed as he left the king. The three travelers found shelter in a fancy guesthouse near the palace. They were met a short while later by a young elvish woman, who bowed politely as she spoke. "I am bid to fetch you to the courtyard. Please follow me."

Da'ad nodded. The courtyard was a large area. It was filled with fine statues and small trees. There was a long reflection pool at its center with an ornate fountain in the midst of it.

The walls of the yard were lined with potted plants, some of them flowering. Large marble columns guarded the entryways, leading into the palace. To the south, a small road led into the marketplace.

The king sat to the north with the queen to his right. Da'ad and his companions were seated to their left.

The men watched in amazement as the yard filled with fine elvish delicacies. Archibald eventually stood to open the feast. As he retook his seat, he turned to Da'ad. "You do remember our traditions?"

Da'ad nodded and took the ceremonial first bite. The others waited for Archibald to partake before eating. Entertainers quickly filled the yard with song and dance. In the background, an orchestra played elvish music.

"We appreciate your hospitality. Tabor is a wonderful place."

Archibald nodded. "We are honored to have you, my friend. Perhaps you should take a few days and rest. I am certain we have activities enough for your enjoyment."

"Of that, I have no doubt."

The king nodded and raised his goblet. "To Thoren Da'ad and his companions. May you find peace on your journey."

"Here, here." the audience chorused. Those with goblets joined in the toast.

When the dancers were finished, other performers acted out scenes of elvish folklore. Their costumes were well made of various fabrics and animal skins. It was easily evident that this was no amateur production. The feast continued throughout the night until most of those present were either too drunk or too tired to carry on.

Riada made merry with the wine and passed out during the final hour. Da'ad and Bek returned him to the guesthouse where they placed him on his bed before collapsing into their own.

***

The sergeant was still passed out by midmorning. Bek and Da'ad groaned as they forced themselves from their mattresses.

"What was that stuff?" Bek asked.

"What stuff?"

"Whatever we drank last night."

"Elvish wine."

"I don't remember going to bed."

"Don't worry. The effects will wear off soon. Just try to move around as much as possible."

"That's easier said than done." Bek rolled slowly onto his front and pushed himself into a kneeling position. A short time later, he stood and held himself up along the wall.

"Try drinking water. It helps clear the wine from your system." Da'ad handed him a wooden cup, from which they took turns drinking until they were interrupted by a knock at the door.

One of Archibald's servants was standing outside. "The king is waiting for you."

"We'll be there just as soon as we clean up a bit." Da'ad glanced toward Riada then over at Bek.

The messenger offered, "I will wait here until you are ready."

"Well, are you ready?" Da'ad asked his friend.

Bek laughed. "Are you sure you want to do this?"

Da'ad nodded. Together they lifted Riada and dragged him to a water trough, beyond the awaiting messenger. They tossed him in, without a word, and watched as he jumped to his feet, swinging madly.

Da'ad lightly pushed him back into the water with a laugh. "Not this time, old friend."

It took a few seconds for Riada to fully gather his bearings. He pondered a fight but quickly reconsidered. Moments later, he joined the others in laughter. The messenger watched quietly as they re-entered the guesthouse.

Once cleaned up, the men followed him to the palace. Archibald was conversing with others when they arrived. "Welcome, my friends. This is Leatis, one of my scouts. He has agreed to take you through the pass. I am certain he will more than serve your needs."

Da'ad extended his hand. "Pleasure to meet you."

Not accustomed to the human tradition, Leatis only took the hand after being prompted by Archibald. "I am glad to be of service. Your reputation is legendary."

Da'ad smiled, chancing a glance at Archibald, as if to ask, *Reputation*?

"Oh yes, the entire city is very familiar with your successes during the goblin wars."

Archibald paused. "Will you be returning when you are finished?"

"Most likely. At least, I hope to."

"Good. I look forward to speaking with you again." With that, the king bowed and returned to the business of state. Da'ad and the others walked to the stables.

"The elf stables are much cleaner than those I'm accustomed to," Bek observed.

"Elves are very disciplined. They do not like filth or clutter," Da'ad replied.

"Admirable trait."

Leatis joined them inside a few minutes later. "I have taken the liberty to inspect your animals. They are in fine shape. Still, I thought a reshoeing might be in order. I completed the task during the celebration last night."

Impressed, Da'ad thanked him. The elf nodded politely. "It was no problem. It is always a pleasure to be of service to the great Thoren Da'ad."

"I appreciate the compliment, but I know the propensity for people to exaggerate."

"The king is neither given to inaccuracies nor to exaggeration."

"No, I don't suppose he is." The men mounted their horses.

"The main pass is far too dangerous for small parties. There are too many brigands too well hidden," the elf cautioned.

"How will we get across then?" Bek inquired.

"There is a second, lesser-known pass through a tunnel in the mountain. It is a short distance above the main pass. The higher ground and dense brush will enable us to watch for brigands without exposing ourselves."

The men rode for hours, reaching the tunnel a little after midday. Leatis dismounted then turned to the others.

Da'ad nodded his approval. The tunnel opening was just high enough for the horses.

"We should continue on foot for now," Leatis warned. The cave was rocky and difficult to traverse. Everyone was relieved to finally reach the other side. "We should be well hidden from the view of anyone below. Let me cover the legs of our horses before we continue," Leatis advised.

"What are those for?" Riada asked, pointing to the leggings.

"This path is overgrown with thorny bibric bushes. The leggings protect the animals from the thorns. I suggest we continue to walk them for now. It may be possible for someone to spot us otherwise."

Da'ad agreed. A few minutes later, Bek asked, "What's that smell?"

"Goblins, or their fecal matter, to be more precise. They often use these rocks to extricate. We should remain vigilant," Leatis observed. The smell eventually gave way to a new stench.

"Goblins?" Riada asked, his hand on his sword.

"No, brigands. They're waiting for something. Someone is coming down the road."

Bek turned to Da'ad. "They're walking into a trap. We should try to help them."

After taking a moment to consider the matter, Da'ad nodded. "Very well. What do you have in mind?"

"I'm not sure. Perhaps if we shoot the leaders."

Riada protested. "We would give away our position and remain outnumbered."

"Wait," Leatis cautioned as he raised his bow. He watched one of the brigands place a trumpet to his mouth.

With hardly a sound, he released an arrow, sending it straight through the head of the brigand trumpeter. Startled, the others turned to see where the arrow came from. They began firing blindly into the rocks as Leatis continued to pick them off like flies.

The clamor alerted the party below to the danger, and several dwarf militiamen retreated into what could best be described as a war wagon. The wagon consisted of thick wooden walls covered with thin metal plating. The wheels were made of wood reinforced with steel.

Once the brigands were scattered or killed, the Paladins turned their attention to the dwarves.

"Everyone all right down there?"

"We're fine! Now be off with you!" a well-armed dwarf replied, giving the idea that he wanted nothing to do with conversation.

The encounter was distasteful yet typical of the dwarves, who were known for their offish ways.

"We ought to get out of here. The sooner the better," Bek suggested.

Da'ad agreed, and the men followed Leatis back to the trail. They reached the path's end nearly twenty minutes later and mounted their horses.

"We will be taking the main trail from here on out," Leatis explained.

It took fifteen minutes to reach the edge of the valley, where the mountains gradually tapered into a series of rolling hills.

The group stopped at a small stream connected farther down with the larger of two rivers in the valley. While resting, Riada noticed a slight glimmer along the opposite side of the road.

He quickly investigated, discovering an odd-looking silver disc partially buried in the sand. It was hidden by small brush and leaves, which he carefully removed.

Leatis followed him and discovered an old stone marker a few feet away.

"What's that?" Bek asked.

The elf glanced up. "That is nothing, merely old spoils from a brigand raiding party. This marker is the real prize."

He handed it to Da'ad, who examined it and remarked, "Curious."

"What do you make of it?" Leatis inquired.

Da'ad flipped it over and observed, "It's covered in some kind of ancient writing. I can't read it, but the back looks to be a map."

He searched the area, pointing out various landmarks that appeared to match the marker. After a minute or two, he began cutting away the brush, exposing a cave. The site had been long hidden from view. After the men cleared it, Da'ad lit a lantern and gazed inside. Leatis examined several odd scratch marks along the surface. "This cave was carved artificially."

"Bring me that silver disc."

Bek struggled to get it free. He brushed it off then handed it over to Da'ad, who studied it for several minutes. "What do you make of these markings?"

"Some kind of instructions, perhaps," Riada speculated.

"Obviously, but to what?"

Da'ad looked around then declared, "I've got it."

Holding the disc up at various angles, he attempted to reflect the sunlight into the cave.

"Help me prop it up!" he called as he aimed the reflected light.

Once the disc was secured, he entered the cave with Leatis. Even with the reflected light, visibility remained poor.

"This disc appears intended to reflect more light at certain hours of the day. Perhaps if we wait until the sun is directly overhead."

Da'ad agreed but insisted, "We really should be going. Besides, as soiled as it is, we won't be getting much more light from it."

Turning his attention back to the cave, he examined the skeletal remains of its only inhabitant.

"What is it?" Riada asked.

"A centaur."

"I thought the centaurs died out more than five hundred years ago. There is no way the contents of this cave are that old."

"Judging by the weathering of the stone, I would guess the cave is no more than half that age," Leatis observed.

The cave was filled with what appeared to be crude furnishings. A large slab, evidently used as a table, sat in the center of the darkened room. It was covered with crumbling parchment .

After a minute or two, Da'ad located a stone box near the back wall. With a little effort, using his knife, he managed to pry it open. There were several thick books and fragments of parchment inside. He carefully removed them and wrapped each tightly in his cloak for safekeeping.

Da'ad turned to the others. "Search the cave and gather everything you can. I want to bring as much as is practical with us."

With great care, Leatis removed the crumbling fragments from the stone slab and used two sheets of paper to prevent them from deteriorating further. He placed the sheets inside a book for transport, then wrapped the book in burlap and tucked it away in his saddlebag.

After looking over the records, Da'ad noted, "Perhaps Archibald will be able to read these."

He carefully re-tucked the books into his cloak and returned them to his saddlebag.

"Tabor has an extensive library with language experts capable of translating nearly any ancient record. We should have all the resources you need."

Da'ad nodded. The group followed the Fern River toward Thornguard, along the edge of the Great Fruited Forest. The city sat at the center of the Valley of Scholars, an easy two days' journey from their present location.

The Great Fruited Forest was an ancient orchard resting to the west. It had long gone wild and was filled with all manner of beasts. To the east was a combination of desert and grasslands. The road offered a fantastic view of the forest. The men watched as a large fruit bear climbed an apple tree some distance to the west.

"We should be careful. There have been an increasing number of forest creepers sighted in the area," Leatis warned.

Da'ad agreed. They camped near the river and followed its banks into the valley the next day.

The Valley of Scholars was a largely dry area. The engineers of Thornguard rerouted the Fern River around the city on both sides. A large bridge extended across the river to the southeast. Two guard towers surrounded the bridge. On its far end, a pair of small cannons pointed outward, away from the city. The cannons, better known as scatterguns, were filled with scrap metal and stones.

The city was surrounded by a large stone wall almost thirty feet high. It had only two gates, the largest to the southeast and the smaller to the northwest.

There was a sturdy dock near the smaller gate but no bridge. Small boats were used to ferry travelers across.

A large barracks was built into the wall. It housed just over 120 soldiers patrolling the wall in rotating shifts of thirty.

The southeast gate was accessible by way of a long, narrow passage. There were openings along both sides of the entryway enabling archers to pick off hostiles.

In the event of attack, a portcullis could be lowered to reinforce the gate. Da'ad looked over the city then motioned for the others to cross the bridge.

He shouted to the guards on the other side, "I am Colonel Thoren Da'ad of Gant, requesting permission to enter!"

An unconcerned soldier waved them across. The inner city consisted of several districts. The southeast area, nearest the gate, was made up of largely stone residences. Most had small shanties outside of them where the smiths produced many of the oddities for which Thornguard was known.

The buildings grew increasingly larger to the north, where the university and most of the government facilities were located. The university consisted of some two dozen buildings, the tallest being the faculty tower at fifteen stories. It was surrounded on three sides by student housing. At the tower's top was a large mechanical clock, which rang twice on the hour.

The city engineers diverted some of the river water into three separate trenches running beneath the streets. The water was used to carry away sewage and other unwanted materials. A large fountain in the city center provided most of the population's drinking water. Unlike the sewers, it was fed by an aquifer.

Not far from the fountain, water was pumped from the aquifer into one of several large towers. From there, it was allowed to flow on demand to all corners of the city using a complex system of pipes and gravity.

Another celebrated feature of the city was the fancy bath-houses located near the northwest corner. The baths utilized large furnaces beneath the ground to create steam and heat. A complex air and ventilation system allowed individuals to regulate water temperature.

The city streets were lined with fancy lamps. The posts rose almost ten feet into the air. The streets were also lined with numerous devices of varying purposes, some built for functionality while others were purely aesthetic. Trees were plentiful on the campus, which included several small parks. There was an artificial pond outside the city administrative building.

Several mechanical statues followed the course of the river, where it flowed beneath the streets. The water turned a series of wheels, which caused the statues to move. Other devices were powered by steam provided by numerous steamhouses.

Da'ad instructed his companions, "We need to find the faculty tower. It should be the tallest building in town." He had no trouble locating it. Several low-level scholars and bookkeepers looked up as he entered.

Da'ad approached an odd-looking man at the front desk. "Perhaps you can help me. I'm looking for Phineus Mibbin."

The man, wearing black robes and a scholar's cap, looked up from his books long enough to scowl. "He's retired. You will most likely find him at his residence."

He was about to draw a crude map in the chalk dust atop his desk when Da'ad interrupted. "Directions won't be necessary. Thank you."

The man nodded, making a slight "hmmph" sound, then returned to his business.

PHINEUS

Da'ad led the others to Phineus's residence, a large stone manor. The house had at least two visible gables with fine glass windows exposed by open shutters on the outside and covered by white curtains on the inside.

He pulled a large rope hanging from the top of the covered porch, ringing a bell inside. They waited about a minute until the door creaked open and a bearded old man peered cautiously outside. He adjusted his spectacles and asked, "Who is it?"

"What's the matter, old man? Don't you recognize your friends?"

Phineus opened the door a little more and cried out, "Thoren Da'ad? Come in. Come in. What brings you here?"

"Just business."

Phineus was dressed in night robes and wearing a thin stocking cap as he gleefully welcomed the soldiers. He quickly beat the dust from a small sofa and motioned for the men to be seated.

"I'm here on behalf of the order of Paladins from Gant. We're looking for a base of operations in the north. We would like to use Thornguard."

Da'ad glanced at a small clock on the wall and watched as it signaled the hour. Phineus's room was filled with such oddities. "Interesting, isn't it?" the old man inquired.

"I built a large table clock some years ago and sold it to a mage who was in town." He paused to adjust his spectacles. "Now what was it you said about the Paladin order?"

Da'ad leaned forward. "Our plan is to use the old monastery outside the city. It will add to Thornguard's security and offer us a satisfactory base of operations. We will, of course, need to renovate the structure. I'd like to take a closer look in the morning and assess its condition. I wonder if you might support us in this venture?"

Phineus nodded. "The matter will need to go before the council. I can see that it is presented but can no longer guarantee approval. I will see what influence I still have in the morning. You might as well ascertain the building's integrity while I take care of business here."

Da'ad thanked him then motioned for his companions to stand.

Before leaving, he paused. "You don't by chance know how to read the ancient centaur language?"

"Kaytire?"

"Yes, I think that's what it is."

"No, we don't have much here for translating uncommon languages. Perhaps the monks in Nellor along the north shore."

"No, thanks. We'll be passing through Tabor on the way back. The elves have an extensive library and several language experts. I just thought since we're here..."

In accordance with custom, Da'ad and Phineus presented each other with a kiss to the cheek before parting.

"I'll see you in the morning, old man."

"In the morning then."

Phineus did not wait for Da'ad, though, when morning came. Instead, he proceeded directly to the town hall where a few of the dozen councilmen lingered in preparation for their daily meeting. The hall, an ornate stone building, was rather large for its needs. It had several rooms, including the spacious lobby where Phineus stood waiting.

The court was comprised of twelve council members and a judge, who sat as the primary authority over all major civil actions. Phineus watched the entrance carefully, hoping to catch Graphius before the session.

Graphius was the current judge, having succeeded Phineus some years back. The two had long remained friends. As he entered, Graphius offered his hand.

"Phineus Mibbin, what brings you here this morning?"

"I have a brief favor to ask."

"Name it. Heaven knows I owe you a few."

"It's not for myself. It's for an old friend. An acquaintance of yours too, I believe."

"Who is that?"

"Thoren Da'ad."

"Da'ad?" Graphius asked, "What's he up to?"

"He's here on behalf of the Paladins of Gant. They are looking for a northern base and wish to renovate the old monastery. He stopped to see me last night."

"It would be nice to have an extra military presence here with all the pirate activity that's been going on. I'll do what I can. Still, I can't promise anything. The council must vote as a body. I'll present your request if you like."

Phineus nodded. "I'd appreciate that, but I think I'll remain here until the vote."

Graphius agreed.

Outside the city, Da'ad was busy inspecting the monastery. He quietly led the others inside the tattered stone building.

Riada shook his head in disgust. "This building should be torn down."

Da'ad offered, "It is in far worse repair than I'd hoped, but it will still meet our needs."

Riada raised his brow as if to ask in what way it would suffice.

"We will need to tear down the original structure and rebuild it entirely," Da'ad remarked.

"Hope Phineus makes out better today than we have," Bek uttered under his breath.

"It will be fine."

Bek leaned slightly against an old support to test its stability. The pressure caused the beam to crack. Part of the wall fell in, forcing the men to back away.

"We should leave here," Riada advised.

All three agreed and quickly returned outside. From there, they assessed the exterior.

"The mortar is eroding between the rocks, and in many places there is little more than gravity to hold them together," Bek observed.

———

While the Paladins bemoaned the ancient structure, Phineus was pleading their case to the council. Graphius officially recognized him, following the minutes. "Ladies and gentlemen of the council, it is my pleasure to maintain the great civic interest that I once exercised as chairman of this body. I come here on behalf of the Paladins of Gant. They have requested permission to build a fort outside our city. It is my belief that by approving this request, we will further secure our territory and interests. The pirates of Caprada are growing bolder and soon will be terrorizing citizens under our watchful care unless we act now to prevent them. Already they infringe on our mining operations near the coast. The Paladins presence will ease the cost of our defense and preserve a greater percentage of our raw assets." Phineus continued uninterrupted for about five minutes.

When he finished, one of the council members stood in opposition. "We cannot permit a foreign army to remain in our territory. How are we to know that their intentions are peaceful? We may be providing them the means to destroy us. I move to vote down this treacherous nonsense before it causes irreparable harm."

Phineus quickly confronted the man. "The Paladins are one of the fairest and noblest fighting forces ever organized. They are no more capable of stepping on our rights than we are of stepping on theirs. I assure this council that if they posed a threat, I would not be here on their behalf."

The councilman reiterated his opposition, after which another stood to support his caution. Following the brief remarks, Graphius called the chamber to silence. "My fellow members of this council, I stand in support of Master Phineus to vouch for the character of the Paladin order. These are good men of the highest integrity, and they will pose no risk to this city. Further, it is dishonest to characterize them as foreign. At least one of their number, Colonel Thoren Da'ad, is a former instructor of our great university. Many of the Paladins originated from these parts. At this time, I am calling the council into chambers."

The entire council rose and proceeded into a special voting chamber. Each member was assigned a separate booth and given three colored stones, representing yes, no, and abstention.

A wooden box was pushed to each booth in order of seniority. The votes were cast by dropping a stone into the hole atop the box. The remaining two stones were deposited into a storage box below. Once the final vote was cast, the box was removed and carried into a counting booth in clear view of the public. There, the clerk tallied the votes, announcing each stone. When he was finished, the judge read the final tally aloud to the audience.

"Seven red, four blue, and two white."

Phineus bowed his head in disappointment. He was about to leave when Graphius approached to congratulate him. Puzzled, the old master inquired, "The blue lost, didn't it?"

Graphius laughed. "Oh that. They rotate colors now. The red stones represented the 'yes' votes."

"Why did they begin that?"

Graphius shrugged. "Why do they begin anything? Someone thought it was a good idea, and no one else objected."

"How often do they change the colors?"

"Quarterly."

Phineus smiled humbly and thanked him.

THE FRUITED
FOREST

Worn by a busy day, Phineus returned home. He was boiling water when the doorbell rang.

Thinking it to be Da'ad, he hurried to answer but found a very angry councilman instead. The man's face was rife with spite.

Phineus motioned inside. "Please, won't you come in and join me for tea?"

"How could you let that army into our city? I intend to see that you get what's coming to you."

The man removed a large dagger and raised it high above his head, ready to strike. Phineus moved backward into the house, his arms raised defensively. The councilman followed aggressively.

"The council has decided the issue. They do not share your irrational fears."

The councilman prepared to strike as Phineus backed into a corner. At that moment, Da'ad burst into the room. "What's this?"

The attacker turned around, dropping his knife, and fled out a nearby window.

"Follow him," Da'ad instructed Leatis while rushing to Phineus's side.

"Are you all right?"

"Yes, I think so. Good thing you arrived."

"Who was that?" Bek inquired.

"His name is Vindor. He's rather new on the council."

Da'ad offered his hand. "What did he want?"

"He called me a traitor and said I would get what was coming to me."

Da'ad turned to Riada. "Help Leatis. Question the suspect, but do not harm him."

A short time later, they heard several faint shouts coming from the street. "Please, please, don't kill me."

"Who are you working for?"

Most of the rest was garbled. Several minutes passed before Riada and Leatis returned.

"He won't be bothering you again. He was in a trance. I brought him out of it, but he has no recollection of who or what sent him. All I could learn is that he did not know them."

Da'ad turned to Phineus. "Perhaps it would be a good idea if I were to remain here tonight. You might give some thought to accompanying us to Tabor."

"I've been meaning to visit there for some time. This may be just the motivation I need."

"Good." Da'ad instructed Bek and the others to return to the inn.

He then turned to Phineus. "What happened with the council this morning?"

"Nothing really. A couple of members objected to the motion but nothing that I would have thought unusual or out of the ordinary."

"I suspect that there is more to this than meets the eye. Did you say you had hot water on?"

"Yes! Yes. I'd almost forgotten. Would you like to join me for tea?"

Da'ad nodded. "I could use a good cup right now."

———

Night passed without further incident. When Da'ad and Phineus reached the inn, Bek was in the stable making preparations to leave. He returned a few minutes later and announced, "The horses are ready."

"Good. I see no reason to delay."

"I can think of one," Riada interjected.

"What's that?"

"Breakfast."

"I suppose we can leave after breakfast, though Phineus and I have already eaten."

"It was only a light meal. I can eat again," Phineus interjected, clearly more interested in the social aspects of the meal than in the food.

As soon as they were finished, the group proceeded to the stables. Their horses were already saddled and waiting for them. Phineus took a moment to hook up his wagon. One of the stable boys did most of the work, for which Da'ad gave him a piece of silver.

The first day of travel was light. The group ventured south along the outer edge of the Great Fruited Forest, never actually entering the maze of trees. Numerous animals called the forest home, the most formidable being either the giant fruit bear or the forest creeper. The forest was peaceful during daylight hours, but after sunset, it would become an uninviting nightmare of screams and shadows.

There were still several hours of daylight left, and Da'ad was not ready to give up for the night. Unwilling to travel deep inside the forest, the group moved south between the trees and the valley. They stopped near the forest's southeastern corner.

The chirps of numerous birds echoed in the air gradually growing silent as the sun set, only to be replaced by the hoots of owls and the haunting howls of distant wolves. Leatis chased away a lone sabercat that strayed too near camp.

By far, the most chilling sound of the night was the haunting shrill of the forest creeper, a strange, occasionally deadly predator that made its home in the deep thickets of the trees. Creepers were nocturnal and seldom left their burrows during the day.

Leatis advised that the group set up obstacles to protect the camp. He placed a ring of bells near the tents then took refuge in a tree.

Da'ad handed him a dish. "Are you sure you want to sleep up there tonight?"

The elf nodded. "Creepers are not known to be forgiving. They have carried off full-grown men. Should one stray near here, I want to be ready for it."

Fortunately, creepers, like many animals of the forest, had learned to stay clear of the road. They preferred the shelter of the trees and seldom exposed themselves in the open.

Phineus sat quietly near the campfire, unconcerned by the dangers of the forest. He threw a bag of yellow powder into the flames and amidst the protests of the Paladins declared, "You go to too much trouble to keep the beasts away. The animals around here have sensitive noses. They hunt by smell. This bag will drive them away until morning."

"That bag is likely to drive me away," Riada protested.

Da'ad chuckled. "Next time you use one of those things, old man, how about a little warning first."

"If you like."

"I would."

From his tree, Leatis sniffed the air and made a funny face. He then climbed down. "I've been listening to the cries of a wounded fruit bear a few hundred meters from camp. It appears to have been injured in a fight with a creeper. If the creeper was hungry enough to attack a fruit bear, it will be hungry enough to attack a man. I suggest we be extremely cautious. I will attempt to locate it. You should do what you can to fortify the campsite."

Leatis sniffed the air again then vanished into the trees. Da'ad and Bek began moving logs around the camp.

Phineus laughed. "Your efforts are for naught. No beasts are coming here tonight."

"All the same, I'd like to be ready if one does."

"Suit yourselves."

Phineus smiled confidently as he roasted an apple over a flame.

The night passed with little more than an occasional howl or distant shrill to disrupt the men's sleep. Bek and Riada were still in bed when Da'ad rose to inspect the camp.

Phineus was fueling the fire. He turned to acknowledge the colonel. "Good morning."

Da'ad nodded. "Have you seen Leatis this morning?"

"Yes, he headed off that way." Phineus pointed to a small path, to the north. "He seemed a bit troubled by something."

Da'ad picked up an apple then followed the path out of camp. He drew a dagger as a precaution but soon put it away when Leatis motioned to a patch of brush. Something was moving in the bushes. The two men listened to a strange groaning.

"That's a giant fruit bear. It was injured during the night. I told you about it."

"The creeper?"

"It's down there. I've been tracking it all night."

Leatis handed Da'ad a bow and said, "Take this and wait in that tree. The beast is probably hurt from its encounter with the bear. I'm going to attempt to lure it into the open. When it crosses that road, I want you to aim for the back of its neck."

Da'ad agreed and Leatis disappeared into the bushes.

As the sounds grew louder, the colonel pulled back his bow-string. A moment later, he heard a loud rustling in the bushes. He pulled the string tight and waited as a brown flash of matted fur and quills crossed his path.

The creeper emerged from a different location than he had anticipated, forcing him to compensate. He winged the beast in the front left leg then attempted to reload, but his arrow fumbled into the path. Realizing it was his last, Da'ad dropped the bow and reached for his dagger.

He was about to toss it when Leatis speared the animal from fifty feet away. "Quick! Help me bury it."

Da'ad rushed from his hiding spot. "Hideous creature. It smells even worse than Phineus's repellent."

"Is that what that was?"

Da'ad nodded, and together they covered the creeper with soil. Leatis prodded him to hurry. "The blood is toxic. When mixed with air, it can kill if the exposure is long enough."

Even given their brief encounter, Da'ad was visibly ill. He managed to throw several handfuls of dirt onto the carcass before giving way to a dizzy spell. Leatis helped him back to camp.

"Your exposure was light. The effects should wear off in a few minutes. Meantime, drink a lot of water and get some rest."

Phineus noticed Da'ad's stagger and asked, "What happened?"

"He is sick from exposure to the blood of a creeper. It will pass."

Da'ad took a seat next to Phineus and began rapidly pouring water down his throat.

Leatis turned to the scholar and inquired, "What was that stuff you were burning last night?"

"It's just a mix of sulfur and various salts meant to repel creepers and other predators of the area."

"Does it work?"

"Absolutely."

"Might I have a look?"

Phineus stood to retrieve a bag from his cart then passed it to Leatis. Da'ad was beginning to feel better. The dizziness had left him, and the sickness in his stomach was down. "Don't spill that stuff. I'm not sure my stomach can take it."

"It won't do much unless you spill it into the flames."

"You heard him. Keep that stuff away from the fire."

Da'ad stretched his shoulders and stood up. "I think I've had enough of this place. Let's eat then get out of here."

"I think we ought to cut a new path around the carcass. We shouldn't travel too close. It will take several days for the toxin levels to return to near normal," Leatis advised.

"I thought we buried it."

"We did, but as the carcass decomposes, the toxins seep through the soil and escape."

"The carcass is somewhat off the main trail. Are there any long-term effects from the exposure we are likely to encounter?"

"Not if we don't stop."

"Perhaps if we speed our pace, we can make it without having to cut another path."

Leatis nodded disagreeably.

"It would take us significantly longer to cut around the carcass. Let's just hurry past it and hope for the best."

The others agreed with Da'ad. They covered their faces and held their breaths. The effects were minimal. Only Riada showed any sign of illness. Curiosity prompted him to test the air.

The group gradually approached the pass, stopping about a mile away. "Tabor is only about a day's journey from here. We should set up camp and proceed the rest of the way in the morning."

Da'ad glanced east and pondered for a moment. "We should continue to the mouth of the pass. I'd feel a lot better if we weren't so close to the forest this evening."

Leatis nodded. "I know just the place." He led the others east for about a mile and stopped with the pass in view. His expression dimmed suddenly.

"Something wrong?"

"I don't know. We had best be setting up camp before we lose the light."

"I agree. Are you sure you're all right?"

"Yes. I sense something, but it has an unfamiliar scent. I am not certain what it is."

THE
NECROMANCER

Leatis sat up late into the night staring at the mountains. He listened to faint sounds unheard by the others.

"What's worrying you?" Da'ad asked.

"The hills are restless. We should not pass this way."

"If not this way, then where?"

"There is a pass to the east. It will add a day's travel but will provide us more cover. It is not unlike the path we took on the way up. I suggest extreme caution. There is evil in the air."

Da'ad nodded sadly then retired. By morning, they began the long trek east. There was a faint smell of death rising out of the pass.

"There was a recent battle here," Leatis observed.

"Dismount and remain as silent as possible," Da'ad cautioned.

The group took most of the day to reach the southern ridge overlooking the pass. From the top of the peak, the men had a good view of the devastation below. The pass was littered with corpses. Several large carts rested on their sides, some of them charred. The only signs of life were a few small shrubs and dozens of vultures feasting on the corpses.

"By evening, the mountain creepers will be here. We are fortunate to have come this way."

Phineus pointed to the field below. "I think there is someone down there."

"You're right. Someone is down there and up to no good from the look of it." Da'ad borrowed a spyglass and looked again. "Necromancers, or worse." He watched as one of the corpses raised its arm and took hold of a vulture by the neck, killing it instantly. Slowly the dead began rising.

Da'ad wiped the sweat from his brow. "We must leave here at once."

The men quickly mounted their horses and hurried down the southern face of the mountain. With the pass behind them, they moved rapidly toward Tabor. Da'ad let out a sigh as they reached the forest. The others shared his sentiment.

"What would the necromancers want with an army?"

"Perhaps they wish to fight a war," Phineus suggested.

"Yes, but whose war? The necromancers have never had any interest in conquest, at least not over land. They must have contracted with someone."

Tabor was still more than an hour away, and darkness was falling quickly. "Let's push forward until we reach the city," Da'ad ordered.

From the city wall, Leatis called to the guards.

"Who is there?"

"Leatis, royal scout and friend to the king. I am escorting Thoren Da'ad and two companions."

"You may enter!" a voice called back.

Once inside, Da'ad followed Leatis while the others took the horses to the stables. At the castle door, several royal guardsmen intercepted the general and his guide. "State your business."

"I am Leatis, scout for the king. Let us pass."

Two of the soldiers escorted them inside and remained until dismissed by the queen. She turned to Da'ad and asked, "Will you take a seat?"

"Thank you, but we really must speak with Archibald."

"I will notify him that you are here."

"Thank you again, my lady."

She smiled very slightly and disappeared into the hall. One of the king's advisors entered several minutes later. "What is your business with the king that it cannot wait until morning?"

Leatis explained in elvish. Despite being fluent in the language, the conversation was difficult for Da'ad to follow.

Satisfied by Leatis's response, the advisor explained, "I will notify the king at once. He will wish to speak with you."

Leatis turned to Da'ad. "I told him of the necromancer."

"Good, that is why we're here."

Five minutes later, the aide returned. "The king wishes to see you. Follow me, please."

Archibald was standing near the door just inside the throne room. "Gentlemen, what is it?"

"The necromancers are building an army."

"You have proof of this?"

"Yes. We witnessed it personally."

"It was dark sorcery, sire. There is no mistake that someone has contracted them to build an army."

Archibald bowed his head in thought. He remained silent for some time. "What did you see?"

Da'ad described the scene, after which Leatis added his own observations.

Troubled, Archibald paced back and forth before consulting his military advisors. When he finished, he rejoined Da'ad. "There is only one place for me to seek advice on this matter, and it is not here. I will leave for Lunora in the morning. I may stop briefly in Freelance. It is possible Frederick will wish to accompany me."

Archibald returned to his throne and dismissed his aides. He then turned back to Da'ad. "I wish to be alone. There is little more to be discussed at this time. I will speak with you when I return."

Da'ad bowed. "There is one more matter. On our journey, we found several old records. I believe they are written in Kaytire, the ancient language of the centaurs."

Archibald looked up. "I should like to see them when I return."

Da'ad agreed, "Certainly," and bowed.

He spent much of the night sitting in his room, pondering. He fell asleep still in his chair and woke just in time to see Archibald leave the city. Following breakfast, he found his way to the library.

It rested along the city's northern edge and was much older than the palace. Still, it was an impressive structure, rising three stories into the air with a fourth beneath the ground. The exterior was covered in vines. The lower two stories were obscured by a thick row of flowering trees.

Da'ad entered through the front door and walked down a wide staircase into a large, dimly lit hall then turned left and entered a somewhat brighter room, where a mildly upset librarian stopped him.

"This is a restricted area! You need to check in over there."

Da'ad entered the other room and found a more helpful assistant who took down his name and pointed him in the right direction. He located Phineus in a side corridor looking over a stack of old books.

"I'm glad to see you've already found your way around, old man."

"Fascinating place. I've been meaning to visit here for some years now. You know, they have records more than ten thousand years old."

"I didn't know that."

"It's true. In fact, I'm told that there is no one alive able to read some of them."

"Dead languages are not that uncommon."

"But languages that cannot be read at all are almost unheard of."

"You may be right. What are you reading?"

"It's an ancient elvish history."

Da'ad shrugged and made a slight umm hmm sound.

"Hold on. The necromancer in the pass was chanting a spell to raise the dead, right?"

Da'ad nodded, uncertain where this was going but far more interested than before.

"It serves reason to assume that the necromancers are building an army. Why would a necromancer want an army unless they were contracted by someone else?"

"That is the big question," Da'ad replied sarcastically.

"There are numerous accounts of necromancers raising armies but none wholly for their own purposes. In every instance, there has been another benefactor, someone exchanging something for the service. The necromancers themselves are driven more by a quest for dominion over death than over the living, yet the army they're raising has no purpose in such a conquest. I fear there is more at play than we know."

"It is very troubling, I admit."

With a nod, Da'ad quietly excused himself and hurried to find Riada and Bek. He located them outside a small pub.

"Sergeant, I need you to rush this message to General Mayweather. Hurry back when you are finished. I might have need of you here." He handed Riada a small folded paper and sent him on his way.

"What's going on?" Bek inquired.

"I don't know yet, but it's almost certainly not good."

"Where did you send Riada?"

"To deliver something to General Mayweather."

Da'ad paused. "I'll be in the room for the next few minutes if you need me. After that, I should be in the library."

"Do you need any help?"

"I might. I need to get those records to Phineus."

"The ones from the cave?"

Da'ad nodded.

Several minutes later, with Bek's help, he delivered them.

"I will ask the librarian to provide me with the necessary resources to translate these," Phineus assured him.

"Thanks. Were you able to learn anything more about the necromancers?"

"No, I've hit a roadblock. There is little or no doubt the necromancers are involved, but we knew that yesterday. Unless I have more to work with, I'm afraid there's little I can do."

Da'ad nodded. "Well, see what you can do with these, and let me know."

After a brief pause, he returned to his room. Meanwhile, Phineus showed the records to one of the librarians.

After a slight pause, the librarian asked, "Do you know what this is?"

"No."

"Are you familiar with the legendary treasures of Reglis?"

"I've heard the myths."

"This text purports to give the location of the vaults of Reglis where the treasure was hidden. You say there were centaur remains in the cave?"

"That is the story I heard. I wasn't actually present."

"The centaurs were quite close to Reglis. It is at least consistent with what we know that they would be associated with the vaults."

"Interesting. When the king returns, let him know I would like to see him, and send for Colonel Da'ad. I would like a word with him."

The librarian nodded then sent an aide to fetch Da'ad.

The colonel was eating when the message arrived.

Bek was seated across from him.

Both men reluctantly halted their meals and hurried to the library. They found Phineus partially hidden behind a stack of books and speaking with a librarian. The noise from Da'ad's entry prompted the educator to look up momentarily. He quickly returned to his work.

The colonel eventually interrupted with a hmm hmm sound. Unable to tear himself from his work, Phineus invited the men to have a seat. The librarian was busily pouring over what appeared to be a crude map. He translated a number of characters on it.

Da'ad and Bek were puzzled by the conversation.

"For someone eager to see me, you're doing your best to pretend I am not here."

"Just be patient. You ought to find this very interesting."

"I've been here for several minutes, and this is the first you've spoken to me."

"I'm sorry. I'll finish in just a bit, and then we can talk freely."

"Maybe we should come back."

"No! This is too important. Just be patient."

After several minutes, Phineus motioned for Da'ad to have a look at the map.

"The text that accompanied this map mentioned the treasures of Reglis. The map appears to show the way to the vaults where the treasure is kept."

Phineus shifted forward as Bek asked, "What's Reglis?"

Da'ad leaned forward. "Reglis was a wizard. He was very close to the centaurs in his later years. The centaurs were said to have amassed a great fortune before the Apaethian War. Fearing the approach of Lothar and his armies, they constructed huge vaults in the mountains and hid the bulk of their wealth. Eventually Lothar came, and when the centaurs refused to aide his conquest, he set out to destroy the race completely. Rumors and whispers were heard of the treasure, but no one ever confirmed its existence, and no vaults were found. Many assume that the treasure was captured by Lothar and used to pay his armies."

Phineus stepped forward. "Others feel that the treasure was never found and that Lothar sought to destroy the centaurs out of spite for their refusal to assist him."

"Most credible authorities believe the treasure's existence to be just a myth that rose up in the years following the centaurs' extinction."

"If the treasure does exist and can be found, then the Paladin order and the elves would be well advised to seek it out before some less noble authority learns of it and acquires it first," Phineus advised.

"What are you proposing, old man? Sounds a bit like a goose chase. We don't even know if there is a treasure, and already you have us pursuing it."

Phineus bowed his head. "There is only one way for us to know for certain. Given the possible alternatives, it is my belief that we should not simply leave the matter to chance. If the treasure exists, then it must be found by someone with the capacity to guard it and keep it safe from those who would misuse it. If it does not exist, then at least we will know."

Da'ad paused then slowly stood. "Very well, old man. When Archibald returns, I will discuss the matter with him. If he agrees and the general allows, then we will pursue this mythical treasure of yours."

With that, he turned to leave. Bek followed. "Why do you keep calling him 'old man'? Don't you worry he might take offense?"

Da'ad smiled. He looked briefly toward the ground and then back at Bek. "I've been calling Phineus 'old man' since before he was old. It might worry him if I stopped." He paused. "Besides, I think if I stopped, he might believe that he really is getting old."

Bek shook his head.

THE LICHE KING

Phineus remained in the library for several hours. It took more than a week to finish translating the records.

Riada returned as work was concluding, and reported to Da'ad.

"The general will be here soon. He is bringing the entire army and seemed eager to discuss the necromancer situation."

"Good. How far behind are they?"

"A few days at most. They could arrive any time."

"Very well. See that I'm notified as soon as they get here."

"Yes, sir."

───◦◦◦───

Several days passed before General Mayweather arrived. He had fewer than a dozen men at his side and brought only six beyond the gate.

Da'ad greeted them immediately.

As they embraced, the commander remarked, "I'm told that you have news for me?"

Da'ad nodded. "I have, and more than I realized."

"That's usually how it works. You want to tell me about it?"

"We had an encounter with a necromancer in the pass. He was raising an army."

"Yes, your message said as much. Have you been able to learn anything new?"

"Not much. The necromancers are unlikely to need an army of their own. Someone else must have paid them for it."

"Clearly."

"What are your thoughts?"

General Mayweather paused. "You have something else to tell me, don't you?"

"I do."

"Then let's hear it."

"We discovered a number of old records in a cave near the pass. They purport to give the location of the vaults of Reglis. There were centaur remains there, and the records are old enough to match up with that period."

Phineus, whose arrival went largely unnoticed, interjected, "I feel that if the vaults can be found, we should make every effort to do so."

"Who are you?" the general asked.

"This is my friend from Thornguard, Phineus Mibbin. He is one of the scholars and a former head of the government there. He has been translating for us."

General Mayweather looked at Phineus. "Have you discerned anything valuable?"

"I dare say so. The records contained a map. It claims to identify the precise location of the vaults of Reglis. If true, we cannot afford to allow the treasure to fall into the hands of just anyone."

"I think we should take the possibility that this treasure exists very seriously. I want you to investigate the matter personally, Thoren. Make what arrangements you must, and take whomever you need."

"What of the necromancers?"

"Relax, old friend. We've plenty of men for both. Captain Balad will lead the investigation into the necromancers. He knows more about them anyway."

"Yes, sir," Da'ad replied coldly.

"Thoren, I know you're a stubborn man, but we've been friends long enough for you to trust my judgment."

"My apologies, sir. I will do what I can to find these vaults."

"I know you will."

General Mayweather turned to Phineus and asked, "Might I speak with you privately for a moment, Mr. Mibbin?"

"Phineus, please."

"Phineus then," the general agreed as he excused Da'ad.

Da'ad joined Bek and Riada for lunch in the palace. Riada sat up. "I understand you've spoken with the general. What did he say?"

Da'ad shrugged. "Not much. He wants us to go after the vaults."

"When?"

"He didn't say, but I think he expects us to do it soon."

"What about the necromancer?"

"He is turning it over to Captain Balad."

"That's kind of him."

"Enough! I agreed to pursue the vaults. The necromancer situation will either work itself out or wait until we are finished."

"Your friend Mr. Mibbin is back." Bek stated, as he watched Phineus enter.

Phineus hurried to join Da'ad as the men finished their food. He ate just a bite or two then rushed to the library for the remainder of the afternoon.

＊＊＊

At dinner, Da'ad informed the others of his plans.

"Nothing is ever as simple as it appears. I want to be sure that we are prepared for anything we might encounter," he cautioned.

"What do you expect?" Bek asked.

"Trouble. The problem is that it takes numerous forms, and I have no idea which face it will show."

Phineus, who arrived late, suggested, "I might be able to narrow the possibilities. We are very near pinpointing a destination."

"That will help."

"You want me to see to the horses?" Bek volunteered.

"Not yet. Let's wait until we know where we're going."

Da'ad turned to Riada. "Sergeant, would you see to it that we have all the supplies we're going to need?"

"Yes, sir."

"Phineus, I need you to make sure we have all of the proper maps for the region. Get them to Leatis as soon as you can."

Phineus nodded, his mouth too full to speak. Da'ad moved on, making only a few more requests before conversation broke into a pair of smaller discussions.

Following dinner, he retired to bed. Phineus considered returning to the library but decided rest was more important.

Bek and Riada remained awake for several hours with General Mayweather. They spoke over drinks at a local pub, discussing just about anything and everything except the business at hand.

Archibald returned the next day and sent at once for Da'ad.

"I hope I did not disturb anything."

"No, I was just grooming my horse."

"Good. I have news, but first join me for a drink?" A servant entered carrying a bottle of wine and several glasses.

"Certainly." Da'ad followed the king to a small table.

Once the glasses were filled, Archibald proposed a toast. "To better days."

Da'ad repeated the phrase, and the men drank. General Mayweather entered near the conclusion of the toast. Archibald stood immediately and welcomed him. "General, come join us." He turned to his servant and requested a fresh glass and a chair.

The servant bowed and disappeared, returning two minutes later with both the chair and a glass. General Mayweather sat and thanked her for the glass.

"I suppose we should get down to business," Archibald suggested. "The wizards warned of more pressing matters than the necromancer." He turned to Da'ad. "Is there more you would like to tell me? Perhaps something about those books you found?"

Da'ad nodded. "As a matter of fact—"

Phineus interrupted, "We've been looking over several ancient records that purport to identify the location of the vaults of Reglis. We even found a map."

Archibald's eyes widened. "The vaults of Reglis! The wizard, Terek Greyscale, told me that the solution to the necromancer problem would reveal itself in another quest. He felt you would be preparing for something by the time I returned but never said what. I am instructed to encourage your pursuit of the vaults and provide you with whatever aide you require, including supplies and two dozen soldiers to assist. If you need more, you have but to ask. Should the treasure be found, send word at once, and I will send wagons and men enough to secure it."

"What would you do with it if it is found?" General Mayweather inquired.

"Unless you have urgent need for it, I suggest we store it here. It will be as safe here as anywhere. I will have my engineers construct new vaults to store it in."

"Agreed. I sense danger in bringing it to Thornguard," General Mayweather nodded.

"If you have need for any part of it, you have but to ask."

"I can't imagine needing that kind of wealth. We are well financed, and a treasure that vast is likely to bring with it plenty of trouble."

Archibald bowed his head. "It will be here if you change your mind."

General Mayweather stood to excuse himself, pausing momentarily. "I think it best that we tell as few people as possible about this. No sense risking loose lips."

Archibald's demeanor changed suddenly. "Elves never have loose lips. Nevertheless, we should be cautious."

"My apologies."

At Da'ad's beckoning, General Mayweather retook his seat, and they discussed the composition of his team. "It's a foregone conclusion that Bek and Riada will accompany me, unless of course, you have some other need of them," Da'ad remarked.

General Mayweather shook his head. "No. You have full authority to choose your team. Select the men you trust most."

"Thank you, sir."

"I have two dozen handpicked men with me now, camped outside the city. The rest are less than a day's journey from here. Let me know who you want, and I'll make certain you have them."

"Thank you. I'll have my list ready by this afternoon."

"I'll place my quartermaster at your disposal. You will have access to my best soldiers and scouts. Leatis will assist you in the selection process," Archibald volunteered.

After a brief pause, the king excused himself to see to other business.

General Mayweather stood next. "I must be getting back as well. Be careful. I have a strange feeling that all is not as it appears."

"I feel it too," Da'ad agreed.

"Send me your list when it's ready."

Da'ad nodded and followed the general outside. He made his list over dinner and sent it before nightfall. General Mayweather sent several of the men that night. The rest arrived early the next day.

With the first part of his team assembled, Da'ad began his inspection of the elves. He relied heavily on advice from Leatis. Archibald sent two of his best historians to assist with cultural and language issues.

Two elvish women were assigned to accompany the party as cooks. Archibald made it very clear that they were both skilled warriors.

Near mealtime, Phineus nervously approached Da'ad with a concern. "I understand that you are still assembling a team to seek out the vaults."

Da'ad nodded.

"If it is not too much trouble, I would like to accompany you. I think you will find that I still have a few things to offer."

Da'ad laughed. "I wouldn't have it any other way, old friend." He paused then added, "Don't sell yourself short. You have a great deal to offer, and I'm sure to need you before this is over."

Phineus smiled. "By the way, General Mayweather is about to leave. I thought you might want to know."

"I'd best go and see him off." Da'ad hurried outside just in time to catch the general overseeing the final stages of his departure. "I hear you're leaving today."

"Just as soon as we can. We've had a little trouble with one of our tents, but we should be under way shortly."

"I'm glad that I at least have the opportunity to see you off."

"So am I. In addition to the men you requested, I will be leaving two ambassadors in Tabor. Should you need to get hold of me, send a message with one of them."

Da'ad nodded. He watched as the general mounted his horse and rode off into the trees.

When Da'ad re-entered the city, Phineus showed him part of an old map. The colonel nodded then led the way to the library, where, with Leatis, they poured over several additional maps.

"I want to move farther south before we head west. I hope to avoid any chance encounters with the denizens of the Blue Mountains," Da'ad cautioned.

Leatis bowed. "If you wish, but my experience is that they seldom stray from their camps. Those mountains are filled with mercenaries, not thieves. They do not bother idle travelers."

"It's bad enough that we have to cross near the Red Cliffs. Let's try to avoid the Blue Mountains if we can."

"It will add another day to our travel."

"Nevertheless, I want to avoid them. I've had a bad feeling about those mountains since I was a boy."

"Very well, we'll go south then."

Bek, who just entered, asked, "What's so special about the Red Cliffs?"

"There are numerous legends that the Red Cliffs of Wyneth are home to a damned race of men." Leatis replied. "The necromancers of Rosewood absolutely refuse to enter the area. Still, there is little solid evidence of any hostile settlements. The pass is riddled with obstacles, caves, and hazards, but travelers routinely take it, and few have reported anything more than an occasional encounter with a mountain creeper."

"There is something in those mountains. I've traveled them myself many times, and always I've felt as though I were being watched," Da'ad interjected.

"Have you ever had any difficulties there?" Leatis inquired.

Da'ad shook his head. "Just a lot of sleepless nights." As the meeting wound down, he excused himself and exited the library, leaving the others to finalize the route. He inquired into the supply situation, at the quartermaster's.

The quartermaster assured him that most of the supplies were already loaded and he would have everything on his list by morning.

Pleased with the progress, Da'ad stopped at the stables to inspect the horses. After fifteen minutes, he left to join the others for lunch.

"So how are things?" Phineus asked him.

"Good so far. I think we should be out of here by morning. I suggest that everyone rest up. It's going to be a long day."

"You still have reservations, do you?"

"Just a dislike for unnecessary travel."

Da'ad dished himself a plate of food and began eating.

"If all our meals are like this, I think I can learn to enjoy elvish cooking," Bek remarked.

Phineus, who preferred blander foods, made a funny face. Following lunch, he returned to the library for several hours. Da'ad did not see him again until late. By that time, most of the significant preparations had been made, and both men were ready for some well-deserved rest.

Da'ad was one of the last to be seated for supper. He cautioned, "Slow down, gentlemen. I don't need any casualties before we get past the gate."

Riada was enjoying a bottle of wine. "You've been fond of the bottle since I've known you. Don't you ever enjoy a clear head?" Da'ad asked.

The sergeant laughed politely, burying the painful look behind his eyes. "I do all right for myself."

Da'ad nodded. "I know you do. You're the best swordsman I've ever taught, and a good friend too, but I worry sometimes about your happiness."

Riada forced a smile. "Why is that?"

"Because I care about you. I don't have any family anymore. War and time have seen to that. In a way, I think of you and Bek as family."

Riada's expression softened. "Sir, I've survived situations no man should be allowed to survive. I should have died many times over, and in this line of work, it's only a matter of time before luck runs out and chance catches up with us."

"That's why you drink then? You're worried about dying?"

"No. I drink to cloud my memory, to hide the pain and dull my senses. I used to look in the mirror at a man I admired. Now I'm almost ashamed. Years of death and devastation have made me a cynic."

"We all grow a bit cynical in this business, but we need not be ashamed of our work. We protect the innocent and make peace possible."

"I said almost ashamed. I just wonder what else I might have become."

"Well, don't wonder too long. You're likely to lose sight of what you might yet be. I've known you for nearly twenty years now. You're a good man, and I'm grateful you made the choices you did. There are few, if any, whose company I prefer when things get ugly."

"Thank you, sir. That means a lot."

"Thank you, and remember, luck only plays a small part in it. I like to think we make our own luck."

"Maybe we do. I'm just not sure I care all that much whether I live or die the next time."

"You care whether the rest of us live or die, don't you?"

"Of course."

"We care whether you live or die."

Riada looked down and mumbled, "I know," then set the bottle aside and excused himself from the table.

———

Morning arrived quickly, and with the team fully assembled, Da'ad inspected the column one last time. Supplies were secured inside the wagons and checked then rechecked. Each member of the team was issued a weapon and armor. For the Paladins, this was an insignificant time since they already had their weapons, but for many of the others, it was quite important.

Phineus, being up in years, was issued the lightest armor available, a fancy leather suit made especially for elvish hunters. The design allowed for greater agility and flexibility but offered only minimal protection. He did not put it on, opting instead to store it.

Most of the elves selected heavier leather or layered linen with thin metal plating. Leatis wore heavy linen with removable plating. He was armed with two long daggers and a pair of bows, one a long bow for distance and the other a hunting bow. He carried a sword, strapped to his horse, but seldom used it.

His helmet was made of fine metal with a thin leather lining placed inside mostly for comfort. It was lighter than the Paladins' steel helmets but offered far better protection than the largely leather helmets chosen by many of the others.

Once the team was properly armed, Da'ad mounted his horse and rode around the column issuing last-minute instructions. Their destination was just beyond an obscure mountain pass near the Red Cliffs of Wyneth, some four hundred miles from Tabor. The pass was unlabeled, though Da'ad referred to it as Dead Man's Pass, an apparent reference to its proximity to the necromancers of Rosewood. It was seldom used, perhaps because of the abundance of superstition and myth connected with the place. Still, the more popular crossing to the west carried the same reputation.

Some of Da'ad's men heard whisperings that the mountains had eyes and saw everything. Others claimed that there were great monsters in the pass. Some even said that it was haunted. The situation was not helped by Da'ad's own reservations.

The cliffs bordered the thick Withered Forest to the south-west, a large area of dry, baked land littered with the remains of ancient trees. There were two major cities in the region. Whispering Pine was a dwarf settlement, slightly northwest of the pass. Rosewood, also known as the city of the necromancers, was just over the ridge, a few miles to the east. The vaults were thought to rest a day and a half's journey to the west of Whispering Pine.

The journey along the southern side of the mountain divide went smoothly. Da'ad was careful to steer clear of the Blue Mountains. As they drew nearer to "Dead Man's Pass," the trees became increasingly less inviting. The pass itself was buried in a thick, unnatural fog. The top of one of the mountains vaguely resembled the skull of an ox rising above the clouds. Concerned by the fog's unnatural hue, Da'ad ordered the team to hold up for the night.

The group set up camp in a good-sized clearing several hundred meters to the south of the pass. Da'ad turned to Phineus. "Hopefully this fog will lift by morning."

"This is no ordinary fog."

"I know."

"What do you plan to do?"

"I plan to sleep on it. I'll decide how to proceed in the morning." Da'ad paused. "I am open to suggestions."

"If I had any, I would have offered them by now."

Phineus glanced at the glowing mist. "We could try the Tibben Pass to the west."

Da'ad shook his head. "No. I thought of that. This fog extends well beyond the Tibben Pass."

"I think I'll consult with the elves. Perhaps they know something we're overlooking."

"Perhaps, but I doubt it."

Strange sounds emanated from the fog throughout the evening. Da'ad spent a wakeful night pondering his course of action. Soon after falling asleep, he was awakened by a loud shrill and the sound of panicked voices. Leatis had matters under control by the time Da'ad left his tent.

"What happened?"

"A mountain creeper broke into the camp. It's dead now. No permanent damage."

Leatis turned to the others. "Help me get it out of the camp and bury it."

After testing the wind, he covered his face and helped move the beast. Meanwhile, Da'ad checked on the wounded sentry. "How are you feeling?"

"It stings a bit, sir, but I'll be all right."

"Have one of the elves take a look at it then get some rest."

"Yes, sir."

Da'ad turned toward the fire and waited for Leatis.

"What happened? How did it get into the camp?"

"It appears to have climbed through the timbers. The dirt mound isn't high enough, and we left too much space beneath the logs."

"Can we fix it?"

"Yes, but I think we ought to wait until morning. It's too dark now."

As Da'ad exhaled, Leatis told him, "Fortunately, mountain creepers are smaller and less toxic than their forest cousins. Everyone should be all right by morning."

"I need to replace the injured sentry. Can you look at his wounds then take his place?"

Leatis nodded.

Da'ad thanked him then returned to bed.

When he awoke, he used the creeper incident as an excuse to remain in camp another day. His men spent much of that time improving the walls around their tents. Da'ad conversed briefly with Phineus. "The fog looks about the same as it did yesterday. I don't think it's going to let up," Da'ad observed.

"I suspect you're right."

"I have to be honest with someone. This fog scares me. There is something in there."

"Have you noticed how it glows?"

"I have. That's no ordinary reflective glow either. Tell the men to get some rest. I'll be in my tent if you need me." Night fell quickly. Though the noises continued, the men were used to them and lost little sleep.

When they awoke, Da'ad ordered the team to take down the tents. "We're moving on."

"Into the pass?" Phineus asked nervously.

"We can't wait here forever, and that fog looks as though it will be around for a while. Draw your weapons and watch for anything out of the ordinary."

"This fog seems pretty unusual," Bek retorted, prompting a dirty look from Da'ad.

"Why don't we take the long way over the mountains to the west?" Phineus asked.

"The trails there are too small for our carts. We would have to leave our supplies behind. The Tibbin Pass and this unnamed road are the only crossings large enough to meet our needs."

Da'ad pulled out several long ropes and ordered everyone, "Dismount and grab hold." He moved along the column, tying the ends together into one long line, then called to Leatis. "You're the best scout I have. Care to take the lead? I'll follow immediately behind you. Take it nice and easy. I don't want any accidents."

Leatis nodded as he took the rope. He used his bow to feel the road ahead. They traveled just shy of four hundred feet when the fog inexplicably lifted, enabling the soldiers to see nearly twenty feet in front of them.

Da'ad noticed movement in the rocks to their left. "There is something out there," he whispered to Leatis.

"I know. I have been watching it since the fog lifted."

"What do you think it is?"

"I have no idea, but it knows we are here, and it is watching us closely. I am certain it will not be long before we learn who or what it is."

Da'ad ordered the group to slow its pace. "Let's move away from the western side of the road. I want to keep as much distance between us and those rocks as we can."

They proceeded cautiously, each man holding tightly to his weapon, anticipating a fight. Strange sounds echoed from the cliffs as the outlines of people emerged all around them.

"Take cover behind the wagons and prepare for a fight, but do not engage unless attacked!"

With his group entrenched, Da'ad watched the strange line of warriors in front of him. For some time, the fog-veiled figures stood motionless. After many minutes, a lone personage stepped forward. His large stature and dark armor stood out. His face was concealed beneath a steel helmet. Only his deep, red eyes were visible. He raised a hand into the air and spoke with a penetrating voice. "Peace, my friends. We will not harm you."

"Then why block our path? Let us be on our way," Da'ad replied.

"In time, you will be grateful for our encounter. We have much to discuss."

"Discuss?" Da'ad asked.

"Yes. I know you, Thoren Da'ad. I know your purpose, but without our help, you will fail."

"You know this? How is that possible?"

"I know many things about you—past, present, and future."

"Identify yourself."

"I am Raelian, King of the Liches, and this is my domain!"

The creature's words sent a chill down Da'ad's spine.

After a pause, Raelian motioned for Da'ad. "Be careful, sir," Bek cautioned.

Da'ad nodded then slowly approached the massive, armor-clad figure, with Riada a short distance behind. Bek eventually joined them, his hand clenched tightly around the hilt of his sword. They stopped several meters in front of Raelian.

"Why are you here?" the Liche King asked.

"You told me you knew that."

"So I do, but do you?"

"I would not have come so far if I did not."

"This is what you believe then?"

"You do not?"

"You are here because it was foretold that you would come. Your purpose is twofold: to find the tomb of Reglis and to free us from our mountain prison."

"You are prisoners?"

"Yes. We cannot leave the mist."

"How are we to free you, and why?"

"You seek the vaults of Reglis. If you wish to find them, I can help, but first you must help me. Show me your map."

Still untrusting, Da'ad refused. He slowly backed away.

"Show me your map!" Raelian angrily repeated. "Do not think me incapable of taking it! I am not interested in your treasure, Paladin! I have information that will aid you. If you value your lives, show me your map."

"I think it likely he already knows our destination. Perhaps we should cooperate." Phineus suggested.

He moved forward and handed Da'ad the map. The colonel reluctantly passed it to Raelian, who opened it and laid it in front of him.

"The treasure is not at the location you seek. Proceed there, but when you reach the tomb, touch nothing except that which I shall tell you. There is a treasure there, but not a treasure to be taken lightly. It is cursed, and great pain awaits those who would remove it. Take only the amulet shaped like this crest." Raelian pointed to a crest on the bottom of the map. "You will find it around the neck of the deceased. When you have acquired the amulet, bring it to me, and I will show you the location of the vaults."

"What is the significance of this amulet?"

Raelian removed his helmet, revealing a faintly glowing skull. His deep-red eyes continued to burn as he told Da'ad, "Years ago, my people were human. A mage entered these parts and offered us eternal life for a price. We paid his fee, and instead of eternal life, he left us in eternal damnation. The mage was part of the necromancer settlement now known as Rosewood. The necromancers deceived us and placed a curse on this land. We are not permitted to tarry in open daylight. This fog protects us while we are here, but it cannot extend beyond the boundaries you see. The amulet will permit us to lay waste to the city of Rosewood and enact our vengeance on those who betrayed us. We shall know no peace until this is done." The creature's voice, which began in deep, penetrating anger, was now nearly a whisper.

"Go now," he told the men as he restored his helmet.

The vast Liche army parted, allowing Da'ad to pass.

As he crossed the Liche's line, he hastened his pace out of the pass then slowed to a gradual stop.

"You're not going to bring it to him, are you?" Bek asked.

"I don't know."

Phineus who had been listening in approached.

"This may be the solution Archibald mentioned. The one the wizards told him about."

"Not likely," Bek scoffed.

Phineus argued his point vehemently until Da'ad intervened. "All right, both of you stop it! I don't know if this is what Master Greyscale meant. Nor do I know what I will do, but I think for now I'm going to proceed as though Raelian spoke the truth."

Bek reluctantly accepted this, leaving Da'ad alone with Phineus. "I don't like the idea of working with these creatures, but I see little choice. If what he said is true, he may have saved us from a terrible blunder," Da'ad told the others.

"Perhaps it is as he said, for the better good," Phineus replied.

"I hope you're right."

DILEMMA AT WHISPERING PINE

With the pass behind them, the group traveled at top speed toward Whispering Pine. The dwarf city was very large but felt like a small town. Its market consisted mostly of tiny tents and temporary structures.

A military barracks rivaled the church as the city's largest building. Thousands of small thatched homes lined the countryside interspersed with the trees. A large stone manor near the center of town served as the seat of government.

The city was surrounded by a rock wall approximately three feet high, parts of which were almost new; other parts were in a state of severe disrepair. Two guards paced back and forth along the wall near the gate, each carrying a sturdy battle-axe.

The usually stingy dwarves were uncharacteristically pleasant. The town's narrow streets were lined with onlookers, all hoping to catch a glimpse of the soldiers. The dwarves produced mostly silver and iron from their mines, which were burrowed deep into the mountains.

Da'ad made a brief stop at a blacksmith's to reshoe his horse and offered an additional sum for minor repairs to his armor.

"It will be better than new when I'm finished," the aged smith assured him.

Da'ad chuckled, at the dwarf's boastful nature. Though skilled artisans, especially in metals, dwarves loved to brag.

There was a slight stench outside. Farm animals were common and walked in and out of buildings freely. The men were pleased by the smell of fresh bread emanating from a nearby bakery.

The dry dirt roads made for a great deal of dust. Matters were not helped by the fact that it had been more than two months since the last rain. As the dust settled, Da'ad made his way to the governor's manor. In contrast with the rest of the city, the manor was in surprisingly good condition. Several chimneys protruded from what appeared to be a new roof.

The stone walls were clean. The grass out front was largely dead, killed by the long dry spell. Most of the water in town flowed from the mountains where rainfall was more plentiful. The city boasted a surprisingly modern aqueduct.

Whispering Pine presented an odd mixture of ancient and modern technologies. On the one hand, most of the homes were quite primitive, and yet the city was filled with modern marvels, such as the aqueduct and the mines.

Poor as Whispering Pine was, its people seemed oddly ignorant of their meager conditions. They paraded about with their chins high, boasting of their plentiful harvests and mineral wealth. While it was true that they had more than they needed of both, they seemed strangely preoccupied with increasing their lot of each. Da'ad was amazed by the unusual reluctance of the dwarves to part with wealth, even to improve their situation.

Many of them lived in poverty, not so much because they could not afford better, but because they would not part with the money necessary to acquire it. Social status in the city was more a function of wealth in the bank than other physical possessions. Da'ad quickly came to realize that the modern aspects of the city existed largely to improve its mining operations.

As he proceeded to the manor house, he was met by a well-armed group of dwarves. They seemed very pleased to see the men and were exceedingly friendly. One, an authoritative dwarf with a long, unkempt beard and shiny suit of armor, smiled disingenuously. "Welcome to Whispering Pine. I am Barigal, governor of these parts."

"We are pleased to offer our respects," Da'ad replied cautiously. He presented Barigal with several gifts, some of them valuable. By far, the dwarf seemed most interested in a tiny sack of gold coins, which he quickly looped around his belt and carried with him. Some of the others carried the remaining gifts to the manor.

"I've ordered a fine feast to celebrate your arrival. You will, of course, make yourselves at home."

"We will do our best," Da'ad promised.

"You get settled then meet me back here. I'll have the feast waiting for you."

Da'ad thanked him for his hospitality, still marveling at the reception they were given.

As they walked toward a dirty-looking inn, Phineus asked, "Rather odd reception for dwarves, don't you think?"

Da'ad nodded. "Yes. He wants something. Now we just need to find out what." He instructed most of his men to set up camp outside the city while he and a few of the others checked into the inn. A short time later, he returned to the governor's manor with Phineus, Leatis, Bek, and Riada.

As promised, Barigal greeted the men with a feast. He appeared to be drunk and made a slight spectacle of himself. It was clear that he could be an intimidating presence when he wanted to be.

Da'ad and his companions were seated around a sturdy-looking wooden table. "This table was built by my great-grandfather more than one hundred and fifty years ago," Barigal boasted.

Da'ad complimented him on the craftsmanship. He did his best to keep the governor happy. There was a very likable side to the self-absorbed dwarf, and he was very generous to the Paladins.

"Colonel Da'ad, is your first name Thoren?" Barigal asked with a laugh.

Da'ad nodded. "It is."

"I knew it. We are honored to have the great Thoren Da'ad in our midst, the man who defeated Ceridus at Fell's End."

"Have we met before?"

Barigal shook his head. "No, but I was involved in the preceding war to drive the goblins from Calair."

He continued his boasts for several minutes. When he was finished, he filled Da'ad's cup and offered a toast. Da'ad humored him, though he was growing tired of such moments and was in no mood for a drink.

He took a brief sip from his glass then returned it to the table. Barigal quickly slurped up the contents of his own goblet, coating his beard with white foam. "I never thought I would share a drink with General Thoren Da'ad, the famous liberator of these parts," he remarked as he poured himself a second glass.

Soon after Barigal's remarks, the food arrived and the men began eating. It was surprisingly appetizing. "I never realized that dwarves were such fantastic cooks."

"My dear Colonel, there are two things dwarves enjoy as much as working the mines: a good drink"—Barigal raised his goblet high into the air—"and fantastic food."

Da'ad nodded politely in passive agreement.

"I trust your travels have gone well?"

Da'ad nodded. "They have." He continued eating, pretending not to recognize the governor's curiosity.

"So you've not said much about your purpose here."

"No, I suppose I haven't."

"Why are you here?"

Da'ad set his fork down and looked the governor in the eyes. "We came in search of a tomb."

Barigal laughed. "There are many tombs in these parts. Whose do you seek?"

"Reglis."

Barigal's silence was telling. He was undoubtedly aware of the wizard's reputation but apparently not of any connection with the region. He made a brief hmm sound and did not bother to inquire further.

Da'ad forced a smile as the dwarf invited, "You will sleep here tonight and each night of your stay."

"You are too kind, sir. I wouldn't think of inconveniencing you. Besides, we've only just checked in next door."

"Nonsense. It is an honor to have you. It would be a great offense if you did not stay. The inn can cancel your accommodations. Besides, you will not find a more comfortable bed anywhere in town."

"I require my associates to remain close."

Barigal's face dimmed slightly. "Surely you don't need them all. Choose those you must have, and they shall stay here with you. The rest may stay in the inn."

Da'ad inhaled deeply, glancing briefly toward the ceiling then back to Barigal. He held his breath as he considered the offer.

"How many can you house?"

"I suppose, I mean, I guess, well, I could house five or six upstairs."

Da'ad rolled his eyes in frustration. He clearly did not want to stay in the manor but saw little option. He sighed. "I will make arrangements for six of my men to join me here."

Barigal grew concerned and began to ask if Da'ad was certain he needed so many but stopped short, realizing that he had already committed.

Da'ad turned to Bek. "Notify the elf scholars to meet us here. Riada, Phineus, Leatis, and the scholars will remain with me."

"What about me, sir? Do you want me to remain as well?"

Da'ad shook his head. "No, I need someone to remain in charge of the camp."

Bek nodded. "Several of the team would like to stay at the inn. What should I tell them?"

"Tell them all right, but I still need people in the camp to look after the gear."

"I'll see to the camp. Not everyone seems interested in the inn anyway. I should have plenty of company."

Da'ad nodded his agreement. Following dinner, he visited the inn for a brief drink, after which he returned to the manor. Phineus was there waiting for him. The others arrived within the hour. Da'ad briefly addressed them.

"As Governor Barigal was kind enough to extend his hospitality, we will be staying here for the time being. I want you to move your belongings in as soon as possible. His staff will show you where to place them."

Da'ad stood as the others hurried to gather their things. He could scarcely escape the governor's company while in the manor and spent as much time as possible at the Toadstool Inn next door. The inn was a dirty, rundown place, but it was quiet during the day.

While Da'ad was seeing to business at the inn, Barigal consulted his librarian, "What do you know about the tomb of Reglis?"

"Mostly rumors and myths. The tomb is believed to be filled with traps and hazards. It has remained hidden since shortly after the wizard's death."

"Yes, that's all fine, but where is it?"

"No one knows."

Frustrated, Barigal muttered to himself, "How am I supposed to impress Thoren Da'ad if I can't find it?"

"What do mean?"

"Never mind!" Barigal shouted as he stormed from the room in search of a bottle.

He settled down at a private bar outside the dining hall and commenced getting drunk. When Da'ad returned, the governor was in a state of semiconsciousness. Da'ad and his companions slipped by unnoticed while Barigal dribbled on about a former love interest.

By morning, the governor was still sleeping off the effects of his binge. Da'ad did his best not to wake him.

He bumped into Phineus, on his way out. "How did you sleep last night?"

"Pretty well. Thank you. You?"

"Oh, it's not as nice as my bed back home, but these feather mattresses are a fair substitute."

Da'ad laughed. "You complain too much, old man. These beds are much better than the hard ground."

"I think you misunderstand my meaning."

"Do I?"

"You do indeed." Phineus scowled.

"Well, best be getting down for breakfast before Barigal tells us what he wants."

"I'm afraid he already has."

Da'ad stopped midstep. "Really? What did he say?"

"He asked a lot of questions while you were at the inn, mostly about Reglis and our purpose in these parts. He was quite intoxicated."

"What did you tell him?"

Phineus laughed. "Oh, not much. His questions were pretty basic. I doubt he has any idea of our true purpose."

"Let's keep it that way. What did he tell you?"

"He offered to assist us in our search for the tomb."

Da'ad's expression turned from one of concern to one of vague curiosity. He betrayed just a touch of amusement as Phineus continued.

"In exchange he wants our help ridding one of his mines of some kind of creature called a mog."

"Oh, that's all. The way he's been going on, I thought it would be something big."

"It may be tougher than you think. Evidently these creatures have metal scales and claws. His own people have failed several times to rid the mine of them. They appear to feed off the ore."

"It's only a matter of time before he asks me about it. I'll consider it then. Meanwhile, see what you can dig up on these things."

Phineus nodded as they reached the dining room. The others joined them a short time later.

When he arrived, Barigal looked ill and complained of a headache. He made another vague inquiry into the Paladins' purpose before sitting down.

"You know, maybe I can help with your quest."

"We'll let you know. There is always a chance we can use good engineers."

"You won't find any better than here." Barigal carried on for several minutes about how great the engineers of Whispering Pine were. When he finished, he suggested, "Perhaps we might make an exchange. We have a bit of a problem, you see, in one of our mines."

"Have you now?"

"Animals, called mogs, have taken up residence there. They feed on the ore."

Da'ad did his best to appear interested. "What is a mog?"

Phineus smiled but said nothing as Barigal explained. "They are fierce beasts that hide in the caverns and feed off the ore. We believe that they have established a nest in the lower caverns, but none of us have been able to get near enough to destroy it. The beasts themselves are nearly indestructible. Their outer skin is covered in metallic scales. The creatures have very long, sharp claws and can rip a steel breastplate in half."

"You've seen them do this?"

Barigal stumbled through his words. "Uh no, not personally, but I've seen the condition of my men when they exited the mine."

"You have this damaged armor? I should like to see it."

"We are skilled artisans, Colonel. We don't leave things broken that can be reused."

"Pity," Da'ad muttered sarcastically. "I should like to see the armor next time. It may tell us a good deal about what we are dealing with. Meantime, we are on a schedule and must continue our journey. Perhaps if we have time, we will give your problem some thought and address the matter when we return."

"We would be most grateful if you do."

"I cannot promise anything. We'll have to see what happens."

Barigal took this as an agreement and celebrated by pouring an entire mug down his throat. He wiped away most of the foam then let out a loud belch. With a look of satisfaction, he laughed and stumbled clumsily from his chair, falling to the ground almost immediately.

Da'ad quickly rose to his feet, fearing the governor had injured himself. His fears were eased by Barigal's loud laughter. Da'ad helped him to his feet and suggested, "Perhaps you should lie down for a while until your head clears."

"My head is as clear as any here."

Barigal pulled away and stumbled through the door, crashing into a suit of armor in the next room.

Da'ad looked at Phineus. "Shall we go?"

"Go where?"

"Wherever you like."

"Sure. Let's check in with the others."

Phineus paused. "Actually, if you don't mind, I think I should like to visit the mine for a few minutes and see what we are up against."

"Sure, if you like. Let me know what you find."

Phineus nodded.

They parted company outside. Da'ad walked to the inn while Phineus went to the stable to inquire about a lantern. The sage stopped to recruit one of the scouts then proceeded to the mine.

Phineus was unable to detect any signs of hostility in the creatures. They seemed shy and kept their distance.

He placed a small amount of diluted acid on the ground near one of them then backed away slowly and waited for it to make contact. The mog quickly reeled in pain. Phineus used a bottle of water to wash away the remaining solution. He then covered the area with dirt. In higher concentrations, he theorized that the acid might prove deadly.

He kept this theory to himself for the time being, fearing that Barigal might abuse it, and spent much of the remaining day alone, making notes in his journal. When he finished, he contacted a smith and presented him with blueprints for a special lantern and two spray devices. The lantern was ready that evening, though the spray devices required numerous custom parts. The smith agreed to make them but would need at least a week. Phineus agreed and promised to pick them up on his return.

Meanwhile, he designed a crude device out of a leather wine pouch. Unlike the custom devices, which would be pressurized, the pouch needed to be squeezed. He filled it with a mixture of mostly water and a small amount of acid then tinkered with his new lantern for several minutes. When he was finished, he woke Da'ad.

"Who is it?"

"Phineus. I have news about the mogs."

"About the what?"

"The mogs. You know, the creatures in Barigal's mine."

"Oh, that. What's the news?"

"I stopped by there this morning after breakfast. There were several of the creatures about. They seemed rather shy and kept their distance. I managed to place a small amount of an acid on the ground near one of them. The effect was interesting but not altogether surprising. They have low tolerance for the solution, and in higher concentrations, I'm sure it could kill them."

"Do you think that will be necessary?"

"No, and I would like to keep that information to just the two of us for now."

Da'ad nodded. "I suppose we should keep that from Barigal." He struggled to dress himself then invited, "Care to follow me to the pub?"

"I'm not really thirsty."

"That's all right. Neither am I, but if we remain here, Barigal is sure to find us."

"Very well. To the pub."

They were referring to the bar inside the inn. Riada was there drinking when they arrived. He waved briefly.

The doorways were a bit short for the men. Da'ad had to duck as he entered. Most of the chairs and tables were also short. It was obvious that the building was not designed to accommodate full-sized visitors.

Da'ad led Phineus to a table in the far corner. Phineus noted that the area was surprisingly clean. Da'ad smiled. "The dwarves here are very finicky eaters. I'm told they take great care in the preparation of their food. Though they clean little else, you will not find a dirty table in the dining area."

"How are their appetites?"

"I've seen few things so large as a dwarf's appetite. You hungry?"

Phineus nodded.

"Wait here. I'll scrounge up a couple of menus."

Da'ad returned a short while later. As they waited, Phineus described his visit to the mine and requested an extra day to continue his studies.

"The mogs are not our problem yet. With a little luck, they may never be our problem."

"If we could only be so lucky. I believe these creatures became our problem the moment we set foot in this place. All I ask is one day. Truly you can spare that for an old friend."

"Does it mean that much to you?"

"I believe it may."

"All right, but day after tomorrow we leave, ready or not."

"Agreed. One thing more."

Da'ad watched curiously as Phineus told him, "I'd like you to accompany me in the morning."

Da'ad scratched the side of his chin. "Very well. Seeing as we won't be leaving, I have no plans."

Their conversation was interrupted by the announcement that their food was ready. "Let me get that," Da'ad volunteered. He returned with two large platters.

"You weren't kidding about the portions. This could feed me for a week."

Da'ad laughed. "There have been many weeks that I wished I could have eaten so well."

"I'm not at all convinced that the mogs are hostile." Da'ad glanced up from his plate as Phineus continued, "It was dark in the mine, but from what I was able to see, they were more afraid of me than I was of them. Their scales appear to be made of silver and not a harder metal, such as iron. I find it difficult to believe they could cut a steel plate in half, as Barigal claimed."

"I'm sure he embellished quite a bit. Dwarves are known to do that."

"I'm certain you're right. I've commissioned the construction of a pair of devices to repel the mogs if necessary. They won't be complete for a few days, but I have a crude leather device we can use in the morning. I intend to fill it with a diluted acid solution in case of trouble, though I doubt strongly we will need it."

"As you noted earlier, I think the less Barigal knows, the better. Knowledge to a dwarf can be a bit like faith to a zealot."

"What do you mean?"

"They never quite know as much as they think they do," Da'ad explained.

"I don't follow."

"Dwarves are quite arrogant beings. Feed into their egos and they will take good care of you, but disagree with them and you'll likely have an enemy for life."

"And that's like a zealot?"

"Zealots often come to take their doctrines for granted. They believe things as much because they want to as for the truth of the matters. The faith they claim is all too often blind. They seldom think to test their assumptions and are all too eager to fault any contrary assumptions."

"Have you known many zealots?"

"Yes. Zealously is part of most everyone's religion."

"I think you take a jaded view of religion, my friend."

"Nonsense. I am very religious. I just don't believe lightly. People should learn to question what they want to believe. I think most lack the faith to test their assumptions. They fear being wrong and prefer ignorance to disappointment. We're so busy molding God to suit us that we forget to mold ourselves to suit Him."

"I suppose you may have a point, but I still don't share your sentiments entirely."

"You don't have to. It's probably for the best that you not. It can be easy, as a cynic, to be bitter and judgmental. I guess I've spent too much time around politics."

Phineus laughed. "Politics?"

"Yes, now there is a false religion if ever I've seen one."

"That I can agree with, having delved into it myself for so long. It's absolutely unbelievable the things people do for the sake of power."

"It's unbelievable the things they believe for the sake of convenience. No one should ever trust a politician."

"I was a politician, you know."

"I'm not pretending there are no honest politicians, but they are the exception. People seem far too willing to believe in the exceptions. Best that they learn to question even the honest leaders than that they believe the crooks to be honest. Besides, power corrupts even the best of men. Without it, one can accomplish nothing. The temptation is to do what is needed to keep the power necessary to accomplish even the most noble of goals."

"I suppose when you put it that way you have a point."

Both men took their time eating. Da'ad quietly paid for the meal before they returned to the manor.

As expected, Barigal intercepted them. Phineus excused himself to his room, leaving Da'ad to entertain the governor. "So, Colonel, what is this I hear about you leaving in the morning?"

"That was the plan. It's changed a bit, I'm afraid. One of our members requested an extra day to take care of a few things."

"Ah, good. That will give us more time to talk."

"What would you like to talk about?"

"Oh, I don't know. Perhaps we can share a drink and see what comes up."

"I'm afraid I've had a busy day and should be getting some rest."

"Of course. I'll speak with you in the morning."

"In the morning then."

Da'ad excused himself to his room after leaving a note for Riada explaining that they would be staying another day. He was not as tired as he let on but lacked the patience for another lengthy conversation.

He was awakened the next morning by Phineus.

"Good morning. You were still planning on accompanying me?"

"To be honest, I really wasn't planning much of anything until you woke me."

"I figure we can eat breakfast then hurry over to the mine."

"Good. Why don't you wait outside while I get dressed? I'll join you in a moment."

They met several of the others at the inn over breakfast. Most of those present expressed a desire to join them in the mine. Da'ad deferred to Phineus, who seemed pleased for the company.

He was eager to test his new lamp. Unfortunately, the mogs were sensitive to the bright light and fled the chamber. With Phineus in the lead, the group made its way deeper into the mine. They found numerous grapefruit-sized spheres along the walls. The orbs were silver in color and appeared to be made of metal.

"Very odd. I wonder what these are?" Da'ad whispered.

"They appear to be eggs."

The mogs became increasingly aggressive as the men approached the spheres. Phineus used his diluted acid to keep them away.

He looked around, noticing several broken shells. "I wonder if they will react the same toward the broken ones?"

"One way to find out," Da'ad replied.

Phineus bent over and collected several of the shells. The mogs seemed wholly disinterested and kept their distance.

"This is consistent with what I expected. The broken orbs have no value to the creatures."

After filling an old burlap sack with the broken shells, Phineus examined one of them. "I'd like to get this outside where I can see it in the light."

"Shall we go then?" Da'ad asked.

"Yes. I'll follow your lead this time."

Once outside, Phineus proclaimed that the shell was comprised of very high-quality silver.

He carried it back to his room for testing.

Da'ad brought a small bag of the discarded shells to Barigal. The governor was drooling over it when Phineus interrupted. "Fantastic news! Just as I suspected, the shells are almost pure silver. Those creatures apparently have the ability to filter out impurities better than we can."

"What are you talking about?" Barigal shouted.

"The orbs. They are eggs."

"Orbs and eggs. Have you lost your mind?"

"I think what Master Phineus is trying to tell us is that the quality of silver in these fragments is incredibly good."

Phineus nodded. "Yes."

Barigal seemed satisfied. "This is fantastic. If we get rid of the mogs, we can collect all of the orbs. The value must be enormous. Now how do we kill these creatures?"

"I'm not certain killing them is necessary. Trained up, they may save you a lot of work. These creatures must absorb some of the other elements from the soil for their more vital functions. They showed almost no interest in the discarded silver."

"You don't mean to leave those things in my mine, do you?"

"Destroying the mogs may be possible, but in the end, I fail to see what we would accomplish," Phineus replied.

"We would rid my mine of those creatures." The idea of leaving the mogs in his mine made Barigal furious.

"We will see what we can do when we return. For now we need to make preparations to find the Tomb of Reglis. I suggest that you leave the beasts alone until we're back," Da'ad cautioned.

Barigal reluctantly agreed.

ASSISTING THE DWARVES

Phineus turned to Barigal. "I must concur with Thoren. I suggest you stay out of the mine until we return."

He suspected the governor already had plans to enter the mine. Unable to do anything at the moment, he kept his thoughts to himself and quietly returned to his room.

The Paladins left early the next morning. The trail to the vaults was overrun with thick vegetation, forcing the men to cut a new path through the brush. The task took nearly two and a half days. Unfortunately, after clearing the path, the group was inhibited further by an uncharted lake blocking access to the mountain.

Da'ad ordered Bek, "Have the men set up camp for the night. When they are finished, have Leatis and Phineus draw up plans for a small boat."

Bek nodded. Phineus began work on the plans, even before the first tent went up. By nightfall, his design was nearly complete. Da'ad looked it over, making a few suggestions, then passed it along to Leatis, who began construction the next morning. It took two days to complete the craft. The lack of sufficient lighting forced Da'ad to wait another before testing it.

While the Paladins waited near the mountain, Barigal was busily laying plans to retake his mine. He located one of Phineus's empty spray devices and filled it with water, which he arrogantly presumed would protect him against the mogs.

When the device had no effect, he was stunned. His soldiers attempted to fight but mostly stumbled around, swinging at shadows and bumping into each other. The scene might have been considered comical if not for the numerous injuries they sustained.

Many blades were broken without ever touching the armored scales of a mog. Several dwarves were banged up so badly that they had to be assisted from the mine. The emerging soldiers and miners told the awaiting crowd of a fierce battle with vicious monsters. The panicked crowd was almost as terrified as the soldiers.

All of the retreating dwarves seemed quite convinced that their tales were true, though none could recall exactly how they came to this knowledge. They described varying monsters of inaccurate proportions. No one seemed to notice the numerous inconsistencies.

In the aftermath of the first failed assault, several bone-headed schemes were cooked up to rid the mine of the mogs. Most of them ended in disaster, with men fleeing the mine in quick succession.

Barigal suffered numerous injuries during this time and had to be assisted to his manor. His once-pristine armor was badly scarred. Convinced that he must be rid of the mogs, he continued to mutter from his bed. He shouted out orders and repeated, among other things, phrases like, "They nearly killed me!" He demanded help into his bed then fought those attempting to help him, insisting, "I don't need any help. I can get in on my own." He was filled with emotions, mostly negative. They twisted his mind and perception, causing much fatigue and confusion.

Elsewhere, Da'ad was facing trouble of his own. His boat was now complete, and after an initial test voyage, his scouts returned with news of a massive dam blocking the river. Unfortunately, the resulting lake completely blocked access to the mountain caverns.

The existence of the dam was an encouraging find, since, in theory, they could remove it and release the water. Unfortunately, it was fortified with brick and stone, packed with clay, and interwoven with logs. Destroying it was to be no small task.

Da'ad consulted with Phineus for over an hour. "The dam might be removed with blasting powder, if we had enough for the job," Phineus offered.

"Well, we haven't. What else can we do?"

"Perhaps if we consult Barigal, he might consent to lend us a pair of his engineers. Of course, it may mean clearing his mine first."

"I'm sure it will."

"I should have a look at the dam myself come morning. That ought to give me an idea of what we will need," Phineus offered.

"All right. Let me know the minute you're finished, and we'll start back."

Phineus nodded.

<hr/>

They met early the next morning. Two of the elves accompanied Phineus on the boat. He spent more than ten minutes sketching the dam and estimating its dimensions, then carefully tucked away the diagram in a watertight bag and rejoined Da'ad on the shore. The boat was secured and hidden beneath the dry grass. Within minutes, the group was back on the road.

Heavy winds had been building along the edge of the mountains. Da'ad was pleased to be leaving. A thick covering of clouds drifted overhead, dropping a downpour of rain and wet snow. The clouds gradually thickened until they completely blocked out the sun.

Lightning burst overhead with such a terrible roar that the ground shuddered beneath the men's feet. The rain gradually turned to hail and eventually flooded much of the former campsite. Da'ad's soldiers were forced to remove several fallen trees. They spent a good deal of time freeing their wagons from the mud. Everyone was greatly relieved to reach Whispering Pine, and no one more so than Da'ad.

He found the streets much quieter than before. There was a large gathering of people near the silver mines. Phineus muttered something under his breath and glanced disapprovingly toward Da'ad. A few minutes later, several well-armed dwarves emerged shaken from the mine.

Da'ad rode forward. "What is going on?"

One of the onlookers, a filthy middle-aged dwarf, raised his head and explained, "It is a competition."

"A competition? By whose authority?"

"The governor's, sir." The dwarf pointed toward a piece of parchment hanging on a nearby tree.

Da'ad read then removed the notice. He quickly rejoined the others and showed it to Phineus. "It appears that Barigal could not wait for our return."

Phineus adjusted his spectacles and took a close look at the parchment. "One thousand gold coins! Barigal must be very territorial in deed. I've never known a dwarf to part with money lightly."

"Nor have I."

"Well, what shall we do?"

"I think I'll have a word with Barigal before someone gets killed."

"How do you know they haven't already?"

Da'ad scowled but said nothing. He begrudgingly led the way to Barigal's manor. Phineus followed closely behind until they were intercepted by several soldiers at the porch. "What do you want?"

"I would like an audience with Barigal at once."

Nervously, a soldier retreated to the manor to inform the governor. He returned a few minutes later. "The governor is waiting for you inside. Follow the servant at the door."

A middle-aged woman greeted them and led the way. The governor was still in bed when they arrived. He was busily shouting out orders. While he seemed quite recovered, he was absolutely convinced that his injuries were still serious. Da'ad saw little point in confronting him directly. He made a brief uhh humm sound and waited to be acknowledged.

Barigal quickly dismissed his nurses. "Come in. Come in." His demeanor changed as he greeted the men. He even forced a smile.

"What happened to you?" Da'ad asked.

Barigal let out a brief laugh. "We went into the mines to have a look around. The mogs attacked us almost immediately with little provocation. There must have been twenty or thirty of them. They were everywhere, thrashing with claws and twelve-inch fangs. We were fortunate to escape with our lives."

Da'ad could not help but to smile at this obviously fictitious tale. "Yes, indeed." He forced back the urge to laugh.

Phineus looked to say something but was silenced by Da'ad. "May I examine your armor, Governor?"

"Certainly. It's in there."

Barigal motioned to the closet across from the bed. Da'ad opened it slowly, revealing the damaged breastplate. He lifted it and examined each dent and scrape. "Are all of these new?"

"Yes. Ordinarily, I would have repaired the damage, but as you can see, I am laid up at the moment. Those creatures did that."

"All of it?"

Barigal nodded. "Yes, they nearly killed me."

Da'ad tossed the armor back into the closet, picked up a sturdy sword, swung it once through the air, then returned it to the closet and turned back to Barigal. "My condolences on your injuries. I am most grateful you are alive."

Barigal smiled arrogantly. "What may I do for you gentlemen?"

"I've come to request a favor, but first, do you have a mace?"

Da'ad's inquiry caught Barigal off guard. He paused for a moment. "Yes, but I've not used it in years." He pointed to a wooden case near the back of the closet. "It's in there."

Da'ad opened the case and examined the well-polished weapon for several seconds before closing the lid. He nodded slightly to himself then placed the case down and closed the closet door. "How large did you say the creatures' claws were?"

Barigal went into a lengthy explanation. Da'ad pretended to listen, though he already knew all that he cared to.

"I wonder if you might spare a few engineers. We've run into a problem. The tomb we are looking for is blocked by a large lake. The lake is held in place by a dam. We need help removing the structure."

Barigal smiled thoughtfully. The look on his face was unmistakable. "Let's make a deal. You get rid of the mogs, and I will see that your dam is removed."

Da'ad nodded. "I'll visit the mine again. If the creatures are a threat, we'll do what we can to remove them, though I strongly suspect that these animals might be a blessing in disguise if you use them right."

Barigal sneered. "I've no use for ore-stealing monsters. Just get them out of my mine!"

"Very well, but they may come back."

"Just get rid of them!"

Da'ad agreed then turned to Phineus and motioned. "I believe it's time to leave. We'll see you in the morning, Governor."

They left Barigal shouting orders at his nurses.

"Surely, you don't believe his story."

Da'ad shook his head. "No, but I see nothing to be gained by challenging it."

"The evidence against it is overwhelming. Certainly, it was sufficient to challenge him. After all, there is always something to be gained by standing up for truth and right!"

Da'ad shook his head. "Not so. We cannot justify our actions solely in the nobility of our cause. There is a time to speak and a time to reflect. Barigal is not ready to listen. Forcing the truth on him now would only cause resentment and lead to unnecessary difficulties for all involved."

Phineus mumbled something to himself, clearly unhappy with the situation. With Da'ad in the lead, they proceeded to the mine where a burly looking dwarf was being carried away. With all of the activity outside, the air was fettered with the scent of animal manure. Phineus covered his nose and took a deep breath. Noticing this, Da'ad smiled.

"Best just grin and bear it. Your nose will acclimate in a few minutes."

Phineus sheepishly uncovered his face and breathed in. They watched as the crowd gradually dispersed, leaving only a few small children.

"Is your lantern finished?"

Phineus nodded. "It's back at my cart. I can retrieve it."

Da'ad agreed, and Phineus hurried after it. He returned a few minutes later, reluctant to show the device.

"Something the matter?"

"You'll not be killing them, will you?"

"Not likely. I just want to have a look. If I'm correct, the mogs must have entered from somewhere deep inside."

"Perhaps I should get the spray canisters, just to be safe."

Da'ad agreed and waited as Phineus disappeared again. The old scholar eventually returned with the canisters and two soldiers. Da'ad led the way inside. The mine was damp and uninviting. Its walls were a combination of packed dirt and stone, held in place by massive timbers. The air was musty and smelled of freshly dug soil.

Phineus lit the lantern and displaced Da'ad in the lead. There were patches of moss covering the damp areas, nearest the supports. The mogs kept their distance and loomed curiously in the shadows.

The men followed the fleeing mogs to a rear chamber; the same chamber where they found the orbs. After several minutes, they noticed a tiny opening in the floor, near where the mogs disappeared.

Da'ad motioned for Phineus to bring the light nearer to the hole. They listened as something scurried away. After observing the creatures for several minutes in a much dimmer light, Phineus suggested they leave. Da'ad followed him out.

"These creatures' mouths are far too small to have caused the damage Barigal claims. This is consistent with the earlier observations and sketches I made. Even if Barigal's people removed the eggs, the creatures could not have caused such injuries."

"They didn't. Barigal's armor bore the scars of dwarf weaponry. One of his own men likely hit him in the confusion. I doubt seriously that the mogs were anywhere near them. Even if they were, their claws are made of silver. There is no way they could have cut through steel."

"Then why didn't you point this out when we were with the governor?" Phineus asked.

"Because, as I told you before, he would not have listened, and we would now be facing an enemy where we might have a friend.

What good would come from alienating the dwarves before asking their help at the dam?"

Phineus remained silent. "Exactly. Nothing," Da'ad said.

"I think you missed your calling. You should have been a diplomat," Phineus retorted.

"I have been, many times. It is often as important to know when to fight as how. A fight avoided may prove a greater victory than a fight won."

Phineus reflected silently on Da'ad's words.

The two men said little else as they approached the manor.

They next met several hours later at the inn. It was midafternoon when they joined each other in the partial seclusion of the bar's northeast corner.

"I have been studying my sketches, and I think it might be possible to block the mogs' entrance into the mine. They will eventually find another way in but not the same way."

Da'ad lifted his head with interest.

"The creatures mouths are far too small to chew through large, rounded bars. Steel may be too hard for them anyway. I think we can fasten bars across the tunnel entrance and seal it off with stone and concrete. Even so, I still believe the best solution would be to tame them and use them to improve the mine's efficiency."

Da'ad shook his head. "The safe move would be to simply seal the mine and let them return in their own good time. I doubt Barigal wants to hear any more ideas regarding taming the mogs."

"I'm sure you are right. Perhaps we should just do it and be done with it."

Da'ad finished his drink, and both men returned to camp. By this time, the others had set up a command tent outside the manor. Most of the men were registered to stay at the inn.

Da'ad met Bek outside. "I took the liberty of checking our gear and registered both of you inside," he told them.

Da'ad thanked him and invited Phineus to accompany him to see Barigal.

Barigal was in his room but no longer in bed. He had accepted that his injuries were not as serious as he once believed and was pacing the floor.

"I see you're feeling better."

"Yes."

Da'ad took a quick look around the room. "What happened to your nurses?"

"I sent them away. As you can see, I am feeling much better now. Won't you be seated?" Barigal motioned toward a small table near the bed and passed out mugs. "Care for drink?"

"Not too much. Thank you." Da'ad raised a hand slowly.

Phineus quietly accepted a full goblet and set it aside, untouched. Barigal poured the contents of his own goblet down his throat with careless haste. He spilled a little down the front of his beard but did not bother to wipe it away.

"Tell me, what have you discovered?"

"I think we can seal off the tunnel where the creatures entered, but it will only be a matter of time before they return."

"How long before you can seal it off?"

"I think we can begin work tomorrow afternoon. We will need a few things though."

"Just name them."

Phineus handed the governor his list with instructions. Da'ad then returned to his room, where Phineus soon joined him.

"Well, I'm glad that's done," Phineus offered.

"You think you can get along without me in the morning?" Da'ad asked.

"Why, where will you be?"

"Right here. I have a few things to see to. I'll try to meet you outside, when you return."

"I think I can instruct your men on what needs to be done."

"Good. I'll see you in the morning then."

They met briefly over breakfast, then caught up with each other again as Phineus was exiting the mine.

"Everything taken care of?"

"Yes, but we could have used your help. Those materials were heavy."

"You were lifting?"

"Not me personally, but I saw the strain on your men."

Da'ad laughed. "A little exercise won't hurt them. Care to follow me back to the manor?"

"You know they will be back, don't you?"

"Fortunately, that's not our problem."

Da'ad knocked loudly and waited. They were quickly brought before the governor, who was in the dining room busily complaining about the food.

One of the servants announced the men, and Barigal quickly stood to greet them. "Come in. Care to join me?" He motioned to the table and watched expectantly as his guests were seated.

Da'ad politely declined an invitation to eat. "About those engineers you promised—"

"The mogs are out of the mine?"

"They are."

"Very well, a deal is a deal. They will be ready when you are. I've already spoken with them."

Da'ad nodded. "Thank you." He stood to leave, but Barigal stopped him.

"I'll have them meet you at the inn in the morning."

He watched as the men exited then called for the nearest servant. "Have the engineers I've selected meet the men at the inn in the morning, but let them know that I would like to see them first."

The servant bowed. Following his conversation with the engineers, Barigal hurried to the inn, where he hoped to catch Da'ad in time for one last drink. When he arrived, he found the colonel busy packing.

The governor waited a few seconds while Da'ad wrapped up a conversation then called out loudly, "Mr. Da'ad, care to join me at the bar?"

"I'm awfully busy at the moment. If you can wait, I'll join you when I'm free, but for one drink only. I need my rest."

"Of course. I'll wait at the bar." He waited for almost an hour, drinking himself into mild frenzy before Da'ad arrived.

Phineus smiled. "I think I had better get some rest. You two have fun."

Da'ad nodded before joining Barigal. "So what are you having?"

"Nothing but the best," Barigal proclaimed loudly, in a drunken slur. He turned the bottle toward Da'ad, exposing the label.

Following their drink, Da'ad retired. Barigal remained for several hours and eventually passed out in a drunken slumber. The barman and one of his guards had to carry him back to the manor.

THE TOMB OF REGLIS

Barigal was still in bed when Da'ad awoke. As promised, his engineers were ready and waiting near the bar. Da'ad was pleasantly surprised by their promptness and quickly introduced himself. Both engineers were dirty and unkempt. The first offered his hand enthusiastically and introduced himself by name. His language was coarse and unrefined.

The second was eloquent and polished, no doubt the product of higher education, almost certainly acquired outside the city. There was an air of arrogance about the dwarves. Still, they seemed strangely preoccupied with pleasing Da'ad.

"I understand that you will be assisting us with the removal of a dam."

"It is an honor to serve the great Thoren Da'ad."

Da'ad raised his hand to halt any further praise. "We have a long day ahead of us, gentlemen, and I really must eat, so if you will excuse me." He walked slowly to a nearby table and joined some of his men for breakfast.

Phineus arrived late and quietly pulled up a chair. After several minutes, he asked, "Have you smelled our engineers?"

"I have." Da'ad looked expectantly at him.

"What do you intend to do about it?"

He shrugged. "I suppose I intend to sleep in separate quarters."

Phineus did not find the remark amusing and protested loudly. "That's easy for you to say, but I have to work with them."

"Well, if it makes you feel any better, then I'll sit in on the meetings with you."

Phineus huffed. His lower lip was partially curled. "It will make me feel a little better, I think."

"Good, then it's settled."

A short while later, one of the Paladins approached from outside. "The carts are loaded, sir. We're ready to get under way."

"Very well. I'll be right out."

The soldier saluted smartly and departed. Da'ad finished the last remnants of his meal and was in no hurry as he stood to leave. Phineus followed him to the door and watched. "Mount up!" Da'ad ordered as he completed his inspection.

The sun was just peering over the horizon as they left the city. Travel was slow and tedious. More than once, the men had to free their carts from the rocks and dry soil. The recent rains loosened the dirt, which frequently gave way under the weight of the heavy carts, creating long, snakelike tracks.

To entertain themselves, the dwarves frequently showed off, a fact that only increased tensions with the others. Several times, the dwarves were asked to bathe. Being stubborn, they disregarded each instruction, though they dared not disobey Da'ad. It was not clear that this was out of respect or fear.

Phineus found it amusing and laughed quietly. He told Da'ad, "Thoren, I think our engineers are more obedient to you than many of your own people."

"Why do you say that?"

"Oh, no reason, really." The look on Phineus's face said otherwise as he turned to leave.

"I have to admit, their behavior is curious," Da'ad wondered aloud.

The dwarves were unusually heavy eaters. At mealtimes, they sat by themselves, not so much for the sake of being antisocial but because they stank.

The odor was most offensive to the elves, whose sense of smell was far greater than that of the men. As the complaints mounted, Da'ad grew increasingly upset.

"Enough!" He halted the row of men and carts. "Have the engineers brought to me at once."

"Yes, sir."

Several minutes later, the dwarves scampered forward nervously.

"Gentlemen, we have a problem. I'm not going to lecture you on how to live your lives, but while you are under my command, you will wash yourselves regularly. Is that understood?"

"Yes, sir," both responded in unison.

"Good. Now, I want you to go to the river and clean up. There will be no supper for either of you until you are finished, and I don't want to hear another word, from anyone, about your stench. Is that understood?"

"Yes, sir."

The dwarves left disgruntled but were careful not to show it. One of the soldiers provided them with soap. They spent nearly thirty minutes cleaning out their badly matted beards. Much of the hair had to be trimmed away. The beards were almost half their original length by the time they were done. The cold water was at first refreshing but quickly became uncomfortable.

While the dwarves bathed, Da'ad addressed the others. "I want everyone to make the engineers feel welcome and included. No more petty complaints or bickering."

He addressed the elves specifically for a minute, warning them against leaving camp at mealtime.

Satisfied that there was no further misunderstanding, Da'ad nodded. "Good, you're dismissed."

Leatis calmly offered his approval. "It will be good to bring everyone together as a team. Spending meals together will be a positive step."

"Not just meals. I want you to see to it that everyone is functioning as a unit before we reach the dam. For the time being, we are not just companions. We are a family. See to it that everyone is united in that pursuit. That's an order."

The elf bowed. For a brief moment, Da'ad swore he could see the flicker of a smile on his face.

With the others gone, Da'ad laid down for a quick nap. He awoke several minutes later. By this time, his tent was up. Most of the others remained near the stream, leaving the camp largely empty.

Da'ad glanced across the way and caught sight of the cooks just finishing with the dwarves' clothing. He turned toward the river where several of the men and elves were splashing in the water.

The dwarves had long since finished bathing but refused to get out until their clothing was ready. The cooks were intentionally taking their time. After a few choice insults from the shivering dwarves, they decided to leave the clothing near the camp's recently constructed fire pit. They remained nearby, knowing full well that the dwarves would not leave the water with women around.

Da'ad quietly excused them then called out, "All right. They're gone. Now come out of there."

He ordered one of his men to fetch a pair of towels. The engineers were relieved to finally be out of the water. They thanked the colonel repeatedly as he shrugged and returned to his tent.

The dwarves settled in near the fire with a bottle of rum, "liquid warmth" as they called it.

At mealtime, Da'ad ate quietly in his tent before joining the others outside. He took a seat next to Phineus near the fire and watched as Riada sharpened a dagger.

Bek eventually sat across from him. "What do you think we'll find when we knock out the dam?"

"No idea, perhaps the vaults. Possibly nothing."

"The Liche King seemed quite certain that we would find something." Phinues laughed.

"I know. That's what's bothering me. I'm not sure I trust the Liches," Bek replied.

Da'ad looked at him sternly. "I'm not sure I trust them either, but for now, this is the only lead we have. Cheer up, Lieutenant. Whatever we find, we'll deal with it accordingly."

Bek forced a smile and then turned as Riada put away his knife.

Da'ad had a slight headache and retired to bed. The trail was moist the next morning when the group broke camp. More than once the men had to dig their carts from the thick mud. Still, the delays were minimal. They reached the lake shortly before lunch, setting up camp near the mountain. Riada and Leatis dug the boat free. It took them several minutes to clean it out.

"I want you to take the dwarves to the dam following lunch. Hopefully we can take care of this thing quickly." Leatis bowed.

The dwarves were still eating when they arrived to look over the boat. "Simplistic, but I suppose it will work."

Leatis frowned but said nothing.

Da'ad motioned with his hand. "Go ahead and climb in." He and Riada pushed off and watched from the shore as Leatis used a long pole to push across the water until an oar became necessary.

The dwarves carefully compared Phineus's drawings to the actual dam. They made numerous notations before tucking everything back into the watertight sack. One of them measured the depth of the reservoir at several locations and then estimated the volume of water.

Once satisfied that they had all the information they needed, they told Leatis to take them back. As soon as the boat reached shore, they hurried past Da'ad toward their tent. Da'ad quietly returned to his own tent, where Bek joined him.

It was mealtime when the engineers re-emerged. "We've considered the dimensions of the dam and feel we are ready to proceed."

"Good. We'll begin in the morning."

Da'ad turned to Bek. "Have the boat ready just before sunrise. Instruct Phineus to accompany them. I'll speak with Leatis. Let's see if we can take care of this thing early."

"Yes, sir."

A short time later, both men joined the others around the makeshift table for a brief game of cards. Da'ad excused himself momentarily at Phineus's request.

"I understand that we're going to blow the dam in the morning," the old man observed.

"I see you've been talking to someone."

"Yes. Lieutenant Bek spoke with me a moment ago."

"Good. I want you to accompany them out. I'll have Leatis meet you in the morning."

On the other side of the fire pit, the dwarves were busily boasting of their skills with blasting powder, each claiming to require less than the other to release the water. Da'ad and Phineus could not help but overhear the proud rantings.

"I just hope they keep their heads long enough to get the job done. I really don't want to do this twice," Phineus remarked.

"Nor do I," Da'ad agreed.

Both men finished their food and retired to their tents.

After tossing for much of the night, Da'ad spoke with Phineus again over breakfast. "I had a rough night last night. My dreams were troubling. Problem is, all I can remember is the sensation of danger."

"I wouldn't read too much into dreams, especially those you can't remember. Probably just some subconscious fear making its way to the surface," Phineus counseled.

Leatis overheard. "Dreams may be very significant. I wouldn't shrug them off too lightly. The wizards often communicate with one another by way of dreams. I am told that there are many beings who use them for various purposes. It may be that some unearthly force is attempting to communicate a warning."

"If that's true, then why don't I recall the dream?"

"I don't know. Perhaps the dream itself is not as important as the caution it inspires."

"I don't need anxiety dreams to teach me caution."

"It may be a mere anxiety dream. I just don't advise shrugging it off lightly. I've known a thing or two of significant dreams in my life."

"Now that you mention it, so have I, but I've always remembered them the next morning, as though I had experienced them in my wakeful hours."

Leatis bowed. "I had best be getting the boat ready."

"I'll join you when I am finished," Da'ad offered.

Following his meal, Da'ad hurried to the water, where the boat was resting near shore. Riada and Leatis were standing above it. Phineus arrived a short time later and took his seat near the front.

The dwarves were making merry at the breakfast table and did not arrive for several minutes. They were somewhat inebriated, prompting Da'ad to caution Leatis.

As soon as the dwarves were seated, Leatis pushed the boat into the water then took his seat inside with the others. Da'ad watched from shore while the others delivered explosive charges along the dam.

The boat was too small to carry them all at once and had to make several trips. Still, the dwarves used far less powder than Phineus expected.

"Are you sure this will be enough?"

"Absolutely. It's probably more than enough. All we really need is to weaken the structure at several pressure points, then let gravity take care of the rest."

Phineus grew upset. He repeatedly cautioned, "Be careful," which only upset the dwarves.

They responded by acting even more reckless than before. Leatis and Riada eventually interceded, insisting that the engineers stop playing childish games and get on with their work.

"Please, just let this work," Phineus prayed aloud as they reached the shore.

The powder kegs were fitted with tiny tubes, attached during the boat's final pass. Each tube slowly allowed gas into a chemical chamber. The chamber acted as a timer, which would eventually set off the explosives.

The devices were surprisingly advanced for Whispering Pine. Originally developed in Thornguard, Phineus had no idea that they had made their way so far west.

From shore, one of the dwarves busily showed off with small amounts of excess powder. "Don't waste that. We don't know yet if we need it," Phineus scolded.

The dwarf responded belligerently until Da'ad intervened. "We don't have time for childish bickering."

It was several minutes later that the first charge sent up a plume of smoke and debris. The dust gradually settled over the water. Several more explosions followed in quick succession.

It was soon apparent that the dam was still in place. Phineus was furious. "I warned you that we needed more powder. Now we will need to go out and do it again."

Da'ad inhaled briefly. "Perhaps you should stay here this time. I'm sure that Leatis can supervise sufficiently."

"Best not send anyone out there right now," one of the dwarves cautioned.

Phineus turned to face him. "And why not? The charges all went off, and the dam didn't blow."

"It will. Just give it time."

Da'ad stepped forward. "Are you certain of that?"

"Absolutely. It takes time for gravity to do its thing. Even now, those supports are growing weaker by the second. When they give out, that entire lake will flood the valley below, and I wouldn't want to be on the water when it does."

"Very well. We'll wait."

Phineus continued to watch with great skepticism. After nearly an hour, the first timbers began to snap, increasing the pressure on the rest of the wall. Within minutes, the entire wall collapsed, releasing the water, just as the dwarves had predicted.

Phineus sneered in disgust. He resented the fact that the dwarves were right. Unable to face them, he retired to his tent.

Da'ad offered his brief congratulations to the engineers and requested that they remain in camp until the water level dropped sufficiently to allow access.

The dwarves agreed.

By late afternoon, the top of a cave was already exposed. Sometime during the night, the water dropped below the floor. Able to access the caverns, Da'ad excused the engineers, who returned to Whispering Pine.

Phineus was eager for a look inside. With Da'ad's blessing, he led a small group into the darkened cave. The rock was wet and slippery. Leatis quickly concluded that it was too dangerous to continue and ordered everyone out.

"Perhaps we should let it air out for a day and try again," Phineus suggested, his voice filled with disappointment.

Da'ad quickly agreed. "Cheer up, old friend. We're getting closer. I understand your disappointment, but this is only a minor setback. We'll be inside soon enough."

"Forgive an old man's impatience."

"There is nothing to forgive."

Phineus returned quietly to his tent to ponder his disappointment while Da'ad spoke with Leatis.

The water continued to drain throughout the night. By morning, much of the entryway was dry, and Da'ad authorized Leatis to take a team inside. He ordered Phineus to remain in camp. After only fifteen minutes, Leatis returned with word that much of the floor was still covered in water. He explained, "I think we're going to need to wait at least a week, perhaps longer. It's solid rock in there, and the water has nowhere to go."

"It's solid rock in the entrance too, but the water is evaporating here."

"It's exposed to the outside air. The air inside is saturated and ventilation minimal. It will take more time for the inner rock to dry."

"Isn't the entire cavern connected to the outside, right here?"

"So far as I know, and it is venting but very slowly. We must be patient."

"All right, but I don't look forward to telling Phineus about this. He's itching for a look inside."

"Would you like me to speak with him?"

Da'ad shook his head. "No, I'll talk to him. I have some work for him to do anyway."

"There's not really much to see yet. Everything is far too wet, and there is a strong musty smell," Leatis explained.

Da'ad escorted the team back to camp where Phineus was waiting. The colonel shook his head as he approached. "You're not going to like this."

"What is it?"

"The interior is still too wet to enter. Leatis recommends that we wait at least a week to let things air out."

"A week is a long time. What are we going to do while we wait?"

"I think I'll have the group work on the camp for a while. In the meantime, I would like you to see what you can do about designing and building some stands for lighting."

"I'll speak with the elves. They should be able to gather the necessary materials."

"Very well, I'll see you at dinner, old man."

Da'ad left Phineus and returned to his tent.

A week and half went by before Leatis reported that the caverns were dry enough to enter. With Phineus hovering near, Da'ad nodded his approval.

"Very well. Let me get dressed, and I'll meet you at the entrance."

Phineus followed Leatis outside while Da'ad struggled to pull on his boots. The dry lakebed was covered with gravel near the edges. The stone made a loud cracking sound as the men walked across it.

"It's still wet in places, so be careful," Leatis cautioned.

Phineus was about to lead the way inside when Da'ad stopped him. "Let Leatis take the lead. I don't need to be carrying anyone out of here."

"At least give him my lantern. It's the brightest light we have and would serve us best in the lead." Da'ad agreed, and Phineus handed the lantern to Leatis. The cave was formed in such a way that even with Phineus's lantern and numerous torches, much of it remained shrouded in darkness. There was still a strong musty smell inside, typical of an area long under water. Parts of the floor remained very wet, making the rocky surface slick and difficult to traverse.

Da'ad's men hammered numerous metal torch holders into the rocky walls. The first chamber was a large open area, apparently of natural origin. The chamber was artificially enlarged, probably on several occasions.

Two of Phineus's stands were placed near the center. The torchlight revealed a small corridor leading up to a large artificial room. The ceiling was well over thirty feet high. The walls were largely smooth and spanned at least one hundred feet in each direction. The room did not appear to have been entirely submerged. Some damp artifacts were scattered near the entrance and in the low-lying areas of the chamber. Even so, most of the room was quite dry.

"The water must have only reached six or seven feet in here," Phineus suggested.

Leatis stepped forward. "There is some evidence of water in here, but I doubt it was ever that high. The watermarks on the walls only reach a foot or two in the lower portions of the chamber. I suspect that most of the room was never wet."

Phineus nodded. "Yes, perhaps you are right. Those are water marks."

"We have been gradually moving uphill, Colonel. I estimate that we are a foot or two above the original lake level right now.

"That would mean that the lake level was higher than we found it at some point."

"Very good, Thoren."

"I don't know where the water might have gone though. The bed is clearly defined and doesn't extend out beyond what we drained."

"There is some evidence that the water may have extended out to our camp many centuries ago. It's very faint but possible," Phineus remarked.

Leatis shook his head. "No, I think these marks were created from a different source." He pointed to a small trickle of water running down the wall.

"An underground spring."

"I suspect that the spring must have caused occasional pooling in the low-lying areas. That's very likely what created the watermarks."

"There must be another passage around here. Look around and see if you can find it," Da'ad ordered.

"It's over here," one of the soldiers called out, nearly a minute later.

Most of the others hurried to the passage. There was a small stairway leading up to a vastly larger chamber. The chamber appeared to be the remnants of an even larger room. Several big rocks covered what might have been an opening to the outside.

The outer wall had a number of small windows cut into it near the ceiling. The windows provided minimal light at certain hours of the day. There was a massive steel chandelier hanging from the center of the room. It was covered in melted wax and cobwebs.

Da'ad's men hurried to hang torches along the walls. The light revealed a great skeleton in the far corner.

"Dragons!" Phineus called excitedly.

"I see the remains of only one dragon," Leatis corrected.

"What's that over there?" Da'ad asked, pointing away from the dragon.

"Cages. They were likely used to store food for the dragon," Leatis replied.

"Food?" one of the men asked.

"Yes. The chamber is many centuries old. Undoubtedly it comes from a more barbaric period when intelligent beings were sometimes sacrificed to pacify the dragon's hunger."

"You don't mean human sacrifice, do you?" Phineus nervously inquired.

"Probably not in this case. The remains here are orc. Nonetheless, human sacrifice has occurred in the past."

"We've found remains of humans, elves, and even dwarves scattered about the chamber. You don't suppose they were all sacrifices, do you?"

"I do not think so. There is evidence of a fight here. Many of the remains are clothed in armor or grasping weapons. Some of them are slightly charred. They appear to have been fighting the dragon. This might be what killed the beast."

"How long would you estimate this creature was?" Phineus asked as he looked over the bones.

"From the look of it, I'd say almost sixty feet," Riada observed.

"Fascinating. The largest dragon observed over the past century was not quit fifty feet long. This skeleton is nearly ten feet longer," Phineus remarked.

"What are you suggesting?" Bek inquired.

"Only that this may be the tomb of some past dragon lord. If we can narrow down the date, it may be possible to say which one."

Leatis interrupted, "Here." He held up a pair of arrowheads and continued, "The presence of spear and arrowheads confirms my suspicion. The men and elves were fighting the dragon. This one is human. Some of the others are elvish. The presence of battle axes implies participation by the dwarves."

"I've never heard of any of these races working closely with orcs," Riada observed.

"They didn't. The orcs were caged. It remains possible that they were already dead. At any rate, they were never released." Leatis pointed to one of the cages. "See there. The lock is still fastened."

"Over here!" one of the scouts called. He moved his torch across the wall, revealing several crude paintings.

Phineus borrowed his lantern back and examined the wall closely. "They appear to depict the battle. This may be a type of memorial." He glanced across the bottom of the wall and excitedly announced, "Yes. Down here. Do you see it?"

"Elvish writing," Leatis remarked curiously. "This is an unusual memorial for elves. One of the men must have written it. Elvish has long been common among the human settlements here."

"It's difficult to make out the letters. Can you read it?" Da'ad asked.

"Partially. It describes how the men and elves slew a dragon named Vort. The beast raided the villages for cattle and people. Evidently, the villagers arranged to sacrifice orcs and thieves to it until a new king put an end to the practice. These soldiers, or at least the humans, were from Grenalt. I think it likely that the practice of human sacrifice was ended when this territory became part of the Grenalt Alliance," one of the elf scholars remarked.

"The battle must have occurred soon after the collapse of the Aepaethian Empire. I never would have guessed that it was that long ago," Phineus noted.

"I suspect that the mountain must have been sealed shortly after the fight. That's probably when the dam was built," Leatis added.

Phineus nodded. "That would have been around the time Reglis died. It certainly fits the prevailing theory. Still, I wonder why they built it."

"Perhaps that was their intention all along and the dragon was in the way," one of the elves suggested.

"Or maybe they just wanted to keep people out of here," Phineus speculated.

"Whatever the reason, we have a job to do, and I suggest we get started." Da'ad motioned to another stairwell. "Shall we check it out?"

Leatis nodded and quietly led the way.

Riada moved forward. "Of course, I'm no expert, but I would swear this stairwell is of dwarf design."

"Your instincts are good, Sergeant. This is dwarf architecture," Leatis explained.

"It's very different from the architecture below."

"The lower caverns were partially created by the mountain and partially by that dragon. The dragon cave was probably carved out well after these columns were set in place," one of the elves replied.

"Strange that the ceilings would be so high."

"Not really. Dwarves often constructed their facilities to accommodate other races. They prefer high-vaulted ceilings and large rooms," Leatis explained.

"It's very well preserved up here," one of the men observed.

The group fanned out among the room's numerous columns. The hall was lined with burned-out torches, some of which the men replaced. "What's that smell?" a soldier asked.

"Yes, I smell it too, a very faint, sickly sweet odor," another remarked.

"I know this scent all too well." Da'ad's jaw tightened. "That's the smell of death. There are bodies near here."

"Strange that in all this time it would still stink," Leatis observed.

"And yet it does. Search the area and see if you can find where that smell is coming from."

"Shouldn't we better spend our time searching for Reglis?" Phineus asked.

"The Liche King said the amulet would be in a tomb," Riada remarked.

"A likely place for an odor like this," Leatis noted.

"Yes, of course. I wasn't thinking."

After a few minutes, one of the soldiers emerged from a narrow passageway and called out, "This way, sir!" He motioned with his hand then re-entered the passage. Da'ad entered a short distance behind. He was led to a dark room, about twenty meters across.

The odor was stronger in the room, and Da'ad was forced to cover his mouth and nose. One of his soldiers choked up and exited. Along the walls were hundreds of corpses, all of them dwarves. They were stacked neatly, one on top of the other. Most of the bodies were dried out.

Phineus peered inside over Da'ad's shoulder. "Do you think this is it? What we're looking for, I mean? Not at all what I was expecting."

"Not what I was expecting either."

Da'ad turned around, facing Leatis. "What do you make of all this?"

"It is definitely not the tomb of Reglis. He was too well regarded to be given a common burial. He may yet be buried elsewhere in these caverns, but we will not find him here."

"Then I see no reason to tarry. Move everyone back to the main hall. Let's have another look around. See if we can't find some record of what went on here."

The elf scholars agreed. "The dwarves were very fond of histories. They often placed them in or near tombs."

The group pressed forward, carefully examining several similar side chambers but found little of interest. There was a table near the end of the hall resembling an altar. It was well made and finely painted with gold leaves. The top opened, revealing a cushioned interior of red satin and a large book. One of the elves removed the book and began turning its pages very carefully. "It is a history, though not likely to be of much use to us."

"Why is that?"

The scholar flipped through several pages before answering. "It's a war journal, written by a dwarf general. The book is dated several hundred years before the death of Reglis."

Phineus stepped forward to speak with Da'ad. "There is another staircase headed up. Perhaps if we follow it, we might find what we are looking for."

Da'ad agreed. The next level was partially lit by mirrors, reflecting sunlight into the chamber through holes in the ceiling. The lighting was short lived, lasting only a few hours each day. It was already fading when Da'ad's men entered.

The hall was well decorated with lavish art and furniture. The expensive décor was a stark contrast with the appearance of lower levels.

Phineus believed this to be a good sign. "Based on the décor, I would wager we're getting closer."

"I'd say that's a fair bet," Riada agreed.

Leatis turned to Da'ad. "This is more what I expected to find surrounding Reglis's tomb, though it is still not quite right."

"What do you mean?"

"Most of these decorations are dwarven. Reglis was a wizard, not a dwarf. While it is possible that the dwarves might have buried him, I doubt they would have honored him as one of their own. This looks to me like a mere ceremonial chamber. Notice the tables and chairs, the dishes and drinking paraphernalia. None of this would fit Reglis's circumstances. They would have found artifacts more appropriate for a wizard, possibly even magical."

One of the scholars agreed. "He is right. This looks to me like an ancient dwarf dining hall used to celebrate the passing of the soul from one life to the next."

The other scholar moved to the altar and examined a large copper statue. There was a plaque fastened at its base. "This statue was erected to honor a great war hero. Ordinarily, the dwarves would never bury one who died of natural causes in a place like this, but this man appears to be an exception."

"That is correct. Normally, only those slain in battle would be celebrated here, but I have heard of situations like this where warriors who distinguished themselves in combat and survived have been granted the honor, in spite of a natural death. Such honors were usually reserved for only the most courageous soldiers. It was said to be a very rare honor, possibly only bestowed twice," the other scholar added.

"If that's true, then it appears we're looking at a depiction of one of the two," Da'ad observed.

"Very fascinating, the ancient dwarf culture. It was strong on honor and discipline."

"What changed?" Riada asked.

Phineus turned to respond. "There are few today who even remember the old ways."

"You've explained the tables and chairs. What about the rest of this furniture?" Da'ad inquired.

"I should think that obvious, sir. The stone benches are lined up in front of the altar for ceremonies. When they were finished with the service, they would join each other at the tables, to our right, and toast the dead," Leatis remarked.

"You studied ancient dwarf culture?"

Leatis shook his head. "Not at all. It just seems the most logical function given the layout of the room."

Phineus was impressed. "He is correct. The ceremony would have been held first, and the tables were used for feasts where toasts to the departed were common."

He picked up a book and turned to the first page. "This is a typical example of an opening toast. 'We who are living toast the honored dead. Until we are reunited in time, may fortune guide our way.'"

Realizing that time was against them, Da'ad ordered everyone to gather what records they could find and carry them back to camp before dusk.

"Do you think the dwarves will approve?" one of the soldiers asked.

"I doubt they even know this place exists anymore."

One of the elves was fascinated with a large book resting atop the altar. Its leather cover was old and weathered. The gold leaf was flaking in places, and the title was worn from the spine. The book measured nearly sixteen inches across and was twenty inches tall. With its binding, it was approximately three inches thick. The spine was broken in several places. The pages were dry and brittle. Much of the ink had faded.

As the elf worked to decipher the first few lines, Phineus joined him. The book was written in ancient elvish, a fact the scholars found odd given its presence in a dwarf tomb.

"The book is an ancient history, largely specific to the region. It was written by one Venton of Turnbull and is at least eight centuries old."

"Take it back to camp with the others. I'm sure it will make a fine addition to the library. We best wrap this up for the night. It's getting late, and most of us haven't eaten since breakfast."

The men gradually returned to the camp, putting out their torches and lanterns as they went. Phineus followed Da'ad outside. "What do you think about our first day?"

"I'm a little surprised. I'm not sure what I expected to find, but I don't think that was it."

"Well, there is still plenty to explore. Maybe we'll get closer in the morning."

"Let us hope not. My expectation is for danger."

"I see. You are quite right to be cautious. Tombs of this nature have often been rigged with hidden traps and dangers. I'm surprised we haven't encountered any already."

"As you've pointed out, there is always tomorrow."

"I had best start work on the records we removed. There are quite a lot of them, and I hope to have them sorted by morning. The elves are probably waiting for me as we speak."

"Very well. I'll see you in the morning." Da'ad took a seat near the fire pit as one of the cooks handed him his supper.

Bek seated himself next to him. "So what do you think we'll find in the morning?"

"I hope we'll find what we're looking for."

"What's that? A dead wizard?" Riada chided.

Da'ad scowled. "Much more than that. I would never have ventured this far for a mere corpse."

"What do think is in there with him?"

"If Reglis is in there, I don't imagine he will be unprotected."

"You think we'll run into traps then?"

"If this is the right place, then not just traps. I think we'll run into much worse."

"Let us hope not."

Unable to finish his meal, Da'ad retired to his tent.

When morning arrived, the team ate an early breakfast and then returned to the mountain. As they walked upstairs, Phineus followed Da'ad. "The records we were sorting confirmed much of what we believed about the upper levels. They were most definitely used for funeral ceremonies."

"Did any of them mention Reglis?"

"Not at all. It's not surprising though. Nearly all of the books were dated before Reglis's death."

As the team entered the upper level, Da'ad ordered them up the stairwell. Leatis led the way. The final floor was well lit by sunlight and required no torches. Bek took a moment to study one of the several holes carved into the floor, where reflected light streamed down to the level below.

"Fascinating feature. Did you know that reflected light has been in use for well over a thousand years?"

Da'ad shook his head.

The floor was only partially covered and had numerous open windows leading to the outside. There were several stone benches resting along the walls. Some of Da'ad's men took a moment to rest themselves. The ceiling was partially open, allowing plenty of sunlight in. Not quite forty feet from the stairs, the room opened enitrely to the outside. The floor continued another sixty feet, ending at a small dirt path that ran around the mountainside.

From the path, Da'ad could see the tops of neighboring mountains to the west. A few scattered trees provided mild shade. There were several small patches of grass lining the trail where it wrapped around the mountain. The path ended at a massive stone door. There were no obvious handles or levers to open it.

Da'ad felt around the frame. "Search for some means of getting inside."

Phineus soon displaced him. "This could be it. What we're looking for, I mean."

He removed a small knife and began poking around the doorframe. After several seconds, he called out, "Here. I think I've found it."

"Found what?" one of the others asked.

"A way inside." Phineus released a lever, revealing a small hidden door.

Da'ad selected the smallest of his men to enter. The soldier took off his armor and carefully squeezed into the narrow passage. He slid inside on his belly. One of the others passed a torch behind him.

"Can you see a lever or anything near the door?" Phineus asked.

"Not yet. My eyes still haven't adjusted."

"Take your time. Let me know when you're ready."

"All right, I've found what might be a lever!"

Phineus asked him to describe it and then instructed, "All right. Go ahead and pull it toward the door. It should enable us to enter."

Moments later the door swung slightly in. "Push on it!" Phineus shouted. Several of the men responded until the door began to open. Everyone looked at each other expectantly.

"Shall we go inside, or are we going to wait here all day?" Riada asked after nearly a minute.

"I thought I'd leave that up to you," Da'ad replied. He ordered two of his soldiers to remain outside and then drew his sword and entered slowly. Riada followed. Leatis entered next, with most of the others in tow.

The walls of the chamber were lined with fresh torches, most of them never used. Da'ad inspected one. "They look all right. Try lighting them and see what happens."

Riada bowed respectfully. Within moments, visibility improved and several oddly shaped trees came into view.

"Trees inside a mountain?" Phineus asked curiously.

"Yes, very curious, indeed," Leatis remarked.

As Phineus used his lantern to examine the nearest tree, one of the Paladins noticed a slight glimmer in the wood. He removed a knife from his belt and attempted to pry the object loose. Something seeped from the wood onto his hands, causing him to back away. "This sap feels like blood."

Leatis hurried forward to examine it. "This is blood."

Da'ad requested an explanation. Both Phineus and Leatis continued to examine the tree for several minutes.

"This tree looks almost human." Phineus gasped as he noticed what appeared to be a face on it.

Leatis approached him from behind. "I believe these trees were once human."

"Good chance of it. I don't think we should tarry any longer than necessary."

Da'ad placed his hand on Phineus's shoulder. "Agreed, but first let's find out what this place is." He excused most of the men from the chamber, sending them back outside. Several of them seemed relieved. Only Da'ad, the two elvish scholars, Riada, Bek, Leatis, and Phineus remained.

They proceeded cautiously past the trees toward a closed door. The door appeared to be made of wood, overlaid with metal, possibly gold. There was an inscription above it. Da'ad held up his torch, enabling one of the scholars to read it.

"Do not remove anything from this chamber except the amulet we were sent for."

"Why? What does it say?" Da'ad asked.

"It is a curse. If we take anything from the treasure, we will become as the trees we just passed."

Da'ad inhaled momentarily then let the air out slowly. "You heard him. Take nothing but the amulet."

The door stuck badly. The men eventually had to pry it, using the hilt of a sword and a large pole. They pulled it open several inches at a time until the opening was wide enough that they could easily enter two by two.

The room inside was small by comparison with the outer chamber. It extended only a dozen or so feet from the door and somewhat less from side to side. The interior was filled with fancy treasures. The room was dark, making it difficult for the men to see the full extent of the wealth inside. Da'ad hung his torch along the wall and replaced another, instantly improving visibility.

There was a large, stone casket across from the door resting along the walls where they met in the corner. With the torches in place, the casket was reasonably well lit. The lid was carved with intricate elvish designs. The two elvish scholars marveled at its detail. They attempted to decipher a number of small markings along the casket's outer edge.

"These markings are a warning to those who would steal the treasures of this room. There is no doubt that those trees were once human. The gem we attempted to remove from one of them must have been a part of this treasure."

"Remember, take nothing. If you find the amulet, let me know, and I will pick it up. Do the markings give any indication of who is buried here?" Da'ad asked.

The elf pointed to another engraving. "This appears to be the final resting place of the wizard Reglis."

"Then this is the legendary treasure of Reglis? I was under the impression it was much larger than this."

"Impossible. This cannot be the treasure of Reglis," Phineus interupted.

Da'ad was about to inquire why not when one of the elves concurred. "He is right. This may be the wizard's final resting place, but this is not his treasure. The vaults are most likely located elsewhere and would certainly be much larger."

"Didn't the Liche King tell us he would show us the way to the vaults after we return from the tomb?" Bek reminded the others.

Da'ad nodded thoughtfully. "Something like that."

"What we are looking at is what the people of the time often termed a funeral offering. It represents only a token portion of the deceased man's wealth and was left behind as a tribute. It is possible, even likely, that this was not even part of the treasure. The peoples of this region may have gathered it as a tribute after the original treasure was hidden," one of the elves remarked.

"That's a good possibility. The original treasure was said to have been hidden by Reglis while he was still alive. It is unlikely, given his character, that he would have reserved anything for his tomb."

"We should remove the cover and have a look at the body. If Reglis did keep anything from his treasure, such as an amulet, it would almost certainly be with the body."

Da'ad and Bek moved to one side of the casket while Leatis and the elvish scholars moved to the other. Phineus remained at the end. Together, they slowly pried the lid upward, loosening it enough that they were able to fit a knife beneath it. Bek seemed a little nervous as they moved the lid to the side, away from the wall. Riada joked to ease the tension.

Da'ad quickly silenced him.

"I have a very bad feeling about this. Something is not right here," Bek interupted as the others inspected the body.

"It's just your imagination," Riada replied.

Da'ad shook his head. "No. I sense it too."

The corpse was dressed in fancy armor and partially covered with a shield on top. The upper shield was inscribed in elvish.

Da'ad read it aloud. "Here lies Reglis, greatest of the wizards." The lower half of the shield was inscribed in a language unfamiliar to him.

"It is written in the language of the centaurs," one of the elves noted.

"What does it say?"

"It says, 'Warning to those who plunder this tomb. Death be a blessing to thee.'"

The elf swallowed nervously. "The treasure is most definitely cursed. Do not touch it."

"What of the body? We need to find that amulet."

"It is probably around his neck. If you move the shield, it should be visible."

Da'ad took a deep breath. "Well, here goes."

He removed the shield, grasping it with both hands, and set it next to the casket lid. As expected, the amulet was visible around the neck. Da'ad looked nervously at the scholars for an instant.

"Raelian implied it would be safe to remove the piece."

Riada raised his brow. "If you believe him, then go ahead."

Da'ad took another deep breath and reached for the amulet. It was attached to a thick chain around the dead wizard's neck. He carefully removed the piece and was pulling it away when the corpse suddenly grabbed him by the wrist. Da'ad panicked, dropping the amulet back into the casket, and then let out a slight yelp. The corpse released him as it sat up, uttering something in a strange tongue.

Phineus translated, "He who carries my amulet shall not rest. Understanding is the key. Great is its power, greater its price."

After issuing its warning, the lifeless corpse collapsed back into the casket. Da'ad quickly reached for the amulet.

Riada watched nervously. "Let's get out of here before we end up permanent fixtures in this place."

Da'ad nodded.

He waited for the others to exit and then tucked the amulet into his shirt and followed. He held his breath momentarily. After a few seconds, he led the others back to camp.

RETURN TO RAELIAN

It was late afternoon when the group exited the cave. Da'ad decided to remain in camp for an extra night. He turned the amulet over temporarily to the elves.

The scholars, including Phineus, studied it thoroughly until night and deciphered several small markings on its underside. The markings were written in a form of ancient elvish, which read, "Wisdom is the key to understanding."

Phineus made a rough sketch of the entire piece, front and back, intending to research it when he returned to Tabor. Unable to decipher anything more, the scholars returned the piece to Da'ad.

Despite his great fatigue and exhaustion, Da'ad spent the night tossing in a state of semiconsciousness. It was as if he were haunted by some unseen force. His attention was constantly taken back to the small amulet now sitting on the ground near his bed. It seemed at times to glow but gave off no light. Da'ad could almost hear it speaking to him.

He attempted to cover it but could not silence its unspoken call. All night, he sensed the strange vibration around him as it filled him with a terrible dread. By morning, the others could easily tell that he had not slept.

Phineus offered to make him a home remedy for sleep, but Da'ad refused. "We need to deliver this piece to the mountains without delay."

⁂

The team traveled for two and a half days before reaching the mountain pass, a journey that would ordinarily take four. Many of the group managed to sleep for several hours at a time in the backs of the carts. Da'ad remained awake the entire distance, never allowing the column to stop for more than a few minutes. He seemed a man possessed as the team approached the pass.

"Are you all right, Thoren? Perhaps I should hold that thing for a while and let you get some rest before we enter the mountains."

"I'll be all right. I think it's best if we get rid of it sooner rather than later."

From a short distance away, Bek called out, "I see the cliffs, sir." He hoped this bit of good news would cheer his restless commander.

Da'ad smiled slightly but said only, "Proceed," in a very exhausted voice.

By nightfall, the party was entering the thick blanket of fog surrounding the lower cliffs. Several troops requested that they be allowed to wait until morning, but in his impaired state, Da'ad insisted on continuing.

Strangely, the fog let up almost the instant they entered the pass. Before long, the soldiers found themselves surrounded by armed Liches. The creatures' eyes glowed eerily as they watched the men.

After a minute, Da'ad recognized the familiar outline of the Liche King, Raelian. The towering figure, dressed in ancient armor, approached slowly with his sword drawn in front of him, his skeletal fingers wrapped tightly around it. His voice was haunting.

"Where is it? Where is the amulet?"

Da'ad did not immediately respond. He waited several seconds before stating in a subdued voice, "It is safe."

Raelian sensed Da'ad's continued distrust. "I have done many things in this world for which I am ashamed, but I have never gone back on my word. Give me the amulet, and I will provide you with what you need." Raelian paused. "We share a mutual enemy, you and I. It is to both of our benefit that we cooperate."

"How can we know you speak the truth?"

"You are a Paladin, Colonel! Trust your instincts." Raelian paused, contemplating something, and then muttered a few barely audible words, after which he raised his head. "I have something for you."

He held out a ring. "Take it. This is the ring of truth. It glows red when the wearer is lied to. Keep it close. It will serve you well on your quest. I would leave you with more, but first I require the amulet. Give it to me!"

Da'ad slowly removed the golden piece from his pocket and glanced at it.

"Hand it to me, Colonel. Your dreams of late have been troubled, have they not? You will find no rest until this item is out of your possession. It is of no use to you. Give it to me now!"

Raelian extended his hand to take the piece. Da'ad hesitated before placing the tiny amulet into the Liche King's bony fingers. As he took possession of the artifact, Raelian smiled deviously. Da'ad seemed oddly pleased to be rid of it.

Satisfied that the piece was real, Raelian looked to Da'ad. "There was a curse placed upon this piece at the death of Reglis. The amulet of Reglis has great power, but those who wield it live a cursed life. It has the power to drive an ordinary man insane. The curse will not harm you further now that the charm is out of your possession."

Raelian attached the amulet to a golden chain around his neck. The Liche King raised a hand high into the air. "Now for the assistance I promised to give you."

Several of his servants approached, bearing gifts, which the king took one at a time and presented to Da'ad. He began with a sword. "Present this to your most trusted deputy. It is made of the strongest steel and will never dull."

He then picked up a shield and passed it to Riada. "Handle this shield with care. It will not only protect you in battle but glows on the underside with a faint green light when an enemy is near."

Da'ad turned the sword over to Bek, who tucked it away. Raelian turned to Phineus with one final gift. "This is one of only a very few copies of the wizard's text. When placed over a text, it instantly renders the words readable to your mind. Keep these gifts safe, and they will aid you on your journey."

Raelian stepped back, bowing slightly as he thanked Da'ad and the others for their assistance, assuring them that they had nothing to fear from him. He then turned and disappeared into the night with all of his followers, dropping something as he left. Da'ad sent Bek to retrieve it.

"It's a small map!" Bek shouted as he picked it up.

He handed it to Da'ad, who observed, "It appears to show the location of the vaults." The paper was old and fragile. Da'ad handed it to Phineus. "Keep this safe."

Phineus placed it within the pages of a large book. He suggested, "We should return to Tabor where I can compare this to other known maps of the area. I should be able to work out the location in a matter of days."

"Very well. Set course for Tabor." The group set up camp just outside the pass.

Da'ad felt much better after a good night's sleep and quickly ordered the team to proceed east along the mountains.

The rains caused the river to swell above its banks, prompting them to move farther south around the floodwaters. This cost the team several hours but was the safest course. They eventually stopped at a tiny fishing village some distance from the pass. Da'ad entered a small shop run by an old fisherman and his wife.

The entrance was obscured by numerous cats resting on the remnants of old fishing gear. An overturned rowboat rested along the outside wall. The wood was weathered and unpainted. From the look of the building, Da'ad could see that it had been repaired many times.

The old shopkeeper motioned for him to enter. The building was very well lit, by both candlelight and at least half a dozen windows, including a strange-looking skylight draped with fishing net. Da'ad paid the man for several dozen midsized fish, most of them caught earlier in the day.

His soldiers cleaned the fish and then turned them over to the cooks for dinner. Some of the men continued watching the mountains near the Red Cliffs. There was an odd weather system forming there. It left many with the unholy feeling that some great curse had been unleashed on the land. Da'ad was grateful to be rid of the place.

THE NEW ACROPILLIAN EMPIRE

As the streets of Acropilla bustled with excitement, a new emperor prepared to address his subjects. Having disposed of an unpopular king, General Parcian Kerr picked up the reins of the empire and promised to rid the nation of crime. He was understandably popular with the masses.

Before stepping outside, he called forward a tall, white-haired man. The man was dressed in modest robes and his face concealed beneath a long, bushy beard. Most of the general's staff believed him to be a soothsayer, though until he approached, none knew for certain. He shook a number of dice and a sack full of charms and then spilled them into a metal dish and began to prophesy.

"I see a vast army under your command. Your name shall be feared in all the land, and you shall never be defeated by the sword."

The new Acropillian leader seemed pleased. He handed the man a sack of gold and smiled. "Thank you for your time."

As soon as the old prophet was gone, Kerr turned to his left and watched as a tall, dark-haired woman entered the room. Her appearance accompanied a sudden drop in temperature. Though it would have been a stretch to call her beautiful, she was by no means ugly. There was something very peculiar about her. She approached the throne and whispered in the general's ear. Many of those present remained wary of her. When she was finished, she departed as quickly as she entered.

General Kerr stood and requested a glass of water. He wet his mouth and then walked to the nearest balcony and waved to the gathered crowd. He smiled and introduced himself with a bit of light humor. The crowd laughed until he raised his hand to silence them.

"My fellow citizens, I have never sought to be your emperor, but as a concerned citizen myself, I will not shirk my duty. Together, we will take back the streets of this city and reclaim a position of greatness among nations."

The crowd cheered, after which Kerr recited part of a lyric commemorating the nation's first leader.

He concluded, "I thank you for your trust and know that together we will shall do great things for this nation. Together, we shall restore prestige to Acropilla."

After waving to the crowd, he re-entered the palace. His troops had been rounding up thieves, prostitutes, and other criminals by the thousands. No one knew for certain where they were taken, but few cared so long as the streets were safe.

Acropilla had once been seat of government for one of the Fairylands' greatest nations. Now it was a nation in decay, desperate for recovery. There was poverty everywhere, and until recently the people had come to expect little relief.

King Reginald, the deposed monarch, was thought of as too tolerant of the petty crime that ruled the streets. He lived a life of waste and excess while his people struggled for survival. It was little wonder that they flocked to support his overthrow.

General Kerr was never the obvious choice to succeed him. Though a prominent military man, the general grew up in the small, obscure provenance of Phalon. His reputation for honesty earned him recognition among the people, and his military prowess made him a favorite among the nobles, many of whom believed they could easily sway his favor.

The general had been far less a champion of elitist rights than expected, favoring more popular policies. Relying on the nobles to fund many of his activities, he largely benefited the working class. Many of the nobles feared him, though few were willing to openly challenge his policies for fear of the people.

Ironically, many of these same nobles had once begged the general to step in. They now believed that they made a mistake and hoped that there was still time enough to correct it. While General Kerr enjoyed great popularity among the people, there remained undercurrents of revolt among the nobles. Still lacking strength enough for a proper fight, most remained silent, biding their time.

General Kerr often spoke of tolerance, but in private, he pushed hard to silence dissention, citing a need for national unity. He asserted that for the nation to become great, its people must see and hear from a common vantage point. Those who challenged him were often run out of town. Many simply vanished, though the general was never directly connected to any such disappearances. Most believed that his overzealous supporters drove them off.

General Kerr was widely regarded as a good leader, acting strongly on his convictions. He was a student of politics and of government, as well as military tactics. His generosity was known throughout the Fairylands. He had even donated financial support to the Paladins of Gant.

Under his leadership, the Acropillian Empire was beginning to enjoy true peace for the first time in decades. The army continued to cart off criminals to unknown locations, presumably outside the city. Few cared what became of the deposed king.

Plans were made to woo powerful allies to the Acropillian cause. Diplomats were sent to all of the major cities, embassies were established, and treaties signed. General Kerr spent much of his time entertaining leaders and high-profile guests. He even sent a dinner invitation to General Mayweather. Kerr had spared no expense and made it clear that he expected all of his guests to have a good time.

General Mayweather was busy when the invitation arrived. It was received for him by a young captain named Vorn. He delivered it that evening with the general's meal. General Mayweather initially shrugged it off but reconsidered at the bequest of his aide.

He sat quietly at his desk pondering the matter for several minutes. The general was not fond of such events and ordinarily would have sent Da'ad, but as Da'ad was absent, he was faced with the task of accepting himself or sending his regrets.

He turned to Captain Vorn. "You come from that part of the continent, correct?" Vorn reluctantly nodded.

"How would you like to take a trip?"

Vorn shrugged with indifference. "If you like, sir." He paused. "Perhaps Lieutenant Orgavire might be a more appropriate choice. I really don't remember much of the area. I was very young when I left." After another pause, he added, "I understand that the lieutenant lived there until recently. I believe he is even personally acquainted with General Kerr."

General Mayweather nodded. "Very well, inform Lieutenant Orgavire to meet me in one hour."

Vorn seemed relieved not to be going. He nodded politely and then disappeared down the hall.

General Mayweather turned back to his desk and began sorting a small stack of papers. His mind was not on the papers. Something was troubling him. Still, he did not know yet what.

Somewhat tired, the general glanced at a large map on the wall. He stared intently at the territory marked Acropilla. His face was contorted with suspicion. He remained in his office for some time until Lieutenant Orgavire arrived.

Lieutenant Orgavire was a thin, pale-skinned man whose features were somewhat sickly. He was healthy enough, though his countenance was very unlike that of a man in his prime.

There was a foreboding look to him, one that seemed to warn, "stay away." With a voice that was raspy and tired, General Mayweather invited, "I am traveling to Acropilla and would like you to accompany me. I understand that you know our host, General Kerr."

"I am acquainted with him."

"Good, what can you tell me about him?"

"Not much that you don't already know. I'm afraid he is a very private man. I merely served under him for a time."

"He has invited us to a dinner. This is purely a social visit, and I would like to keep as low a profile as possible."

"I understand."

THE FALL OF ROSEWOOD

Near the Red Cliffs, a tempest was growing. Thunder and lightning roared across the sky. Rain poured down on the land, forming a vast network of streams and mud. The mixture of water and the red soil closely resembled a great sea of blood.

The Liche King, Raelian, rallied his followers with repeated calls to arms. So terrible was the sound of his voice that the earth trembled when he spoke. With great force, he wielded the amulet of Reglis, announcing, "Make haste, my friends, for tonight vengeance is ours! Take no prisoners. Let none survive. Destroy every building and slay every beast until the city of the necromancers is no more!"

He looked at the amulet and whispered, "Now, little treasure, let your mist free us from our mountain prison." As he led the Liche hordes toward the unsuspecting city of Rosewood, the sound of their feet echoed through the mountains like drums.

"Destroy them all!" the Liches shouted as they marched mercilessly. It took the necromancers only moments to realize that something was wrong. Within minutes, the city of Rosewood was preparing for war. Its citizens hid behind their fortified shelters. Vast hordes of skeletal warriors, ghosts, and the undead gathered to the west, forming a wall between the approaching liches and the city.

❦

Elsewhere, in a dark dungeonlike room, a witch opened a secret chamber and stood above a round reflection dish. She moved her right hand over the water and watched as an image formed across its surface. A badly scarred face appeared.

"Why have you summoned me, Colonel?"

"My lady, Rosewood has come under siege. I haven't determined who is attacking, but some of the residents did mention the name King Raelian. Does it mean anything to you?"

The witch stepped back momentarily. "So the Liches have escaped their mountain prison." She returned to the dish and ordered, "Get your people out of there, Colonel. Your mission in Rosewood is over. Return at once."

"That may not be possible at the moment. Word has reached us that the pass is blocked. We may have to hold out until the fighting is over. I will summon you when it ends. We believe that they are still a day or more away."

The witch moved her hand back over the water, erasing the image. She stood silently for several seconds then ran her hand slowly over the dish again, until the water turned black and a deep penetrating voice emerged.

"Why have you called?"

"Forgive me, Master, but something has come up."

"What is it?"

"Rosewood has come under seige. It seems Raelian has escaped his prison and is moving to destroy the city."

"My sources informed me that something was happening there. Raelian must have acquired the Amulet of Reglis. We will no longer be able to rely on the necromancers. Begin work on the Mantra at once."

"Yes, Master."

Rosewood's preparations continued for two days until the massive Liche army appeared on the distant horizon. Word of its approach was quick to reach the ears of the city's defenders. They rushed to assemble the elders and called on the spirits of the dead to defend them, but neither those spirits nor the vast skeletal army were any match for the rage of the Liches.

The battle commenced for several days as Rosewood was slowly but completely devoured by the vengeance of Raelian. True to their oath, the Liches slaughtered every living creature. Noble as the necromancers' defense was, it proved futile. In the end, none survived. Prisoners praying for mercy were given none.

When the last of the necromancers was dragged from his hiding place, Raelian raised the amulet high into the air and proclaimed, "Now the deed is done. Now, we may rest at last. Search their archives. Destroy all records of their experiments. Topple their buildings, and lay waste to this land. From this day forth, let nothing grow here. May this land be forever cursed to remain dead and desolate."

In Thornguard, General Mayweather was eager to get under way. He rode with a half dozen others. Lieutenant Orgavire remained somewhat isolated, riding several lengths behind the rest of the company.

Eventually, General Mayweather's party reached the pass, where they happened upon a wounded soldier crawling frantically along the road.

"Sergeant! Take someone and see to that man."

The sergeant nodded and rode quickly in the company of another. They lifted the man onto a horse and rejoined the others.

The general approached the wounded man. "What happened?"

The soldier's words were broken by frequent gasps mixed with incoherent utterances. It took several minutes for him to get out the words ambushed and orcs.

The Paladins could make little sense of his speech beyond that. They treated his injuries as best they could. After several minutes he began to recover his bearings.

"What happened?" General Mayweather asked again.

"Our convoy was attacked."

With some effort, the wounded soldier pointed to the south, his hand shaking badly. "The goblins, they ambushed us."

The Paladins looked up and noticed several goblins moving in the distant rocks. The creatures were watching the group closely.

"Load him onto a horse, and we'll retreat to the hills."

The rocky and forested terrain provided some cover. General Mayweather ordered his soldiers to pick off the goblin leaders if combat became inevitable.

"What of the convoy?" one of the soldiers asked.

The general's face grew dim. "We cannot help them."

The Paladin's flight was swift, and the goblins quickly lost sight of them. General Mayweather was a master of camouflage and kept his troops well hidden until nightfall. The goblins were easily discouraged and soon gave up. The general, on the other hand, was not so easily discouraged.

From a distance, he pursued the beasts back to their camp. The Paladins picked off a few stragglers. After the goblins retired, the soldiers entered their camp. The night sky was clear but with no moon. the goblins never knew the Paladins were there.

After making an inconclusive inspection, General Mayweather quietly ordered his soldiers to withdraw. Satisfied that the goblins posed no further threat, the Paladins continued their journey.

The rescued soldier was slowly improving. He was lying on the ground with several blankets atop him, pretending to be asleep, when several of the Paladins interrupted his rest.

"Where are you from, soldier?" Lieutenant Orgavire asked, his bony hands gripping the end of a whittling stick.

The soldier, appearing far more alert than before, looked up from his bed. "Hult," he replied quietly.

His answer intrigued General Mayweather, who asked him to repeat it. "That's one of the Acropillian states, isn't it?"

The soldier nodded.

"What brings you this far north?"

"General Kerr sent a gift to King Geoph of Meno. We were returning after delivering it when the goblins ambushed us."

"How many were in your party?" one of the paladins asked.

"Just under a dozen."

General Mayweather pondered for a moment. "It seems strange that the goblins would attack such a small party with such a large force. This implies some intent."

One of the Paladins nervously approached. "Goblins do not usually attack generic military targets. They tend to prefer merchants and lesser-armed targets that yield a better payoff. Someone must have wanted that party attacked."

The wounded soldier leaned forward, resting his elbows on a rock. "We were insignificant militarily and carried no dignitaries or valuables worth capturing."

General Mayweather quietly scratched his chin. "Interesting."

"Our party was delayed in Meno, and we were anxious to get back."

General Mayweather nodded thoughtfully. "And the goblins took nothing of significance from the battlefield?"

"No, nothing."

***

The group stopped at Tabor, the next day, to drop off the wounded man before proceeding to Acropilla. Da'ad and his companions had only recently arrived. General Mayweather spent most of a day, filling him in on the strange events in the canyon and discussing matters too secretive to share with others.

Toward the end of their conversation, he handed Da'ad a folded piece of parchment. "Be careful."

Da'ad tucked the paper away, pretending for the time being that it did not exist. The general smiled and extended his hand, pulling his friend toward him for a parting embrace.

The next morning, General Mayweather left Tabor. It took just under two weeks for his party to reach Acropilla. Meanwhile, Phineus and the elvish scholars remained busy pouring over the liche king's map. The geographical points on the map were not difficult to match up. Of greater concern were the potential hazards of the region. No one wanted to walk into a trap.

Phineus's face grew weary from the long, sleepless hours. If not for the insistence of the elves, it was doubtful he would have slept at all. The wizard's text made translation unnecessary. The only real burden was locating the information. He so enjoyed the text that he used it to read even languages he was fluent in.

Da'ad and his companions remained with the elves for another week and a half. During that time, Phineus finished deciphering the map. He was busy studying other books when Da'ad joined him unexpectedly.

"Come here." The sage motioned with a sweep of his arm. "I want to show you something. It took me all week to realize that there is nothing in this library regarding the location of the vaults of Reglis. The few rumors and guesses that I came across proved very unhelpful."

Phineus motioned to the Liche King's map, which rested on the table. There were several dark markings around the edges.

Da'ad was about to inquire about them when Phineus explained. "The map was partially written in dead man's brush, a type of ink that only becomes visible when heated. The problem is that the parchment is also susceptible to heat. As you can see by the browning of the paper, I had to be very careful. Even a few degrees warmer than necessary and the map would have caught fire. It's an ancient technique that pirates used to hide their wealth. Based on the consistency of the ink, they could control the heat necessary to discern it. They carried special devices for revealing it. I found one in the museum last night and put it to use this morning."

Da'ad looked at Phineus curiously. "How come you didn't just use the wizard's text?"

"The text only translates. It doesn't make the unseen discernible. Here, I'll show you."

Phineus removed the text and held it over the map. Both men were surprised when it actually appeared to restore some of the damaged markings.

A little embarrassed, Phineus proclaimed, "Curious."

"Looks like you took the long way about it."

Phineus looked up, bewildered. "I had no idea it could work this way."

"That's all right. At least there is enough of it left to read."

The embarrassed scholar said nothing. It took him several minutes to realize that Da'ad was still in the room.

It was only when the colonel inquired, "What do we know about the location?" that Phineus acknowledged his presence with a quick glance.

He rotated the map, providing Da'ad with a better view. "The site is not far from the tomb where we retrieved the amulet."

Da'ad raised a brow. He moved closer for a better look.

"The vaults are just the other side of Rosewood."

Da'ad did not appreciate the irony of this revelation. He was disturbed at the prospect of passing through Rosewood, so near the necromancers. Still, he felt the urgency of duty and quietly whispered, "Gather the troops. We move out tonight." There was little enthusiasm in his voice, only a cold sense of dread forged by experience.

Something felt wrong. He had no idea what was bothering him, only that he had felt this way before and it warned of danger.

Da'ad picked up a quill and paper. He wrote with great urgency, folding the paper carefully before sealing it.

He spent the next several minutes supervising preparations for the journey. Before leaving, he whispered something in Archibald's ear and handed him the sealed envelope. Archibald tucked it away and nodded, saying something in an equally hushed tone. The secretive nature of their communication was cause for great speculation. Most who witnessed it suspected that Da'ad was writing to General Mayweather for instructions.

Meanwhile, General Mayweather arrived in Acropilla, where he gradually made his way to the palace. The Acropillian Palace was a large, ornate building with eight tall towers spaced between massive stone halls and courtyards. There were red flags atop each and several sentries standing guard at each entrance. Unlike Tabor, there were relatively few trees in the city.

There was a forest to the north, but vegetation was sparse elsewhere. Only a handful of cactus and several large patches of dry grass covered the royal lawn, the result of a mild drought. Only a generation earlier the lawn had been lush and green with flowering shade trees interspersed among the many well-tended gardens.

Whatever eyesore the exterior now presented, it was easily contrasted by the beauty and splendor inside. The inner walls were decorated with fine art and expensive furnishings. Servants were busily cleaning in preparation for the evening's events. General Kerr quickly recognized the Paladins and hurried with open arms to greet them. Normally a stern man, he was unusually laid back and quite jovial on this occasion. He appeared to have been drinking, though his faculties seemed in order. After introducing himself, he smiled. "Would you like a tour of the palace?"

General Mayweather was about to accept when a heavily armored soldier interrupted. He was covered from head to toe in dry mud and bore the look of battle about him.

"What is it?" General Kerr asked.

The officer stretched out his hand, revealing a small note. "Sir, this just arrived from our western agents." General Kerr glanced at it briefly then hurried from the hall, leaving General Mayweather wondering what had just happened.

A few minutes later, one of Kerr's aides entered. "General Kerr sends his regrets that he has been unavoidably detained for the evening. He looks forward to joining you tomorrow at the feast. I am instructed to set you up with the best room in the house. You need only to ask the servants, and they will bring whatever you require."

"When we reach the room, do you think you can have a quill and some paper sent up?"

The aide nodded. General Mayweather's attention was briefly drawn to a darkhaired woman, who passed behind them and disappeared through a doorway.

"Who was that?"

"Who was who?" the aide inquired.

"That darkhaired woman. She entered there."

"Must have been Skarra. She moved in about the time the general took up residence."

"You know anything more about her?"

"Not much. She keeps mostly to herself, though I have noticed Lord Martz with her quite a lot when he is in town."

"Martz?"

"Yes. He's a hunchback. A rather cruel man, if you ask me. He commands one of our armies."

General Mayweather seemed intrigued as he followed the aide to a fancy guest room.

The room was well furnished with fine tables and other furnishings, including a rather large feather bed. The bedposts were made of cedar wood, fitted with fancy brass ends. The bed was hand carved and laced in gold trim.

"You may also use the room next door. There are two beds in there, and I will have the maid prepare a third room downstairs by this evening."

With that, the aide departed. General Mayweather sat down at a large desk. A moment later a well-dressed man entered the room with the paper and quill. After accepting the items, the general unrolled the paper and began writing.

***

The Paladins arose the next morning only to learn that General Kerr had left the city and would not return until just ahead of the promised dinner.

The dining hall was very large and located in the center of the castle. It had a high stained-glass ceiling and was draped with red pennants and tapestries. The hall was lined with large wooden tables, all of them covered in platters of fruits, salads, and fancy delicacies from across the Fairylands.

Atop the center table sat a large boar surrounded by vegetables. It was coated in red wine and wildberry garnish. The Paladins were quickly greeted by one of the many servants welcoming guests. They were led to a table, near the center of the room. A short while later, a servant filled their goblets with wine.

Several minutes passed before General Kerr arrived, an event which momentarily ended all conversation. The Acropillian leader quickly took his seat at the head of the center table. He whispered something to one of the servants, and within seconds, General Mayweather was invited to take the seat next to him. The Paladin leader paused before accepting.

The conversation in the hall gradually picked up again until General Kerr ceremoniously stood and in a powerful voice announced, "Gentlemen, welcome to Acropilla. I hope you will forgive my absence of late, but I am afraid, it is sometimes the nature of government to require our attention when it is least convenient. I do not expect any further interruptions, so please drink up and make merry. This feast is as much to celebrate you as myself." Following his brief remarks, he retook his seat. A short time later, one of the delegates rose to offer his praises. Several others rose in quick succession, adding their own sentiments.

When the final admirer concluded, General Mayweather inquired, "Pardon my curiosity, but how have you been able to manage the large numbers of criminals removed from your streets?"

"I'm happy to discuss that matter more fully, one on one, but the short answer is that most are banished from the territory on pain of death. We do imprison the more violent individuals and use some of the lesser criminals on work details. In this way, we allow those who are not likely to repeat their offenses to redeem themselves and prevent those who are the greatest threat from causing further harm. Those in between are allowed to live elsewhere in the land, so long as they are not found in our territories again. It saves money on incarceration, man power, and food and has proven very effective thus far."

General Kerr continued to answer questions and accepted the frequent praise of his guests throughout the evening. Following dinner, General Mayweather returned to his room. He quietly sat and began writing in a small journal.

Meanwhile, General Kerr spent time reacquainting himself with Lieutenant Orgavire. They talked mostly about the past. Orgavire seemed reluctant but polite.

He eventually excused himself. "General Mayweather wants to get an early start back to Thornguard. I really must get some rest."

"Of course. I'll speak with you again in the morning."

Orgavire nodded and then hurried to his room.

———

True to his word, Kerr met the Paladins the next morning. He shook hands briefly with General Mayweather then cornered Orgavire near the horses.

"It was good to see you again, Naisin. Are you sure you won't reconsider returning to the service here? I could enlist you as a captain if you liked."

"I appreciate the offer, but I'm happy where I'm at."

General Mayweather pretended to be unaware of the conversation and said nothing, though not a word of it went unnoticed by him.

Meanwhile, Da'ad and his company were passing near the Red Cliffs. It was a clear day, and the cliffs were no longer shrouded at the base. They sped their pace through the pass and set up camp near Whispering Pine.

Whispering Pine was bustling with activity. Barigal was out of the palace. His aides were busy securing the grounds and took little notice of the Paladins except to send them away. Several women were seen hurrying across streets, some carrying small children. The dwarves were worried. Their men were dressed in armor and preparing for war.

Bek motioned for Riada to come forward. "What do you make of this?"

"I don't know."

Riada rode ahead and stopped a dwarf soldier. "What's going on here?"

"A vast army of demons has destroyed Rosewood, and the king believes that they may attack here."

The soldier looked to Riada expectantly, but the sergeant hurried away to report. Bek was uncertain what to make of the news. He suspected that the Liches destroyed Rosewood. He sent Riada to inform Da'ad about the rumored attack. Da'ad immediately reassumed command. "The Liches' business in these parts is done. They will not attack. You may inform the dwarves that they've nothing more to fear. I will speak to Barigal personally if he does not believe you."

Da'ad sent Bek to deliver the message. He returned twenty minutes later. "I've spoken to the governor, and he is reluctant to believe me."

Da'ad bowed his head for several seconds then looked up. "I'm going to speak with Barigal. I want you to take command again until I return. It shouldn't be more than a few hours."

Bek nodded respectfully. Da'ad mounted his horse and rode slowly into the city. He returned two hours later, while most of the company was eating, and pulled up a seat next to Bek. "The crisis is over. The dwarves are now satisfied that they are not about to be destroyed."

"How did you manage that?"

"Once Barigal finished reciting his fears, I explained that the Liches had a blood feud with the necromancers and destroyed the city for the sake of revenge. He remained uneasy until I told him that with Rosewood's destruction, the Liches were finally free to enter the afterlife."

"And he believed you?"

"Not exactly. I finally gave him a worthless trinket and told him that it possessed magical powers that would prevent the Liches from entering the city."

"That he believed?" Bek seemed amused.

When morning came, Da'ad directed his party beyond the ruins of Rosewood. What remained of the city was littered with the rotting corpses and skeletons of both the cities' defenders and its attackers. The air was wrought with more than the mere stench of death. It emanated with some unseen evil. Da'ad's soldiers surveyed the damage for several minutes then moved slowly in the other direction. Both men and elves began to chatter lightly amongst themselves, speculating as to the cause of the great devastation.

The once-thriving city seemed utterly void of life. Even the soil appeared dead. Most of the smoke was settled, and the ruins were eerily quiet, though several of the soldiers swore they could hear voices. So strong was the foreboding that even the wolves and scavengers avoided the place.

The Paladins made haste and did not set up camp until they were well clear of the battlefield. They eventually found a flat piece of land for their tents and began removing rocks and other debris. Phineus surveyed the area and pointed to a distant hilltop as the likely location of the vaults.

"Let's get the tents up, and we'll explore the hill tomorrow," Da'ad declared. The Paladins spent most of the night listening to the sounds of crickets. A few birds scurried about the outskirts of the camp.

When morning arrived, Da'ad sent a pair of scouts to survey the hill for signs of human activity or structures. They found nothing. He ordered his troops to pack up and move the camp closer to the hill. He then motioned to Phineus. "Come with me. I want to know everything you can tell me about this hill. Why do you think the vaults are there?"

While Da'ad consulted, his soldiers cleared the dead wood and other debris from the new campsite. The hill was covered with green grass, which greatly contrasted the dry, rocky soil surrounding it.

Da'ad sat himself on midsized stone and stared at the mound for some time. He instructed Phineus and the elves, "I want you to scour that hill for any sign of an opening. I'm convinced that one exists. The question is where to find it."

"If there is one, we will find it," Leatis assured him.

"Good. See to it."

He returned about an hour later with Phineus and one of the elf scholars. Phineus explained that the vaults were not in the hill. He showed Da'ad a clay marker covered with characters and used the wizard's text to translate them.

"We found this during our search. The disc gives odd coordinates that don't match the terrain. According to these markings, the vaults are directly beneath our camp."

Da'ad considered the matter. "Well, it's worth a look. Have the men search for any kind of hidden entrance within the camp. Let me know at once if they find anything."

"The entrance should be signified by a marker that closely resembles this one. The marker will be more permanently affixed to the land and may possibly be fastened to a stone concealing the entrance itself," Phineus explained.

THE TREASURE MAP

With Da'ad's permission, one of the elves cast a simple revelation spell, turning up a small stone slab a few inches beneath the soil. The slab was smooth and plain faced. It was solidly fixed to the ground. Da'ad ordered several of the soldiers to break it up with hammers. After a few swift blows, the sandstone split apart, revealing a small opening. It took several minutes for the team to clear away the remnants of the stone, exposing the entire opening. When they were finished, one of the elves dropped a torch inside. Riada affixed a rope ladder and dropped it down the hole. Several of the soldiers then entered.

Da'ad turned to Phineus. "I want you to remain at the surface until I call for you." Two of his soldiers, one Paladin and one elf, remained above to secure the entrance. Bek was left in command of the camp. Most of the others joined Da'ad inside the darkened chamber.

Even with several lanterns, the men had difficulty finding their way. The path was lined with the skeletal remains of what appeared to be large centaurs. The remains were still covered in armor, and there were signs that the individuals might have died in the cavern.

One of the elves found and lit a row of lanterns along the southern wall. This dramatically increased visibility. Da'ad dusted away cobwebs from the remains of one of the corpses. He lifted a shield, examined it closely, and then put it back. Many of the cobwebs still housed sizable spiders.

"Stay clear of the bugs," Da'ad cautioned. With a motion of his hand, he led the team down the narrow passage until they reached a pair of large metal doors.

There were two very prominent keyholes in the doors. Lacking the key, Da'ad motioned to one of his men. "Fetch Phineus." He turned to examine the centaur remains more closely. When he finished, he addressed the others. "Search for a key. These doors were installed by a wizard, and without it, I would not want to walk through them." He quietly pondered, If I were a wizard, where would I hide it?

On his arrival, Phineus immediately began thumbing through notes taken from various texts in the elf library. "This hall doesn't resemble anything near what I imagined the vaults would look like. The notes just don't fit."

"Perhaps they were meant for the tomb," Riada suggested.

"I don't think so. We should be cautious." A few minutes later, one of the Paladins spotted a key in the hand of a dead warrior at the opposite end of the hall. As he moved to take hold of it, the skeleton came to life, closing one hand tightly around the key and using the other to thrust an old sword into the man's arm. With a holler, the soldier released the key and stumbled back in shock. The skeleton withdrew the sword and returned to its restful position.

Da'ad and the others hurried to the wounded man's side. One of the elves whispered a minor healing incantation to disinfect the wound. Phineus poured alcohol onto it and used a torch to heat and cleanse it. The wound was quickly bandaged and the injured man assisted back to camp.

Da'ad removed his sword and used it to shatter the skull of the skeleton. He then scattered the remains and retrieved the key from the floor. The others were unsure what to expect and were greatly relieved when nothing happened. Da'ad confidently returned to the doors with the key in hand.

He held it up. "Try this."

Phineus nodded as he inserted it into the doors and quietly opened them. Da'ad entered first, followed by Riada and two others. Phineus slowly worked up the courage to enter behind them.

There was a musty smell in the air, almost like rotting wood. Still, what wood the men saw did not appear to be in any state of decay. The objects in the room looked to be little more than faint shadows. It took several seconds for the men's eyes to adjust.

Two wall lamps were visible near the doorway. Riada lit them both, revealing several other lamps nearby. One by one, he lit them all. The light revealed a large, sturdy table with a map carved into it. There were no other furnishings. The musty smell quickly faded, almost as if there were some unseen airflow into the room.

With lighting in place, the men could see nearly everything, including the intricate detail inscribed and painted on the walls. The massive wooden framework around the room was of superior quality. The room was very sturdy, leaving little doubt that it was built to last.

The ceiling was supported by three massive beams held in place by more than a dozen large support columns. The columns were made of wood but painted to resemble marble. Each was decorated with fine metalwork, mostly gold, made to resemble vines, reaching up to the high-vaulted ceiling. Da'ad ventured a guess, "I'd wager we are under the hill right now."

Phineus quietly concurred. The walls of the room were decorated with faded murals, barely visible in places. Da'ad examined the table and turned to Phineus. "It appears we have more to do."

Phineus nodded as he hurried to copy the map onto a piece of parchment. Some of the soldiers looked disheartened by the find, but Da'ad seemed pleased.

The Paladins quickly returned to camp and waited out the night. Phineus and the elvish scholars spent much of the evening poring over their maps copied from the table below. A final map was fashioned in the daylight the next morning. After examining it for some time, Phineus informed Da'ad that their destination was almost certainly the Wizard's Cove near Lunora.

"It appears that Reglis hid his wealth right under the noses of the very wizards he disassociated himself from."

A stone-faced Da'ad said nothing for several seconds. "Can this be?" he eventually asked. He turned to Leatis and inquired after the soldier, who was wounded in the chamber.

Leatis perked up. "He is recovering well. It will be several weeks before his arm is fully healed."

Da'ad breathed a sigh of relief. Though he was a natural speaker and usually confident, he hesitated, even stuttered slightly. "We'll be headed for Lunora."

"What's the matter? You seem a bit unnerved at the prospect of seeing the wizards. Are they not our allies?"

"They are. My fear is not of Lunora but of someone in Lunora."

"You don't think we have enemies there, do you?"

Da'ad shook his head. "Not as such. I'm sure you have nothing to fear."

He was reluctant to elaborate, and Phineus thought it wise not to probe further. He quietly excused himself to speak with one of the elves. Da'ad began looking over the campsite as soldiers packed for the trek.

He instructed them, "We won't be traveling past the cliffs this time. I have business to see to in the marshlands east of here. We'll travel along the north side of the mountains until we reach the southwest corner near the marshlands. I'll leave Lieutenant Bek in command and take Riada with me."

He turned to Phineus and Bek. "I have business in the marshes. I need to consult with someone before I rejoin you. I should only be a few days. Have the company set up camp at these coordinates and wait for us."

When he finished, he was rejoined by Phineus. "I've known you too long to think that you will tell me what you are up to, but I am going to ask anyway."

Da'ad smiled and gently patted his friend on the back. "Very well. I will tell you."

He motioned for Phineus to follow. "I was asked to visit the marshes by General Mayweather. He fears that something terrible is going on in the southern lands and wants us to seek out information on a particular spell from an enchantress in the marshlands. I am afraid that I cannot tell you any more than that."

"It's all right. You've said enough." Phineus extended his hand and locked it with Da'ad's momentarily.

The group took three days to reach the southern edge of the marshlands. Like the ruins of Rosewood, the marshes were a strange, dark place. They were home to many creatures, good and bad, not all of which were known. The waters were covered in algae and other small leafy plants. Several strange trees rose up from the bogs, twisting and tangling in a fit of insanity. They seemed to caution, "Beware!"

In the distance, the soldiers heard the hoots of an old swamp owl. They were nearly drowned out by the croaks of large frogs and the buzzing of swamp flies. Several of the men grasped the exposed portions of their bodies in mild pain after being bit by the massive flies. Large reptiles wrapped themselves around small stumps and rocks in the water. A short distance in front of the group, a crocodile vanished into the swamp.

"Watch your step," Da'ad cautioned.

As the men walked, birds scattered in all directions, cooing madly. One of the men spotted the large skeletal remains of an ancient creature, possibly an extinct relative of the dragons. The skull and backbone were visible, but many of the other bones were still buried or missing. A few small fragments of the larger arm bones were partially visible above the mud. The skeleton was both frightening and awesome.

After gazing at it for some time, Da'ad turned to Bek. "Take the company along the southern edge of the marshlands until you reach the eastern corner. I want you to move just south of the mountains and wait for us where we agreed."

"Yes, sir. How long will you be?"

"I shouldn't be much longer than a week. It's possible we may even get there before you." Da'ad turned to Riada and motioned with his chin. "We may as well get going."

They avoided the water as much as possible and moved gradually north, stopping near a small dock. Da'ad rang an old copper bell atop a severely leaning post and waited. Everything about the place was in decay. Several patches of rotten wood were clearly visible along the dock. A small wooden boat rested at the far end. A number of makeshift planks and patches covered the old structure, presumably to fix the many holes that were almost as numerous as the planks.

While the men waited, an elderly ferryman slowly emerged from his shanty some distance from the dock. Dressed in tattered clothing, he was in no hurry. His jacket was covered in so much dirt that it was impossible to tell its original color. The holes in his pants were covered over with repeated layers of worn patches.

When he reached the men, he stretched out his hand and requested, "Fare please." His long, bony fingers clenched greedily to the coins Da'ad placed within them. The old man sneered with selfish delight as he pocketed the money and invited the men, "Have a seat in the boat."

The pier was covered with hazards. Da'ad watched his step carefully, hoping to avoid them. The old man slowly untied the boat and stepped in just behind his guests. He used a long, narrow pole to push away from the dock. After drifting a few dozen feet, he placed it back in the boat, lifted a small wooden oar, and then paddled slowly into the fog. Visibility in the middle of the bog was limited to a few feet. It decreased to a few inches as the boat neared the shore.

The old man nudged his guests slightly. "Here you are, as promised. Shall I wait for you, or can you find your own way back?"

Da'ad turned in the direction of the man's voice, barely able to make out his shadow. "We won't be returning this way. Thank you."

He and Riada watched as the man retreated slowly into the mist. An eerie feeling crept over them as they peered into the thick forest. The fog, which completely concealed the path, seemed alive with spite. Da'ad crouched to feel for the trail with his hands. Riada did the same.

By the time they escaped the fog, they were covered in the equally thick darkness of the forest. With barely a glimmer of light passing through the trees, the men struggled to ignite a torch. Its light served only to prevent them from banging into large objects.

"We cannot be far off course. We haven't been lost long enough. Walk slowly in that direction while I move in the other. Sooner or later, one of us will have to stumble upon it."

The colonel carefully wrapped a stick in dry cloth and lit it using Riada's torch. The two men traveled a combined distance of several hundred feet before Riada shouted, "I've found it!"

Da'ad hurried to his side. "Good job." Keeping close to the ground, they struggled along the path until they spotted the faint outline of a cottage. Its details were obscured by the dark but grew clearer as the men approached.

Its walls were made of stone, cemented together in hardened mud. The roof was covered in wood shingles draped with moss. Small ferns and plants grew along seams. Smoke billowed from a chimney on the far side. The front door was old but solid. The windows were obscured by dirt on both sides. It appeared to have been layered on intentionally.

A short distance away, the men spotted a fully clothed skeleton clenching the handle of a large ax. The blade was buried deep within a tree stump. "Poor fellow must have been struck down very suddenly," Riada speculated.

"This is a dangerous place." Da'ad motioned to the door.

"Where exactly are we?"

"This is the home of the enchantress Izell. Say nothing. I will do the talking, but keep a good hold on your weapon."

"Who is Izell?"

"She is no one to be taken lightly."

Da'ad gave three solid knocks on the door. The faint creaking of floorboards grew louder until at last it swung open.

On the other side, a very old, wrinkled woman stood, wearing an expensive, light-colored gown. Her hair was gray and matted. Her face and hands were filthy, and yet her gown was unblemished. There was something odd about her eyes, though Da'ad could not say what. She was both present and yet aloof, her faculties appearing simultaneously good and amiss. The contrast intrigued Da'ad.

"Who are you?" she asked in a surprisingly soft yet distrustful voice.

"We were sent by the general to acquire this spell." He handed her a note and waited for her to examine it.

"The general? Has he no patience?" she replied, somewhat annoyed. "Very well. Come inside."

Her house was littered with scrolls and books, strewn about in no particular order. The lighting was sufficient, though less than the men desired. They glanced quickly around the room. It resembled a chemistry lab, covered in flasks, potion-making equipment, and odd mixtures. The table in the middle of the room contained a large open book. Cobwebs covered the corners of the ceilings and the rafters.

Da'ad spotted a nearly empty bookcase in the next room covered by a thick layer of dust. The dust was partially disturbed near the edge where a lone book rested. The woman quickly fetched it and handed it to Da'ad. "Tell the general that the spell is complete. My sister has the original, as agreed, and will deliver it when she arrives. Now since I have no further business with you or the general, I will entertain you no longer."

She dismissed the men in a rather impolite manner, making it very clear that she did not wish to be bothered again. Her abrasiveness made Riada nervous. "I'm glad to be out of there. Something about that woman scares me."

Da'ad just smiled as they moved east along a clearly marked yet overgrown road. The path was littered with the remains of numerous animals. "There is a chill in the air. I think we're in for a rough night," Da'ad warned.

"I think you're right. Should we bunker down?"

"I think we had better. We'll be running out of time soon."

They spent about fifteen minutes setting up camp between a pair of large boulders and then covered up as best they could and waited out the storm.

As they were resting, Riada made an attempt at conversation. "What is that book she gave you?"

"General Mayweather gave specific instructions to bring this to the wizards. He told me not to mention his name and to refer to him only as the general. He was not clear about his reason, but I suspect he expected her to mistake us for someone else."

"Do you think the others will have to wait long before we catch up?"

"No. I suspect we may even get there before them. Now I suggest that we get as much rest as we can. We still have a long walk ahead of us."

THE WIZARDS OF LUNORA

Da'ad reached the rendezvous point, almost two days ahead of Bek and the others. When Bek arrived, he instructed, "Have the men get some rest. We'll continue in the morning." It was raining lightly, and he was uneasy about something.

"Still concerned about someone in Lunora?" Phineus asked.

"I am."

"You're certain we have nothing to fear?"

"You haven't."

"I've seldom seen you like this. Mind telling an old man who it is that has you so unnerved?"

"No. Perhaps I'll talk about her some time, but for now I need my rest." Da'ad stood up and retired to his tent, leaving Phineus alone near the fire pit.

As time went on, Da'ad grew increasingly restless. Leatis brewed him a natural tea to calm his nerves. By the time they reached the Mystic Forest, Da'ad seemed weakened almost to the point of collapse.

Riada boiled pine bark and several native mushrooms mixed with squirrel meat. "Try this. It will help you relax."

"What is it?"

"Just an herbal soup. It won't hurt you."

"What about the meat?"

"That's squirrel. I usually use rabbit, but in a fix, squirrel will do."

Da'ad cautiously tasted it. "This isn't half bad."

"Thanks. My mother used to make it when I was young."

"My compliments to your mother."

"Thank you, sir." About ten minutes later, Da'ad was sleeping soundly. He awoke the next morning very well rested.

The forest was pleasant but with an air of mischief about. The smell of the deep-green pine was deceptively calming. A few songbirds chirped happily atop the massive trees as the men passed below.

"Stay alert. Appearances can be very deceiving here," Da'ad cautioned.

A few miles into the forest, the men were buzzed by a group of curious pixies. The sprites flew in circles above the men's heads for several seconds and then lost interest and returned to their nests.

The forest was teeming with life. Even the trees had personalities. Many of them were covered in an assortment of vines and moss, including a variety of wild grape. The ground was covered in dry needles and pinecones, interspersed with colorful mountain flowers.

Many of the men stopped to sample wild berries. They watched a unicorn dash across the path in front of them. Strange vibrations emanated with unheard music blanketing the forest like a quilt of peace.

Riada quietly cleared his throat. "We must be getting near."

The silent music had the unnatural effect of placing the men at ease. It was as if they were being swallowed in pure joy. A voice in their minds whispered, "You are safe here." Many of the men heard it.

A new flutter of young pixies busily laughed and played nearby. Some of them flew down to question the men. Da'ad politely declined their inquiries. Phineus, on the other hand, seemed pleased to speak with them.

"Fascinating, these pixies," he remarked.

As the team exited the woods, the pixies retreated back to their nests. Da'ad spotted a small pool in the distance and pointed. "There, that is where we're going."

As the group approached, they saw a young couple resting near the opposite shore. They periodically tossed tiny stones into the water and watched the men with great interest. The woman stood to greet them. "Have you business here?"

"I've come to speak with the council on behalf of General Mayweather."

The young man moved to her side. "What would you see them about?"

"I have been instructed to deliver a book of spells."

"May I see it?" the woman asked.

"No. It is for the council's eyes only. I will deliver it to them."

Within a matter of seconds, the pool and the couple vanished. In their place stood an immaculate gate leading into a massive city. The gate opened slowly, revealing the very impressive streets of Lunora.

The city walls were covered with intricate murals carved into the stone. The streets resembled a massive museum filled with fine sculptures and artistic fountains. Even the street lamps were made to impress. The bases of the lamps were made with fine marble, capped off with painted metal. Each lamp was decorated with a variety of potted plants, creating of the street a massive hanging garden. The city employed numerous gardeners to look after the grounds. Like the Mystic Forest, Lunora was filled with energy.

Several of the men stopped to admire a massive golden fountain pouring water into the stone pool beneath it. The fountain consisted of several masterfully crafted animals, all seemingly leaping from the center of the pool. Water flowed from the mouths of each and was swallowed up and recycled within a hidden chamber below.

As the men admired the piece, a young sorceress approached from behind. "It serves as the primary water source for this quarter of the city."

Da'ad immediately turned. The sorceress was beautifully dressed in a flowing white gown accented with golden trim. She smiled as he recognized her.

Her dark-brown hair was braided with colorful flowers and capped with a jeweled comb in back. It was held up by a fancy hair net made of fine golden chains. Her beauty was almost hypnotic and easily captivated many of Da'ad's companions. Her manners were refined yet betrayed a quiet confidence. Da'ad shifted nervously, as she approached.

"Jeinan?"

His voice sounded of both surprise and fear. He was not the sort of man to fear lightly, and Phineus found his behavior very intriguing. Nothing about their hostess seemed the least bit intimidating, except perhaps her great beauty, and Phineus knew all too well that Da'ad was not the sort of man to be intimidated by that. Da'ad looked as though he had seen a ghost, and just maybe he had—a ghost from his past. He remarked, "Jeinan," this time a bit louder than before.

Her smile broadened. "Yes, did you think me dead?"

"No, it's just that I thought you would look much older. I haven't seen you in nearly a decade, and yet you look as though you haven't aged a day."

"Thank you. You're probably right. As a wizard, I do not age the same as you do." Still smiling, she moved to embrace him, kissing him lightly on the cheek. Realizing the awkwardness of the situation, she whispered, "Relax. We are not enemies."

Da'ad pulled away, still very nervous.

Jeinan's smile broadened as she raised her hand in a strange motion, brushing her fingers across the left side of his face and whispering something into the wind. He soon found his anxiety replaced by a deep sense of peace and inner confidence.

"Feeling better?" she asked.

"Yes. What did you do?"

She smiled, preferring not to answer. A moment later, she beckoned, "Welcome to Lunora. What may we do for you?"

Her interest in Da'ad fascinated Phineus, who failed to understand Da'ad's behavior and found the entire situation curious. "I need to speak with the council. I have a book intended for them. It is most urgent that they receive it."

"Very well. Follow me into the park."

"How do you know this young lady?" Phineus asked as they followed.

Da'ad was about to answer when Jeinan interrupted. "Now what is this book you mentioned?"

"It's a spellbook. I do not know much about it except that General Mayweather indicated that use of the spell would be quite problematic."

"I seem to recall you were once a general. What happened to you, Thoren?"

Da'ad's expression dimmed. "Times change."

She nodded solemnly. "Indeed." She was about to say something more when a group of tree pixies interrupted. The tiny sprites fluttered about like bees, whispering in her ears as they passed. Jeinan's expression changed quickly to one of concern. "Something has happened outside the city."

"What?"

"It seems imps have infiltrated the forest."

"Imps, this far south? That's unheard of," Da'ad scoffed.

"Yes, it is rather suspicious. The imps are feeding on wild game and have already destroyed almost an acre of forest. Unlike the northern salt flats, they can do a lot of damage here. They must be stopped and soon."

"What do you need?"

"The council is not interested in what it considers petty matters like this. They would eventually exterminate the imps, but not before the creatures cause irreparable harm to the forest. I need someone to find their lair and destroy it before that happens."

"Where are they now?"

"I knew you wouldn't let me down. You always were a hero, Thoren. Do you have a map?" Da'ad nodded and had Riada retrieve it. She looked it over. "I'll provide you with a more detailed map." She then motioned for her servant. "Return to my home and retrieve the forest map from my desk, and bring it to me quickly."

"Yes, ma'am."

Her servant returned a few minutes later with the map in hand. Jeinan opened it and pointed to the approximate location of the imps.

"These imps are well traveled. How do you suppose they got here?" Da'ad asked.

"There are many wizards in Lunora. Not all of them share our values. This may be a simple child's prank, or it could be something more devious."

"I think we should be able to take care of a bunch of imps without much trouble."

"There is a complication. The imps are holding several tree pixies captive in their lair. Try to free them first."

Da'ad nodded.

"I'll take your book to the council while you deal with the imps, unless, of course, you would prefer to wait."

"No. I think it best to get this to the council at once." Da'ad handed her the book and bowed.

"You will recognize the imp lair by the large mound of rock and dirt surrounding it. There will be few trees still standing. Imps are known to dislike them. Please try to destroy the entire colony so that we won't need to do this again."

"I doubt you'll have to. I will need a few things if you can get them for us."

"Name them, and I'll see what I can do."

He gave her a list then removed the map from his belt and pointed. "Have your people meet me here."

With the arrangements made, Da'ad turned to address his company. "We have a job to do, gentlemen. Let's get to it."

While Da'ad was busily pursuing the imps, Jeinan delivered the book to Terek Greyscale. The entire wizard council was gathered and could not help but to take note of the delivery. Terek excused them immediately and hurried the book to his office.

While he studied its frail pages, a lone wizard slipped away to deliver a message of his own. He slowly dipped his finger into a large reflection dish and waited. After several minutes, an image formed of a dark-cloaked woman hidden in shadow.

"What is it?"

"A group of paladins and elves arrived a short time ago."

"What of it? Lunora entertains many people."

"They carried a book. I thought perhaps it might be important. It was delivered to Terek Greyscale by the sorceress Jeinan."

"Describe it."

The wizard did his best to describe the book. As he did so, the witch seemed slightly unsettled.

"So Terek Greyscale has found himself a copy of the Mantra. No matter, it cannot help him. Follow these paladins and find out their business. I sense they may be trouble."

"They may be pursuing the Vaults of Reglis. We heard rumor some months ago that the location of the vaults might have been discovered."

"Find out for certain and let me know."

"One thing more. Our efforts to undermine Master Greyscale have hit a snag. The paladins are outside the city as we speak. They are making plans to destroy the imps. I no longer believe

Master Greyscale will become involved. We will need a new plan of attack."

"Patience. Our efforts against Terek Greyscale can wait. Right now we must stop these paladins. This is not the first of our plans that they have interfered with. Find out what you can about them and let me know."

———✸———

Outside the city, Da'ad's group proceeded west until the forest thinned into a massive clear-cut region. Most of the vegetation was uprooted. The trees were torn from the soil. The area was strewn with massive stumps and partially stripped logs.

The nearer the men came to the lair, the more the forest seemed to darken. This was, despite the fact that it was midday, and there were no longer any trees to block out the sun.

Da'ad suspected that his soldiers were sensing the darkened presence of the imps. There was a strange foreboding in the air, as if the trees were somehow crying in pain. While many of the men fidgeted nervously, Da'ad remained calm. He positioned his soldiers like an artist applying paint to a canvas, each stroke a work of genius. With a motion of his hand, he called forth the Lunorians and their oil drums. About two hundred meters from the edge of the forest was the dirt mound surrounded by large stones. Da'ad took shelter behind a pair of uprooted stumps and observed the mound for several minutes.

Many of the logs and stumps were charred. Smoke billowed from beneath the ground where the imps were still attempting to burn out the roots of fallen trees. Da'ad and his men watched as several dark-colored creatures feasted on the carcass of a small deer. They tore at its flesh like vultures and resembled tiny humans, with the exception of their nearly black skin and the shapes of their heads and faces.

Imps were notoriously filthy creatures. Their faces were covered in the decaying flesh of several past meals. Fortunately, they seemed unaware of Da'ad's presence. He motioned for Leatis.

"I may be able to dispatch them for you. They probably keep the pixies near the opening. If that is the case, I should be able to free them, and we can begin destroying the lair quickly."

Da'ad agreed. He watched in amazement as Leatis and the other elvish scouts dispatched more than a dozen imps in under five seconds. Within twenty seconds, they reached the opening.

As Da'ad signaled for the Lunorians to pour the oil into the lair, Leatis and the elves plugged the entrance with a large stump. They next turned their attention toward a second mound, a sort of back door, several dozen feet from the first.

When the Lunorians arrived, they temporarily removed the stump and poured oil into both holes. Several imps attempted to escape but were quickly cut down by the elves. Both mounds billowed with dark smoke as the Lunorians ignited the oil. The ground temperature rose rapidly, forcing the soldiers to retreat. The entire lair was destroyed within minutes.

Having successfully dealt with the imps, Da'ad returned to Lunora, where he found Jeinan waiting just inside the gate. "The imps are gone."

"Good. Now we can get on with our business. I've delivered the book as you asked."

"What did they say?"

"Not much. They haven't had a full opportunity to look it over yet. I'm assured that once they do, they will summon you to the chamber to discuss the matter more completely. Meanwhile, I've been instructed to present you at a dinner in your honor if you will follow me to the community center."

Da'ad nodded. He glanced across the street then followed her around one of two massive statues near the front gate. "I'm guessing this is more than a mere statue?"

"It is, but then you've been here before and probably know that."

"I may have been here previously, but I've never asked before."

Jeinan was slightly amused by his ignorance. "This way, if you will."

The park was filled with activity. Many young people, mostly students, spent their afternoons reading on the lawn. Some relaxed near the park's decorative fountains.

"Busy out today."

"The park tends to be busy this time of day. Students are studying for their exams. It's a strenuous time for a lot of people." Jeinan gave Da'ad an obvious smile then turned toward the community center and entered with a slight bounce. The center was a fanciful, stone building with arched spires rising into an attractive entryway. Its main hall was very large and filled with elaborate tables.

Da'ad was quickly greeted and shown to his seat by a portly looking mage whose opinion of the colonel was exceeded only by his opinion of himself. The other members of the group quickly followed. A tall wizard at the table's head smiled as the last of Da'ad's companions was seated. He welcomed the men and elves and then turned to Da'ad. "Thank you for joining us this evening. Master Greyscale had hoped to be here but regrettably could not spare the time. We trust that you will forgive his absence. He still hopes to speak with you while you are in town. You may expect him to call."

As he concluded, the wizard raised a hand into the air, and with a wave, the table was filled with fabulous foods. He smiled. "Eat heartily, my friends."

Da'ad glanced toward Jeinan, who was seated across from him. "Eat up, Thoren. We planned this for you."

"And a grand meal it is. It's been some time since I've eaten so well."

The portly wizard next to Da'ad sat up and cleared his throat. "I regret that you could not meet the entire council today, but I assure you they all wished to be here."

An elderly wizard seated next to Jeinan quietly adjusted his spectacles. "You will have the opportunity to see Master Greyscale tomorrow. He wanted a chance to look over the book you brought with you before calling on you. The rest of the council will consider the matter in chamber the next day. You will likely be called upon to testify, if you are still in town. Jeinan can fill you in on the protocol."

"I have no prior engagements to speak of at the moment. I see no reason why we cannot remain a few days."

"Good. I trust Jeinan will entertain you sufficiently in the meantime."

Da'ad was about to respond when Jeinan interjected, "I am happy to show him around, though this is not Thoren's first visit to our city."

"You've been here before?" the older wizard inquired.

"Yes, several times, but that was many years ago."

"Well then, I'll trust Jeinan to refresh your memory." The wizard raised his goblet. "A toast to friends, old and new. May your journey be a safe one."

"Here, here. So how many wizards are on the council?"

"Thirteen. You see seven of them here. You will meet the others soon enough. Master Greyscale is looking forward to speaking with you."

"And I with him. Are the members of your council chosen at large?"

"Not exactly," the wizard next to Jeinan replied.

Jeinan explained, "The council is chosen by its sitting members. Others are entitled to nominate individuals for the service, but the final say belongs to the council itself."

"Are appointments for life then?"

"Not necessarily. The council chooses its members and can release them. Most often, this occurs following a prolonged absence. Occasionally, a released member may be later reinstated." Da'ad nodded thoughtfully. He finished his meal and then watched one of the wizards stand and wave her hand across the table, causing the dishes and food to vanish.

Jeinan stood and motioned for Da'ad and his companions to follow her. She led them to a fancy bed and breakfast. Da'ad thanked her and was about to take his leave when she leaned forward and kissed him gently on the cheek. "It is good to see you again, Thoren. I will be by in the morning to escort you to the council. If you need anything, just ring the bell, and I am assured, by your host, that they will take good care of you."

"Thank you again."

Jeinan nodded and then waved as the men entered the inn.

Riada settled into a large wooden chair in front of a tall oak table near the bar, where Bek was waiting for him with a pair of wooden dice. Several of the others gathered around to participate in the game. Having little interest in gambling, Da'ad retired to his bedchamber.

Several minutes later, Phineus tapped on the door. He entered and seated himself at a small table near the bed. Da'ad laughed. "I should have guessed you would drop by."

"If you want me to leave—"

"No. I just expected you to stop by. What's on your mind?"

"Funny you should ask. I was going to ask you the same thing. You still owe me an explanation."

"Do I?"

"I did ask, and you left me hanging. I suppose I can guess the who, but I still have no idea of the why."

Da'ad muttered something under his breath before looking up. "I suppose it's inevitable. Might as well tell you."

"It is clear she still has strong feelings for you."

"Yes. That's what's worrying me."

Phineus threw him a funny look. "That she cares about you? Here, all this time, I expected you feared the opposite."

"I guess I just feared seeing her, period. We last parted on awkward terms. As I recall, she was quite upset."

"Do you want to talk about it?"

"No, but maybe I should. She was infatuated with me years ago. This was just before I married Sela. She knew we were engaged and tried to talk me out of it. We had been friends for about two years but we were never romantic. I was courting Sela for most of that time. She used to flirt a lot, but I never really thought much of it at the time. When I announced my engagement, she became upset. I thought she would get over it, but it became clear that I needed to leave the city. I didn't return, until now. There is more to it than that, but I really don't want to get into the details."

"That's all right. It isn't necessary. I must say, though, I'm surprised by your brief account. While it is clear that she still has feelings for you, she doesn't seem the vindictive type."

"No, she doesn't. Perhaps time has healed the wounds. At least, let us hope so."

"How do you feel about her?"

Da'ad was surprised by this question. He stumbled over his words for a second or two then replied, "It's in the past, and that's where it belongs. Besides, I swore off love when Sela died, and in my current situation, I cannot entertain thoughts of romance. They are contrary to the bylaws of the order."

"There are several married men under your command."

"Yes, but they remain celibate while on active duty, and most are fortunate to see their wives more than once a year."

Phineus stood. "Well, best be getting along. It's late."

"See you in morning, old friend."

"Yes. You will join us for breakfast, won't you?"

"I'll be there."

A short while after Phineus left, Da'ad gave in to his exhaustion and fell asleep.

It was midmorning when he finally awoke. He would have slept longer but for an unexpected visitor. Jeinan knocked loudly and then invited herself into his room.

Da'ad squinted. "Shouldn't you have waited to be invited in? This could have been an embarrassing moment for us both."

"I'm sorry, Thoren. It was an oversight. Given the hour, I expected you would be awake already. I was hoping we might speak privately."

"All right. Just give me a moment to freshen up."

Jeinan agreed and stepped outside. She re-entered when he called and then moved gradually toward him until she was near enough to wrap her arms around him.

Da'ad pulled back a bit. "What was that for?"

"I thought you could use a good hug about now. It's been a long time, Thoren."

"Yes."

"I heard about Sela. I am very sorry."

Da'ad remained silent. The thought of Sela's death pained him greatly.

Jeinan placed her hand on his shoulder. "We've a big day ahead of us."

"Yes. I suppose we should get ready."

She smiled, took him by the hands, and then led him out the door, past the common room.

Riada watched them breeze by. Phineus entered a short while later. "Have you seen Thoren? He was supposed to meet me for breakfast."

"He and the lady Jeinan just rushed past. You can still see them through the window."

"She seems friendly."

"Yes, very friendly," Riada agreed.

"Remind me to speak with her when they return. I've a good many questions to ask."

Riada nodded passively. Phineus took a seat on the other side of the room and poured himself a small cup of tea.

Somewhere outside, Jeinan was questioning Da'ad about recent events. After telling her about the necromancers, he asked, "Are you familiar with the vaults of Reglis?"

"That's a funny question to ask a wizard. Why do you ask?"

"I'll get to that in a moment. First, what do you know about them?"

"I know what every wizard knows and perhaps a bit more. Reglis was a member of the council who left the city more than a millennia ago. During his lifetime, it is believed he acquired a large number of artifacts, including some he created himself. He had a falling out with the factions on the council and swore he would have nothing more to do with them. A short time later, he left Lunora for good. He was quite wealthy, and, near the end of his life, he swore openly that he would never allow the political factions on the council to acquire that wealth. As promised, he took his wealth with him. Legend has it that he constructed several massive vaults and hid all of his possessions inside. No trace of the vaults has ever been found."

"Do you believe the legends?"

Jeinan nodded. "Many legends are just that, but Reglis was wealthy. He did possess many magical artifacts, and in the years since his death, not one of those artifacts has ever been found. They must be hidden some place."

"What would you say if I told you that I might know where that place is?"

"You haven't found the vaults, have you?"

"Not yet, but I think we're very close. We have some reason to believe that the vaults might be beneath Lunora itself."

Jeinan laughed. "That's unlikely. What makes you think so?"

"We found several records in a centaur cave. Those records purported to identify the location of the vaults of Reglis. When we arrived at the location, we found a tomb, wherein we believe Reglis was buried. Though not the vaults, the tomb did provide an interesting artifact, which we delivered to the Liche King in exchange for a map. The map led us to an underground chamber near Rosewood, where we found a large wooden table bearing a map of Lunora on its face."

"Could you describe the table for me, please?"

"It was a large wooden table about three feet high, possibly as long as ten feet and six or seven feet wide. It appeared to be made of walnut or some other dark wood."

Jeinan asked several specific questions and then explained, "Remember I told you that Reglis possessed several powerful artifacts?" Da'ad nodded. "One of those artifacts was a table, the Table of Armicet. It is said to be capable of showing any location in the Fairylands in great detail. You say you saw Lunora on its face?"

"We did."

"It is possible that you were seeing only the last location requested of it and not the location of the vaults. Still, if the vaults exist, that table may be the key to finding them. I should like to visit the chamber with you."

"You mean return to Rosewood?"

"You want to find the vaults, don't you?"

"If they exist."

"Good, then we must return. I'll speak with Master Greyscale. I'm certain that the council will approve my request to join your party, now."

"Request?" Da'ad asked, somewhat surprised.

"Yes. You do see the advantage to having a wizard in your company, don't you?"

Da'ad nodded.

"Good. I intend to assist you with your search. The council is already aware that you are looking for the vaults. They initially refused to offer assistance when Archibald was here, but I think the discovery of the table will change their minds."

"And if it doesn't?"

"Then I will still join you. The most that can happen is that I lose my seat on the council. It's really more a matter of prestige than anything else."

"How long have you been on the council?"

"A few years now. Long enough to know that it isn't all I once thought it would be."

Da'ad had little doubt that the services of a wizard would be invaluable to his company. The thought of Jeinan joining the team was a little intimidating, but for the sake of his mission, he would set his personal feelings aside. There was no doubt that she was an accomplished wizard with much to offer.

He knew her presence would increase the odds of success and quietly told her that her assistance would be greatly appreciated.

Jeinan chanced a quick glance toward a large ornate sundial a short distance from the street. The dial consisted of a granite patio, approximately twenty feet in diameter, with a pointed piece in the shape of a sail rising out of its center. It was constructed in such a manner as to allow precise calculations of time and day based on the positions of the sun, moon, and certain stars. There were additional poles located nearby that contributed to the dial's accuracy. Noticing her efforts, Da'ad removed a small pocket watch.

"We still have a few minutes. Perhaps we could get something to eat?" Jeinan suggested.

Da'ad nodded, though he was not hungry. Jeinan led the way to cozy restaurant near the park. They ordered light so as not to miss their appointment. Unfortunately, the meal only awakened Da'ad's appetite. His hunger stirred for the remainder of the morning, leading to some embarrassingly loud stomach noises.

The Lunorian council met inside a large spiraling tower. The white stone of the tower was unspoiled. A pair of sturdy marble columns supported the entryway. "I don't recall this building being as impressive the last time I saw it."

"It has been enlarged slightly. They added two stories to the top since you were here last."

"It is an architectural marvel. What's inside those top two floors?"

"We're going up there. That's where the council convenes."

Just inside the entryway, a lone clerk checked in visitors. He recognized Jeinan instantly. "You have a guest today, my lady?"

"Yes. This is Thoren Da'ad. The council is expecting us."

He motioned for them to proceed. "Are you feeling athletic today, or shall we take the teleporters?" Jeinan asked.

Da'ad glanced at the spiraling stairwell. "I think the teleporters will be just fine." He cautiously followed her into the chamber where they were instantly transported to the top of the tower. Da'ad glanced out of the nearest window, admiring the view. It went on for miles.

"It's beautiful, isn't it?" Jeinan observed.

"Yes, it is."

"Many times when I'm troubled, I come up here and stare across the forest. It's so peaceful and relaxing that I can forget about my problems."

The conference room was well decorated with fanciful artifacts. At its center was a massive wooden table of fine quality. The entire council was seated around it, except for Jeinan, who entered with Da'ad. She quickly found her seat. Master Greyscale was seated at the head of the oval-shaped table. He rose to welcome Da'ad and beckoned him to take a seat at the opposite end of the room.

An older-looking wizard near Da'ad's seat welcomed him politely as "General." Da'ad nodded, choosing not to correct him.

Master Greyscale quickly announced, "We have much to discuss today. Let us begin."

Da'ad looked around at the very diverse gathering of individuals. It was easily apparent that the council consisted of wizards of many different backgrounds. Some seemed quite pleasant while others were shrouded in darker qualities. All seemed very interested in the spellbook.

"Do you know what this book is, Mr. Da'ad?" one of the wizards inquired.

Da'ad shrugged. "I know it's a spellbook. It must be rather important or General Mayweather would never have requested that I deliver it here."

"It is," Terek interrupted.

He turned to a portly looking wizard at his left and nodded. Da'ad recognized the man from the feast.

"This is a copy of the 'Lizard's Mantra,' an ancient spell of such evil that it was banned before it could be used nearly a millennium ago. All known copies were destroyed."

Terek stood up with his hands on the table. "I fear it may already be too late to prevent the spell's use. The consequences on its victims will be terrible. Its magic will introduce to the Fairylands the lizard race, and they shall become a scourge on all humanity. They may even threaten the gates of Lunora itself before this fight is over."

An eerie silence overtook the room. Terek quietly referred to several parchments spread out across the table in front of him. It was clear that no one on the council was truly familiar with the text. Master Greyscale quoted from several of the writings of Reglis the only known records describing the spell in any detail. Reglis was believed to have prevented its use when it was first introduced.

After Terek finished, the council broke into a heated debate. Da'ad remained seated and listened. Occasionally, he was asked a question or two by members of the council. His answers were unsatisfactory, as he knew even less about the spell than those questioning him.

By the end of the meeting, they failed to settle on a single course of action. Da'ad left with Jeinan, unsure what to make of the experience. As they prepared to exit the tower, Terek called after them. He spoke in hushed tones. "Colonel, there is a power rising in the land that is fully prepared to use that magic and may already have done so. We must prepare for the worst."

"I will inform General Mayweather when I see him."

"No need. The general already knows."

Da'ad bowed and followed Jeinan outside. It was not long before another member of the council stopped him. "Congratulations on your pursuit of the vaults."

The wizard had a dark aura about him. There was a bit of smirk behind his smile, and Da'ad hesitated to trust him. The mage seemed eager to please, almost too eager for Da'ad's comfort. Until now, Da'ad was unaware of the council's great interest in his pursuit.

He quietly thanked the wizard and was about to leave when the mage placed a hand on his shoulder to stop him. He spoke in very hushed tones. "Should you happen to locate the vaults, I would like to acquire a piece that is believed to rest there. It's a medallion with an odd-shaped ruby in the middle." He quickly described the piece and then concluded, "This item is very important to my work. I will gladly reward you for your efforts in retrieving it."

"I will consider your request, but I make no promises."

"Good, I hope you do. I look forward to our next meeting."

"Perhaps you should tell me more about your interest in this piece?"

The wizard's face grew pale. "Meet me later at my abode." He explained how to find the house and then excused himself abruptly.

———

Elsewhere, at that moment, another of the councilmen carefully touched the tip of his finger to a reflection dish and waited until a hooded woman appeared in the water.

"Have you discovered their destination?" she asked.

"Yes. They are headed toward Rosewood. Thoren Da'ad is leading them."

"Good. You've done well."

As soon as the conversation was finsished, the woman excused him and passed her hand over the water to summon the darkness. A deep voice resonated from the basin.

"Why have you summoned me?"

"Terek Greyscale has acquired a copy of the Mantra."

"It matters not. There is nothing he can do to stop it."

"Also, a group of paladins is pursuing the Vaults of Reglis. They delivered the Mantra and interferred with our plans to remove Master Greyscale. I sense they may be trouble."

"Where are they heading?"

"The ruins of Rosewood."

"Good. They will find a surprise waiting for them when they arrive."

"Thoren Da'ad will be accompanied by one of the wizards."

"They will be destroyed. No magic or power of your world can defeat what I will send for them."

"What of the paladins' protection?"

"It means nothing. Their oath cannot save them."

THE DARK MAGE

Outside the tower, Jeinan patiently waited for Da'ad. She was frustrated by the council's inability to reach a consensus and unaware of Da'ad's recent encounter with the dark mage. Da'ad shared her concerns but not the magnitude of her feelings. He seemed unsure about the council's failure and wondered aloud, "Could Lunora be a divided city?" apparently unaware that Jeinan was listening.

"It can, and it is. There are several factions in Lunora right now. Only two of them are represented on the council. Fortunately, Master Greyscale still has the support of the majority of the council. The only way he is likely to lose it is if the conflict escalates to assassination, an unlikely scenario since his majority is solid enough to maintain control, unless they assassinate three or four members at once."

"A possible scenario, though not a very effective one. The sudden mass assassination would likely result in the disbanding of the entire council and very possibly all-out civil war."

"Unless that is their goal, but the factions on the council are too well known. They are too ambitious and would not risk such an open power grab. I do not believe that conflict of a military nature would be to their advantage. If assassinations on that scale occur, it would likely be caused by an outside faction."

"Experience has taught me that humans seldom do anything that doesn't at least appear to advantage them. Since we are on the topic of the council, I just had an interesting encounter with one of your companions."

"Really, who would that be?"

"A tall, gangly fellow dressed in black with a very dark presence."

By Da'ad's description, Jeinan recognized the mage at once. "Zarg! What did he want?"

"He asked me about some medallion that he says is supposed to be in the vaults. I think he wants me to retrieve it for him. I'm supposed to stop by his house."

"Zarg has always been ambitious, and I've never really trusted him, but I don't think he's a danger to us." Da'ad pondered the matter. Seeing the strain in his face, Jeinan asked, "Something the matter?"

"No, not really. I'm just trying to decide whether I should meet with him or not."

"If you like, I can cast a spell and spy on your meeting. Of course, physically, I would be nowhere near you, but I would be able to observe from afar everything that happens."

"Does that mean that you think I should go?"

"Let's just say that I don't think Zarg intends to harm you, and certainly not before you retrieve this medallion."

"I suppose I should at least hear him out. Can you listen in on conversations?"

"With a great deal of effort, it is possible, but it takes tremendous concentration and focus. If I am to listen in, I won't be able to observe much."

Da'ad glanced at her. "One more thing. How do I find his house?"

"Just follow me, and I'll show you." A short while later they arrived at a dimly lit corner. Jeinan glanced up at the nearest lamppost. "They need to replace the wick. Even magic lanterns require occasional maintenance. Zarg's house is on your right, another block down, third house from the intersection. I think it best if you continue alone from here."

"I'll meet you back here when I'm finished."

Da'ad turned to leave. The lighting in front of Zarg's house was perfect, yet somehow the building seemed shrouded in shadow. Da'ad thought this odd. He was filled with anxiety as he walked toward the front door.

Zarg resided in a quaint little cottage made of white stone, making its darkened face all the more ominous. It was not the house Da'ad imagined it would be. If not for the strange shadow on its face, the cottage would seem quite cozy.

There was little or no space between the houses. Da'ad took a deep breath and knocked. He could see by the windows that the front room was poorly lit. After a moment, he heard the clicking of bolts and locks. He moved back from the door as it slowly creaked open.

To his surprise, there was no one on the other side. He entered cautiously and then paused. The house felt much larger than it appeared from the outside. There was no sign of Zarg or anyone else. Da'ad took two steps into the room and called out, "Hello!" He waited a few seconds then noticed a tiny glowing ball appear through a closed door on the other end of the room. Recognizing it as a wizard's escort, he followed it to the door. The door opened on its own. Da'ad followed several meters behind the sphere. It floated through a narrow hall and vanished into another closed door.

Da'ad made his way to the door but hesitated before turning the knob. He was still contemplating the matter when the door opened by itself.

"Come in!" a voice called out.

The room was small but by no means tiny. There were several shuttered windows along the walls. The fireplace was lit and partially blocked by a large, overstuffed chair. Da'ad approached the chair from the backside. The fire was the room's primary source of light. It burned well, though the logs did not appear to be consumed by the flames. This fascinated Da'ad. He took a moment to study the phenomena then turned to his right and examined the back end of the chair.

Moments later, Zarg invited him, "Do be seated, Colonel."

As Da'ad moved past the chair, he recognized Zarg buried deep in its overstuffed padding. The wizard motioned to the other side of the fireplace, where another similar chair was waiting. Da'ad slowly seated himself in it and studied a large bookshelf along the wall. It was filled with curious artifacts and books, most of which were obscured by the room's dim light.

Zarg smiled as he introduced himself. He noticed Da'ad's fascination with the fire. "Remarkable, isn't it. It is a simple spell."

He stood and approached Da'ad with his hand outstretched. Da'ad also stood and took the hand cautiously. With the formalities out of the way, the mage motioned to a small table beneath one of the windows. It was surrounded by a pair of wooden chairs. "They're not as comfortable as the lounge chairs, but they should suffice for our business." He led Da'ad to the table and removed one of the chairs, inviting, "Please," before seating himself.

"Now what is so important about this medallion you want me to bring back?"

Zarg took his time, answering. "Do you know what that medallion is, Colonel?"

Da'ad shook his head. "No, I'm afraid not, but I would love for you to tell me about it."

"Good, then tell you I will. This is a copy of a protection amulet, enchanted by Reglis centuries ago. The original renders the wearer immune to harmful spells. Certain other types of magic become useless in the wearer's presence." Da'ad watched his ring, but nothing happened. Zarg noticed the shift in his attention. "Everything all right?"

"Yes, I'm fine. Thank you. Please, go on."

"Reglis is rumored to have locked its powers when he hid it away. This makes it largely useless to the average person, but I can unlock the magic for you."

"For me?" Da'ad asked, puzzled.

"Yes, for you. You have many challenges ahead of you, Colonel. Some of them will be quite trying. You will need all of the help you can get if you are to prevail."

"What is your interest in all of this?"

Zarg looked at him curiously. "My interest? Let's just say that I am an ambitious man and expect to be in the council's graces when you prevail."

Da'ad again looked at his ring. "Why all of the secrecy?"

Zarg's face grew cold as he stood up. "Quickly. We're not alone." He led the way into another room. "Someone is attempting to spy on us. We are safe here. You will forgive me, Colonel. I did not think anyone else was aware of our business. I am afraid you may be in greater danger than I thought. This is all very strange and, I assure you, quite unexpected. We shall have to use great caution."

Da'ad appeared unconcerned. "About the secrecy?"

"I've already intimated the reason, in part. There is treachery in the air. I cannot say for certain from whence it comes, but I feel it very clearly. Not even the council is without its spies. Without this amulet, I fear you will fail."

"They say that Paladins live charmed lives. Magic cannot directly harm us so long as we are in the order."

"Perhaps, but I caution you, take nothing for granted, not even your affiliation with the Paladins. Remember that a skilled wizard may strike at you indirectly with great effectiveness, and should you ever be cast out of your order, the danger grows."

Da'ad bowed his head thoughtfully. Everything about Zarg seemed to warn against trust. Still, he could not help but to believe the warning. His instincts told him that Zarg would play a relevant part in his coming quest. "Very well then. I will retrieve your medallion, but I must warn you, do not cross me. I can make a reputable foe, even for a wizard. You do not want me as your enemy."

Zarg smiled deviously. "No, you are correct. I do not, but then, I've always thought that making enemies lightly was a fool's game." As Da'ad stood to leave, Zarg leaned forward. "Colonel, I will be honest with you. I am a shadow mage. This means that I can peer into the shadows of what may be. If you prevail in your journey, you may well save the entire civilized world." He smiled again. "If you wish, I would be happy to accompany you on your journey. My services may prove of some use."

"Thank you. I'm certain you would be of great value, but the lady Jeinan has already requested to accompany us."

Zarg seemed pleased. "Yes, I had forgotten she made that request. Jeinan is quite capable of providing any assistance you might need. Clearly, if she is accompanying you, my services would be better applied here."

He motioned for Da'ad to follow him back to the other room. "Our spy has gone. Please be careful. I've no idea who they are or how much they know of our plans."

Da'ad thanked him politely as Zarg walked him to the front door. He felt torn. Something about Zarg made him very uneasy. He did not want to trust the shadow mage, yet his instincts told him that much of what Zarg said was true.

Once outside, Da'ad hurried to find Jeinan. She was near where they last spoke, pacing, with a look of worry on her face.

"Thoren, I'm sorry. I should have been more careful."

"It's all right. He doesn't know it was you. I don't believe it was your fault anyway. Zarg seemed prepared for an intruder."

"That would mean he was expecting something like this."

"I don't think he expected it so much as he planned for it. He indicated that there is trouble afoot. He even suggested there may be spies on the council."

"It is a possibility. There have been several rifts, and ambitions seem poised for a power play. Perhaps what they dare not do directly they may ask another to do for them."

"Zarg seems to think it goes deeper than petty politics."

"Do you trust him?"

"No, but I can't say I doubt him either. My instincts tell me that much of what he said is true. Besides, this ring is supposed to glow red in the presence of a lie. I don't suppose he could have found some way to trick it?"

"May I see that?"

Da'ad quietly removed the ring and placed it in her hand.

"Where did you get this?"

"During our recent travels, we happened upon the Liches. Their king presented me with several gifts for services rendered. He said the ring would glow red when in the presence of a lie." Jeinan continued to study it intently. "Is everything all right?"

"The ring is legitimate. I cannot detect any hints of curses or dark magic in it. By all accounts, it appears to be what you described. Have you shown it to anyone else?"

"Only those who were with me when I received it."

"Good. The fewer people who know about this, the better it is for us." She paused for thought. "I've never heard of Zarg's medallion, but if this is what I think it is, then you really have something. I'm just amazed that the Liche King would part with it."

"Do you think that Zarg might have countered its powers?"

"I know this ring. Its power is far too strong to be countered by any spell I've ever heard of."

"Perhaps we should get out of the street."

"Yes, of course. I'll accompany you back to the inn."

"I'll notify the others that we leave day after tomorrow."

"I'll meet you at the gate. Some of my staff will accompany us."

"Will that be necessary?"

"Yes. If we find the vaults, I will need someone to notify Terek. I'll also need someone to transport the table back to Lunora once we are finished with it."

"Do you think that's wise?"

"I trust my staff completely, and Terek will not allow the table to be misused once it's placed in his care."

"You trust Master Greyscale then?"

"Yes, with my life. He's been like a second father to me and is probably the only person on the council whose ambitions are largely selfless. Surprisingly, that is likely the reason he was chosen to lead the council."

"All right, bring as many people as you need, but only those you trust," Da'ad cautioned.

As they reached the inn, he wished her good night and offered to walk her home. "You need your rest. We've a long journey ahead of us, and it may be some time before we see the comforts of home again," she relied.

Da'ad bowed and stepped inside then watched from the window as Jeinan disappeared. He was joined by Phineus a few minutes later while entering his room.

"May I come in?"

"Why not? Have a seat."

Phineus pulled up a chair. Da'ad sat on the bed. "How did it go with the council?"

"About as I expected, except with a twist."

"Twist? Is that good or bad?"

"I'm not sure. Not surprisingly, the council is buried in politics. They'll eventually come around, but there are significant danger signs. I've some reason to think there may be one or more spies among them."

"Why do you think that?"

"I was told by one of the councilmen. Jeinan seems to think it possible, and what I witnessed in the chamber may even make it likely."

"What do we do about it?"

"Nothing yet. We've other business to see to first."

"The vaults?"

"That's certainly part of it. Once we find them, I can begin work on the other part."

"What would that be?"

"I'd prefer to keep that private for the time being. It's nothing personal. I just can't take the chance that someone else might be listening."

Phineus nodded and scratched his chin. "So how are you and Jeinan getting on?"

Da'ad sat up. "She still has some of the old feelings. For my part, I wish she hadn't, but she's been surprisingly low key about it."

"Is she really coming with us?"

"Yes, and she'll be bringing some of her staff. We leave day after tomorrow."

Phineus stood and walked to the door. "Well, best be getting to bed."

Da'ad joined Bek and Riada for breakfast the next morning. They talked about many things before Da'ad informed them of his plans to leave the next day.

"I suppose all good things must end," Riada lamented.

"We've a lot of work ahead of us, and we've delayed long enough. It's time to get going again," Da'ad explained.

"Is the sorceress really coming with us?" Bek asked.

"The lady Jeinan will be joining us." Da'ad paused to taste his food. "Do either of you know where the library is?"

"I thought you were the one who has been here before. I've certainly never seen it." Bek shrugged.

"Libraries aren't my hobby, sir. Still, I thought it might have been near the gate."

"No, I don't think so. That's one of the few places I would remember seeing it."

"Why not inquire of Phineus? He's probably been there since our arrival."

"Not a bad idea, but I think I'll go looking for it on my own first."

"Suit yourself."

Da'ad finished eating and then excused himself, with no idea where he was headed. The streets were quiet, as it would be several hours before most of the shops opened.

Most of the others were eating, when he returned. "I see you went for a walk. How was it?" Phineus inquired.

"Good."

Da'ad noticed Bek, conversing with two of the elves near the bar and apologized to Phineus before joining them. "Do you have a moment?"

"Sure. What's on your mind?"

"I'd like you to see to it that the team is ready to leave by morning. I've a few things to do in town."

"When will you be back?"

"I'm not certain. It really depends on how successful I am."

"Well, everything will be ready by this evening. When morning comes, we'll only need to make our way to the horses and carts."

"I appreciate that." Da'ad turned to track down Phineus. He found him a few feet away, glancing out the window. "You busy today?"

Slightly startled, Phineus turned around. "No, not at all. What did you have in mind?"

"I thought we might drop in on an old friend. That is, if you care to join me."

"Why not? Who did you want to see?"

"Gradon Treyor."

"Gradon? Is he in Lunora?"

"He is, and I intend to pay him a visit."

"But he is not even a wizard. Gradon never showed any interest in Lunora when I knew him."

"When was the last time you saw him?"

"I admit it's been a while."

"Yes. Well, he wrote me last year. He wanted to let me know that he was interested in settling down. Evidently he has a girl with him. He wrote to tell me that he purchased a shop and was planning to settle in permanently."

"Who would have figured it?"

"Shall we get going?" Da'ad asked.

Phineus nodded. "Hard to believe Gradon is settled in Lunora. He never liked to stay anywhere very long. You say he wrote to you?"

"He did. He wanted some advice and needed to let me know how to get in touch with him. Unfortunately, I couldn't help him."

"As hard as it is to imagine him settled down, it's even more difficult to think of him being in love. Gradon never spent more than a minute conversing with any girl in his life. I had the feeling he found them uninteresting."

Da'ad smiled quietly. He paused at the street corner and checked his direction. "This way." He motioned as he led the way to a curious little shop. There were no signs out front. The window was full of old books and oddities. "Shall we go inside?"

Phineus opened the door and waited. The door collided with a small chime, alerting the merchant that someone was entering. A young girl glanced up from behind the front desk where she was arranging books and asked nervously, "May I help you?"

"Flora?" Da'ad asked. The girl nodded, a bit more nervous than before. "Is your uncle in?"

Without taking her eyes off Da'ad, she made her way into the back. "Uncle, there are two men here to see you."

A short time later, a very thin gentleman entered the room, squinted a bit, put on his spectacles, and stared at Da'ad. After a few seconds, he called out, "Thoren? What brings you through my door?" He scarcely took a step before adding, "And Phineus Mibbin. I dare say, I never expected to see you here."

"Nor I you. Can it be that you're settling down in one place now?"

"It was necessary. My brother died, and I've been caring for my niece for about a year now. She's a good girl and deserves better, but even this is better than a life on the road." Gradon turned back to Da'ad and asked, "So to what do I owe this surprise?"

Da'ad offered his hand. "Business mostly."

"Only mostly? Tell me, Thoren, what else is on your mind?"

"I need some information."

"I do have a lot of that. Perhaps if you tell me what you are looking for, I might be able to help."

"You always did cut to the point. I need to find out about an amulet. I'm told that it was created by Reglis, and though I've not seen the piece, I have seen what I believe to be an accurate replica. The piece is supposed to be a protective charm against hostile magic. The wizard Zarg has the replica. I thought perhaps he might have purchased it here."

Gradon shook his head. "No. I seldom deal in replicas. Zarg comes by periodically, but he did not get that piece from me. Perhaps I can look it up in the back since the piece is known."

"You've heard of it then?" Phineus asked.

Gradon shook his head. "No. But it is known to Zarg, and he must have learned of it somewhere. Since Reglis wasn't around to share the information, I would wager he learned of it in a book."

"I would say that's a good guess. Do you think you can find it?"

"I have access to the same books Zarg has. If Reglis created the item, it should be listed. Can you describe it for me?"

"It is about this large"—Da'ad held up his hands in a circular shape—"golden in color, with a red stone, perhaps a ruby, in the center."

Gradon handed him a slate. "Sketch it for me."

Da'ad made a quick sketch. Gradon looked it over, asked a few questions, and then proceeded to the back room. He was gone barely two minutes when he returned with a dusty old box. "Let me do some digging around. I should know something by tomorrow afternoon. If you stop in then, I'll let you know what I find."

Da'ad shook his head. "We'll be leaving in the morning. I was hoping you might know something now."

"You can come into the back room and wait. I do have some idea what I'm looking for."

"How long will this take?"

"No idea."

Gradon spent almost an hour digging through books, with no success. When he eventually found a reference to what he believed to be the item, it was very abbreviated.

"This could be what we're looking for."

"I'd like to be certain. What does it say?"

"It appears Reglis did indeed possess an amulet as you've described. Of course, it doesn't tell us anything you don't already know."

"No, but it does confirm a few things. That will do nicely. Thank you. I would appreciate it if you do not mention this to anyone. If anyone asks, tell them this was a social call."

Da'ad handed Gradon a small purse and bowed his head. "Your secrets have always been safe with me," Gradon agreed.

"Thanks again."

Phineus remained behind for several seconds, unaware that Da'ad had gone, and then politely excused himself. Once outside, he found Da'ad leaning against a post. The old man placed a hand on it and rested. "I thought you mentioned Gradon had a girlfriend."

Da'ad laughed. "You assumed that's what I meant. I said only that he had a girl with him. I referred to his niece."

"You knew I misunderstood."

"I strongly suspected it."

After pretending to be upset, Phineus laughed. They remained under the light post for about a minute and then started back toward the inn. Da'ad eventually returned outside and sat in a wooden rocker overlooking the porch. He threw his feet up on an old apple crate and closed his eyes. Without realizing it, he drifted off to sleep.

When he awoke, someone was calling his name.

"Thoren, are you all right?"

Da'ad slowly opened his eyes to the blurred figure of Jeinan standing above him.

"I didn't mean to interrupt your sleep. It's just that I thought you might like to have dinner with me tonight, being that we are leaving in the morning and shan't be back for some time."

Da'ad stumbled over his words. He stood up slowly and stretched his arms. After a brief silence, he asked, "What was that?"

Jeinan laughed. "I just came to invite you to dinner. There is a nice little restaurant near here. They make very good venison steak."

"Sure, why not?"

"Great. Let's get going."

"Do you mind if I get cleaned up first?"

Jeinan looked at his unkempt hair and his shirt. "That's probably a good idea. I'll wait for you here."

As Da'ad hurried to his room, Jeinan entered the common area and took a seat on a small sofa. Phineus was reading across the way from her.

He glanced up long enough to recognize her. "How are you today, my dear?"

"Just fine. Thank you."

"Are you waiting for Thoren?"

"Yes, I am."

"Quite a fellow, Thoren. He's a good friend, very loyal you know."

"Yes, he is."

After a brief pause, she explained, "I knew him when he met his wife. I guess part of me was disappointed that it wasn't me. She was a good person and very good for Thoren. I was very distraught to learn of her death."

"As were we all." Phineus was about to say something more when Da'ad arrived. "Well, it's been a pleasure speaking with you. Enjoy your outing."

"I'm sure we will," Jeinan replied.

She turned to Da'ad. "You look very nice. Much better than a moment ago."

So will we be going anywhere special?"

"I hope so. I have a very nice place in mind."

"Where's that?"

"It's a surprise."

"Don't let it be said I never appreciated a good surprise." Da'ad motioned with his hand for her to lead on. They eventually stopped at an empty lot. There were two small towers touching either side of it. Between the towers was a faint glow.

"Why have we stopped?"

"We're here. Move into the light, but be careful. It can be a little disorienting."

Da'ad was puzzled but did as she asked. He stepped into the light and felt momentarily as though something were pulling at him. He blinked for just an instant and then realized that he was no longer between the towers.

He was standing in a fancy waiting room of what appeared to be a restaurant. Jeinan arrived a few seconds later.

"Where are we?" he asked her.

She smiled as she moved toward an attentive-looking waiter. "This is the restaurant I wanted to show you."

They heard numerous faint voices through the walls but saw only the waiter. He greeted them pleasantly.

"Have you a reservation?"

"Yes."

"Is this your first time dining here?"

Da'ad was about to answer yes, but Jeinan cut him off. "No."

"Good. Welcome back."

The waiter led them through a narrow doorway at the end of the hall. "Would you like to choose a theme, or shall I recommend one?"

Da'ad glanced at Jeinan.

"What do you have available?" she inquired.

"We have the Baths of Covent, the Games of Tempest Mair, or the Showers of the Mystic Forest."

Jeinan frowned. "When do you expect the Morning Gardens to be available?"

The waiter turned toward a small desk and opened his book. "We should be able to set up the Morning Gardens for you. It may take a few minutes."

Da'ad followed Jeinan back into the waiting room. About five minutes later, the waiter returned. "Your booth is ready. Follow me please."

"This is a fantastic setting. I'm certain you'll love it. The gardens are based on the ancient Gardens of Behl, near the present city of Freelance. It's one of the more pleasant settings I've ever seen."

Da'ad's interest was piqued. He nodded approvingly. "How's the food?"

"Wonderful. They have a venison steak to die for. You'll love the setting—a garden paradise with the warm sun shining over the horizon and a cozy breeze rustling through the trees."

Da'ad was about to comment when the waiter motioned toward the booth. The tabletop was made of polished marble. It was set with two silver trays. There were two menus resting near the trays. A massive candlestick held half a dozen lit candles at the table's center.

"The gardens will form in a moment. When you are ready to order, just write the numbers of your selections on the pad and place it on the tray. If for any reason you need me, tap twice on the candlestick with your spoon. I should be here within two minutes. Also, if you wish to interact with characters from the garden scene, let me know."

"That won't be necessary. Thank you."

"Very well. Enjoy your meal."

Da'ad watched with Jeinan as the dark ceiling gradually grew brighter until it resembled the morning sky. The sun appeared on the eastern horizon and began to rise slowly. There were numerous flowers and plants sprouting from the ground. A midsized gazebo appeared around them.

The sound of songbirds echoed through the air. "Impressive," Da'ad remarked.

Jeinan smiled. "Do you really like it?"

"I do. This is very pleasant. Thank you."

"Have you glanced at the menu yet?"

Da'ad suddenly remembered he was in a restaurant. "Not yet. I guess it slipped my mind."

Jeinan laughed. She wrote down her selection and placed the paper on the tray in front of her. Da'ad watched it vanish. In its place, a large tray of food appeared with a bottle of wine and two glasses.

Da'ad quickly browsed the menu and made his own selection as Jeinan poured the wine. When his food appeared, he glaced at it. "It certainly looks good."

"Go ahead and taste it. You won't be disappointed."

Da'ad slowly cut a small piece from the steak and lifted it to his mouth.

"You're right. This is superb. My compliments on your choice."

Jeinan smiled proudly. She slowly raised her glass. "To a successful journey."

"Here, here."

"Perhaps someday I'll show you the Baths of Covent. You get to soak in a warm sauna, surrounded by huge columns, beautiful art, and fancy gardens."

"Sounds interesting, but I think the present setting suits me fine."

Jeinan laughed lightly to mask her disappointment. "Perhaps someday you'll change your mind. It's a fantastic experience. I highly recommend it."

"Perhaps someday." After eating, Da'ad accompanied her for a brief turn about the garden. When they returned to the table, Jeinan tapped her spoon twice on the centerpiece.

"So what's the damage?"

"It's compliments of the council. They authorized it last night. It's their way of wishing us well on our journey."

"Was it their idea then?"

"No. The idea was mine. I mentioned it to Terek last night. He thought it was a good one and insisted on paying for it. Officially, of course."

Da'ad nodded as he put away his purse. When the waiter appeared, Jeinan handed him a sealed envelope. "The council will be covering the cost today." The waiter bowed and thanked her politely. He then raised his hands and clapped. As he did so, the garden disappeared.

"If you will now follow me, I will show you to the exit."

Da'ad and Jeinan both stood and walked to the teleporter. By the time they reached the lot, the daylight was nearly gone. Streetlights provided some illumination.

Jeinan smiled as she took Da'ad by the arm. "If we start back now, we may just have enough time for tea."

"Thank you for dinner. It was just the excursion I needed."

"I know what you mean. I often feel the same way. It is quite relaxing. Still, it gets expensive if I visit too often. I try to limit myself to just one visit a month."

They continued to converse until they reached the house, a large, stately manor. It was well furnished, both inside and out, and surrounded by large lawns on three sides. Trees and other plants blocked out much of the view from the street.

This was not Da'ad's first visit to the estate, so he said nothing of its grandeur. He was reluctant to go inside. They spent only a few minutes sipping tea before he stood to leave. "I really must be going. I've a few things to take care of before morning."

Jeinan leaned toward him as he prepared to leave and kissed him lightly on the cheek. Her kiss caught him off guard. He stumbled backward a step or two and then attempted to speak but could not for several seconds.

"What was that for?" he eventually asked.

Jeinan's expression was one of satisfaction and conquest. "Old friends and new futures. Good night, Thoren."

THE WRAITH
AND THE TABLE

D a'ad returned to the inn just in time to catch Bek on his way upstairs. "Lieutenant! Do you have a moment?"
"Yes. Everything is loaded and taken care of, just as you asked."

"Thank you. Were there any problems?"

"No, sir. Not a one."

"Very well. Carry on."

Da'ad paced the lobby for several minutes before retiring to his room for the night. When he awoke the next morning, he joined the others at the breakfast table then inspected the carts and animals outside.

Bek caught up with him, a short time later. "We've finished inspecting the line. There were a few minor problems with some of the spare parts, but everything is in order now."

"Thank you, Lieutenant."

Jeinan arrived a few minutes later. She was wearing a thick traveler's cloak over her gown.

Her bodyguard, a tall, serious-looking woman, helped her down. She had little need for a bodyguard but kept one anyway, mostly because it was fashionable among the Lunorian elite.

As she stepped away from the coach, she began issuing last-minute instructions to her staff, many of whom would soon be returning home. Her bags, consisting of two large trunks and a tent, were loaded into a large covered wagon. She took a seat atop the wagon next to the driver, waved good-bye to her coach, and then bowed her head respectfully as Da'ad approached. "I am ready to get under way as soon as you are."

"We just need to take a final roll call and we'll be ready. Are all of your people here?"

"They are."

"Good. I'll check back with you as soon as we are finished."

There was quite a crowd gathered to see them off. Several members of the council were present. In the distance, Da'ad spotted Zarg watching from a rented balcony. Terek Greyscale was much nearer watching with several of his aides from a neighboring porch. A group of small children handed out flowers to the soldiers, some of which transformed into tiny birds and flew away. As the last cart exited the gate, the city began fading from view. It was quickly replaced by a grand illusion.

Da'ad approached Jeinan's cart on horseback, hoping for a word with her. She was more than happy to indulge him. "It's been some time since I've left the city. I've been itching to get out for quite a while."

"Then I guess you have your wish. I hope it's all you want it to be. We'll be on the road for a long time."

"Life is never boring, Thoren, when you're around. I'm certain I'll be just fine."

Da'ad saluted politely and then rode ahead to check on the rest of the column. It took several days to traverse the forest. The group was slowed by the number of large carts in their company.

In the evenings, they set up camp along a small river. Jeinan often provided entertainment, performing magical light shows over the campfire. She used her hands to manipulate the size, color, and shapes of the flames. Her use of magic boosted morale. Phineus, like many of the others, was quite captivated by the shows. He made several attempts to duplicate the effects with science, having limited success with the size, color, and brightness but never with the shape of the flames. Still, the men found his achievements fascinating.

Many of those in the company played cards around the fire in the evenings. Da'ad seldom participated and was usually one of the first to retire. He shared his tent with Riada and Phineus, though Phineus sometimes preferred to sleep in his cart.

The only other large tent in the group belonged to Jeinan. Being a lady in a camp full of men, she appreciated the privacy her tent afforded but spent little time there other than to change or sleep. She much preferred to socialize and, unlike Da'ad, spent most of her time surrounded by others.

Leatis was frequently absent from camp, preferring to scout the path ahead. He seldom used a tent, and though no one knew just how far he traveled, he always seemed nearby when needed.

At night, the campfire remained a popular setting. Many of the men shared ghost stories over a bottle of ale. Some played cards while others watched. Phineus often found time for conversation, particularly with the elves.

Jeinan ceased her magic shows when the group reached the Red Cliffs. She began spending much of her time soliciting conversation with Da'ad. When she could not converse with him, she was often conversing about him. Phineus spent a fair amount of time collecting plant and soil samples. Jeinan occasionally assisted, though she clearly did not share his passion for geology.

The fog, which concealed the region the last time the Paladins visited, was completely gone. The air was filled with moisture and a slight chill. By evening, heavy winds entered the pass.

They funneled through the mouth of the canyon, leading into the northland. In order to avoid them, Da'ad ordered his team to set up camp near the mountains some distance to the west. The men and elves built a rock wall about four and one half feet high around the tents. It was fortified with dirt and mud.

Even Leatis stayed within the walls during the night. The howl of the rushing wind created an eerie sound as it echoed through the pass. It masked the far more chilling sounds of the mountain creepers. A few hours into the night, Da'ad was awakened by the sound of Leatis's voice calling out. "Colonel, something has entered the camp! We must investigate."

"What is it?" Da'ad called as he reached for his weapon. Unfortunately, Leatis was already gone.

Da'ad did not expect to find much when he emerged from his tent. To his surprise, he saw a giant fruit bear in the midst of the camp. Several of his men were preparing to engage it, though Leatis believed it best to wait.

The bear was standing on its hind legs and seemed largely ignorant of the men. It was at least nine feet tall. As his men surrounded it, Da'ad noticed Jeinan standing a few feet in front of the creature. She was wearing a hooded cloak for protection against the elements. The bear was making several soft growling noises but gave no indication of hostility.

Leatis motioned for Da'ad. "I think it best that we take a wait-and-see approach. The bear has not attacked anyone yet, and unless I miss my guess, the lady Jeinan appears to be conversing with it."

Da'ad motioned for his men to back away. They watched for several minutes as Jeinan continued her communication. Her mouth was moving, but in the wind, Da'ad could hear nothing. There was a nervous tension in the air. No one knew quite how to respond.

After a few minutes, the bear lowered itself onto all four legs and galloped out of camp. Jeinan turned toward Da'ad as the rain streaked down her cheeks like giant teardrops. He at first believed her upset but soon discovered otherwise. She attempted to address him, but in the heavy wind and rain, he failed to understand. Realizing this, she motioned toward her tent and then escorted him inside. "There is a creature waiting for us on the path ahead."

"The Liche King! We crossed their path before."

Jeinan shook her head. "No, something more evil. The bear told me he felt something there."

Da'ad perked up. "Then you were conversing with that bear."

"Yes, I summoned him to scout the road ahead. I've felt something that has made me uneasy of late and thought it best to find out more about what is out there before we encounter it."

"So what should we expect?"

"From the bear's description, it sounds like a phantom or specter of some kind, possibly left over from one of the necromancers' twisted experiments."

"Should we go around another way?"

"We can't. The specter is positioned too near our destination. There are no other routes that avoid it."

"Then what do you suggest?"

"I think we should play things out for the time being. If its intentions are hostile, I should be able to provide us with some protection, at least long enough to make our escape."

"What if it pursues us?"

"It won't. It can't. The range of a specter of this type is limited. It is likely that there is some physical object, possibly a bone, which ties the creature to this world. It will only be able to travel a limited distance from that object."

"You're certain?"

"I am."

"Good, then we will proceed in the morning. Make sure you are prepared to defend against this thing, whatever it may be."

"I will be."

As Da'ad turned to leave, Jeinan called, "One more thing, Thoren. I'm sensing something else."

Da'ad paused and then turned to face her. "More danger?"

"I don't think so. This feeling is peaceful. It has a familiarity to it, as though I should recognize the presence."

The revelation stunned Da'ad. "Yes, I've felt it too. It is almost as though Sela were here again."

"Perhaps she means to protect you from something."

A thoughtful look crossed Da'ad's face as he turned to leave. Phineus and Riada were both sleeping when he reached the tent. The camp was calm now. Only the night watch remained outside.

Da'ad lay down quietly so as not to disturb the others. He reflected on Jeinan's words, wondering to himself what might be waiting for them.

The group returned to the road early, the next morning. The wind died down, and the team made surprisingly good time through the pass. Their pace slowed as they moved from the rocky pass into the saturated lands of the north. Many of the wagons became stuck, some of them repeatedly, in the thick mud.

Though it was clear that the storm had crossed the mountains, most of the water appeared to be related to runoff. The group continued to struggle for about half a mile until the road improved. The valley was filled with a strong foreboding, which only increased as the group neared the ruins of Rosewood.

Da'ad was forced by a series of equipment malfunctions to halt his team along the outskirts of the dead city. They reluctantly set up camp. Only minutes after finishing, strong winds knocked down and damaged one of the tents. It took an hour to repair the damage. Such mishaps continued for the entire duration of their stay.

Several members of the group were spooked by an ominous shadow that appeared unexpectedly around the camp. One of the cooks sensed something in her tent and refused to enter. A soldier injured his ankle responding to her screams.

Strange reports continued to reach Da'ad throughout the night. No one slept much. There was a midnight report of a goblin raider. Another soldier reported a creeper in his tent. Both sightings were dead ends. There was no evidence that anything was ever there. Phineus reported seeing his dead brother's decaying form chiding him for past transgressions.

When Da'ad inquired about the matter, the old man responded, "My brother died of natural causes nearly ten years ago. Up until now, I've always considered the relationship we had to be a good one."

"That was not your brother. I think it's time we leave this place."

"I heartily agree. I'm not sure how much more of this my aged heart can take."

Following his conversation with Phineus, Da'ad paced about the camp for almost an hour. By sunrise, only Jeinan appeared to have slept well. Da'ad, who had somehow avoided the sightings directly, spent the better part of the night responding to others' terrifying encounters. He briefly spoke with Leatis. "Anything to report?"

"Only that there is most definitely a hostile presence in camp. If we do not leave this place soon, I fear we may have more than ghost sightings to worry about."

"Jeinan assured me that she could handle any spekter we might encounter."

"I would that this were a mere specter. We need to leave here. It is no accident that this creature is pursuing us."

"Have the men take down the camp, and let's get everything ready to move out as quickly as possible."

Leatis nodded. The mishaps continued to plague the group as they packed.

Desperate, Da'ad pleaded with Jeinan, "Is there anything you can do to stop this?"

She nodded, reciting a brief incantation, and then said, "This should help a bit, but it's surprisingly difficult to counter this creature."

The group broke camp with great difficulty and proceeded to the hill. Jeinan's spell appeared to help. The strange sightings declined both in number and intensity.

Da'ad refused to stop until they were well clear of the borders of Rosewood. By this time, his group was only a few hundred meters from the hill. They were tired and beaten and had to stop.

Though there were still several hours of good daylight left, Da'ad chose not to enter the chamber right away.

Most members of the group slept better than the previous night. Still, there was a strange evil lurking like a thick haze just outside the camp. Da'ad watched it for a time as it hovered just out of reach of the tents. It was little more than a shadow, yet its presence was very real.

Like most of the others, Da'ad remained uneasy about it. When the morning came, he shared a meal with some of the others and then sought out Jeinan for advice. Surprisingly, she was still in her tent when he found her.

He hesitated before announcing himself and then heard a voice, too faint to make out clearly.

"Hello. It's Thoren. Is everything all right?"

"Come in."

Jeinan was hidden in the shadows along the far wall. She was seated on a blanket with her legs crossed and appeared to be in a trance. Her face was strangely contorted as if taken with madness. Da'ad remained near the door.

Looking at him, she called out, "Welcome," in a very distorted voice, not fully her own. There was an unusual smirk on her face.

"Who are you?" Da'ad asked.

He almost hoped she would not answer and was secretly relieved when Phineus opened the door behind him before she could. Almost immediately, Da'ad felt a dark presence seize upon him. It was as though something were attempting to destroy him from within. After fighting it for several seconds, he lost consciousness. He felt a deep despair, as if he were about to cease existing.

He found himself surrounded in darkness. The despair continued to build until he could take it no longer. Just as he was about to succumb, he saw a faint glow, which grew gradually larger. His hope increased with the light, until he could feel the darkness releasing him.

Soon, his surroundings came back into focus. He saw Jeinan lying on the floor along the far wall. Phineus was kneeling above him. Unable to stand, Da'ad called out, "See to Jeinan!"

Phineus quickly complied. Jeinan awoke, moments later. She had no memory of the morning's events.

"What is the last thing you recall?" Da'ad asked her.

"I remember waking up for breakfast. I was about to get changed when I noticed a strange shadow in the tent. It started moving toward me, and then everything went blank. The next thing I remember was seeing Phineus hunched over me."

"Do you know what caused this?"

"The shadow had all of the characteristics of a wraith."

"A wraith?" Da'ad and Phineus responded in unison.

"Yes. It must have been summoned to stop us. Ordinarily, I would have suspected the necromancers, but under the circumstances, that seems unlikely. Someone else must have summoned it."

"You mentioned that these creatures have a limited range. Can we find whatever is holding it here and destroy the object?"

"Ordinarily, I would say yes, but wraiths are not like other specters. They are bound only by the spell that summoned them."

"Who would want to summon such a creature to attack us?"

"I've no idea. Had I known we would be facing a wraith, I would never have advised you to come here. That creature should have destroyed us."

"What caused it to leave?" Phineus asked.

"I don't know. It is unusual for a wraith to flee like that." A thoughtful look crossed Jeinan's face. She turned to Da'ad. "I have one thought. Recall when I told you at the cliffs I sensed another presence?"

"I do."

"I still sense it. You have a protector."

"Do you mean to tell me that we are still not alone?" Phineus asked.

"That is precisely what I'm saying. When the wraith attacked Thoren, it was confronted and driven off by another presence."

"Is that theory or reality?" Da'ad asked.

"It's speculation, but it is the only explanation I can think of."

Da'ad nodded. "It is possible. If true, it certainly explains a few things." He recounted seeing the light appear as the darkness began to release him.

When he was finished, Phineus assisted him back to his tent. There was no further sign of trouble for the remainder of the day. Da'ad put off entering the chamber for another day and spent much of the afternoon in bed. Jeinan too spent an unusual amount of time resting.

———⟨∞⟩———

By the next morning, both were fully recovered. There was no further sign of the wraith, and the entire camp was benefited by a peaceful evening. Breakfast was refreshing. Da'ad took his time eating. The cooks prepared a fine meal, and he wanted to savor every bite.

Following breakfast, he ordered, "Let's get to the hill. I want that chamber opened."

He sent Leatis and Riada with two others to prepare the opening. They reached the site nearly five minutes ahead of Da'ad and removed the wooden planks from the hole.

Jeinan was the first to peer into the dark cavern. She cast a spell, which lit the chamber below. A rope ladder was secured at the top and lowered. Da'ad was the first one down, followed by

Leatis, Riada, two Paladins, an elvish scout, and Jeinan. Several others entered later. Da'ad led the group toward the large doors at the end of the hall. They were locked again, and the key was conveniently located in the hands of one of the centaur corpses. The colonel motioned for the others to back away and then raised his sword. Jeinan stopped him and uttered a small enchantment. She then took the key from the hands of the corpse without incident. With a smile, she handed it to Da'ad. "There are always simpler ways of doing things."

He inserted the key into the doors and unlocked them. A cool breeze rushed through the chamber, stirring up dust as the doors opened. Da'ad waited several seconds for it to settle before entering.

Jeinan followed with several of the others in tow. She extended her lighting spell to cover the newly opened room. The remnants of the team's old torches were visible along the walls. The old wooden table was resting quietly in the center of the room. There were no other visible furnishings.

Many of Da'ad's companions sat down on the massive stone blocks that supported the pillars. Jeinan moved quickly to examine the table. The tabletop was flat and no longer had a map upon its face. She uttered something, and the table began to morph, revealing valleys and other large features, including a city near the edge.

Phineus studied the features intently. "Fantastic! This is the pirate city of Verne. It is about two hundred and fifty miles north of Thornguard."

"Then that is where we will find the vaults of Reglis," Jeinan declared.

"I'm afraid Verne is not among the more hospitable places on earth. It is a slum city filled with thieves and outlaws and has caused much trouble for Thornguard of late," Phineus remarked.

Jeinan nodded. "The vaults are beneath the city somewhere. We must travel to Verne if we are to access them."

This was a surprising development. "Why would Reglis hide the bulk of his wealth in a pirates' den?" Da'ad asked.

"You're thinking about this all wrong. The city may be a pirates' den now, but that was not always the case. When Reglis was alive, Verne did not exist. There was another city in its place, one inhabited by the centaurs. The city was devastated during the war that wiped out the centaur race, but it remains very possible that the vaults are still hidden and undisturbed there."

"We lack the numbers necessary to secure the treasure, even if we should find it. With so many thieves and cutthroats, we might be better off if we did not," Da'ad speculated.

Jeinan disagreed. "The pirates are not well organized. They may feed off others, but they are not terribly loyal or intelligent, and I believe we will be able to handle them."

"You mean to fight the entire city?"

"Not at all. Even a wizard cannot handle so many without significant risk. It would be unwise to make the attempt. I am merely alluding to the fact that Reglis was no fool. He was very skilled in the shadow arts and would not have neglected to plan for our present situation, which he very likely foresaw. Reglis would never have hidden his vaults for all to find. We should have little trouble entering unseen."

"All right. We'll make the attempt, but at the first sign that we are in over our heads, I mean to withdraw."

"The pirates will not be a match for you with a master wizard at your side, at least not if we avoid a direct fight."

"That is a fact that I do not believe should be well publicized right now. The less the pirates know about us, the better."

"I will honor your wishes. I see no reason to let them know of my skills. If we are cautious, Verne should prove to be little threat to us."

"Perhaps, but I want to draw as little attention as possible. It's likely that with a group this size, we cannot avoid attracting some, but I don't think it wise to draw any more attention than necessary."

"I agree. No point making our job more difficult than it is."

Da'ad turned to Phineus. "Make a sketch of this map. Have the elves assist. I want as much detail as you can manage, especially of the city."

Phineus agreed and began work immediately. He sent Leatis to fetch the elvish scholars. Together they made three rough sketches of the map, each focusing on different parts of the city. This sped their work considerably. When they were finished, they combined their drawings into a single detailed map, showing what they believed to be the precise location of the vaults.

Jeinan returned to the camp and called on her staff. "When the scholars are finished, I want you to retrieve the table and load it onto one of the carts for delivery to Lunora."

"The table will not fit out the entrance."

"Perhaps you should disassemble it and bring it out one piece at a time," Da'ad interrupted.

"That won't be necessary. Come and get me just as soon as Phineus and the elves have completed their work."

The scholars continued their work for several hours. It was nearly lunchtime the next day before their map was ready.

Phineus remained with the table until Jeinan arrived. He was curious to see how she intended to remove the piece. She pulled out a small object from her travel bag, whispered something, and then threw the object against the far wall. The wall gradually opened into a stairwell wide enough to safely remove the table. With help from several of the Paladins, Jeinan's staff carried it to an awaiting cart. She accompanied them up and then supervised as they secured the cargo. Da'ad watched from a distance as the cart disembarked. Jeinan retained only her handmaiden for the trip to Verne.

It took mere minutes to pack up the camp and get underway. The journey was a tedious one. The group encountered a goblin raiding party several days in. No one was injured, but several of the carts were damaged, resulting in mild delays. Two days later the goblins returned. Jeinan scared them off with a simple spell, ending the raid quickly.

"I don't think we will have any more trouble from them," she told Da'ad.

"I hope not. We have more important things to concern ourselves with."

"Such as?"

"Such as reaching Verne. There is still a good distance until we reach the city. The forest ahead is full of creepers and other dangers. After that, there is the Great Inland Desert."

"I can keep the creepers away, and the desert won't bother us so long as we travel at night." The desert was by far the greater obstacle.

Taking her advice, Da'ad refused to travel during the day. He had his men set up camp before sunrise each morning. They made every effort to camp near large rock formations so that the camp might be protected from the desert winds and sand.

Water was readily available from several varieties of cactus and other desert plants. The desert had no permanent settlements, and food was scarce. Da'ad avoided the largely friendly nomads since some of the tribes were hostile and the worst were known to be cannibalistic.

As a result, they had to rely on lizards and edible cactus to supplement their supplies. No one was permitted outside the camp during daylight. By choice, most remained inside their tents.

Vegetation was more common along the desert's northern ridge, a rocky region often traversed by merchants. Da'ad followed it for several days, along a small, intermittent stream. The waters were low but still very much in season.

Da'ad's sleeping disorder worsened with the daylight. His thoughts often wandered as he would stare meaninglessly at the tent ceiling, sometimes for hours. On one such occasion, he stood up to look at the desert sands. They seemed to call to him as depression took hold of his mind. Though he knew not why, he felt compelled to venture out into the scorching sun.

———

In a distant corner of the continent, a conversation was concluding in secret. The darkened water of the reflection dish vibrated with evil.

"How could he defeat the wraith?"

"There is greater power surrounding this one than I expected. You must destroy him."

"The desert sands will take him. Even now, they call to him. He will not be able to resist them. Soon he will be lost in the desert and we will be free to plan your return."

———

Leaving the camp unnoticed, Da'ad scampered eastward with a scarf around his face to protect his eyes, mouth, and nose. He was oblivious to his surroundings as he pressed forward in an easterly direction. Some distance in front of him, he thought he could see someone approaching. She was calling out to him. His skin burned in the midday sun. He used his hands to shield his eyes from the whirl of particles and belting winds.

Even so, his vision was blurred and his eyes swollen. He fell repeatedly into the vast dunes. Once his strength gave out, he collapsed then, with tears in his eyes, looked up at the oddly clear personage before him. "Sela," he gasped.

She smiled warmly as the desert vanished from view. Only her personage remained as he floated across a vast plane of light. Though she said nothing, the love in her eyes was unmistakable. Da'ad found a peace he had not felt since she left him. Somehow he could feel his body slowly releasing him. Much to his surprise, he found himself fighting it. Just as he was about to give in, he felt the sensation of moisture on his lips. Though he heard no voice, his wife appeared to whisper farewell. He watched as she slowly faded from view.

Alone in the darkness, he could hear faint sounds like voices. They gradually grew clearer. Someone muttered, "Quickly. We must get him back to the tents."

He felt someone lifting him and then recognized Bek's voice. "Keep giving him water."

As Da'ad reached the camp, Phineus called out, "Is he dead?"

"Not yet, fortunately. I think we found him in time."

Da'ad could hear Jeinan calling out in the distance. "Quickly. Get him inside." After that, the words faded into mumblings and then silence. The faint light between his eyelids again turned to darkness until he saw only Sela. She seemed very real to him. He could feel her gentle touch and the warmth of her lips on his face. Even the scent of her hair seamed real. At that moment, she was more real to him than any living being.

She knelt beside him and carefully placed his head in her lap. He relaxed as she brushed his face gently with her fingers. "Thoren, our time together is limited. Soon, I must return to my rest."

"Let me come with you."

"I cannot. I am here only as a protector. Your work is not yet finished. Be patient, my love. In time, we shall be together again."

He was about to speak when she cut him off. "Time is short. Listen carefully. When you reach the city, look to the sun for guidance."

"What do you mean?"

She smiled and then repeated, "Look to the sun for guidance. I can tell you no more."

Sela's image faded until Da'ad saw only blurred darkness and then a tiny flicker of light, almost like a candle. He was awake, though he knew not where. His eyes hurt as he struggled to make out the shapes inside Jeinan's tent.

"Where am I?"

He felt the light stroking of a hand across the side of his face and heard Jeinan's voice. "You're going to be all right. Just relax. You need rest."

Her voice was unusually strained. Even in her hushed tones, Da'ad could tell she was troubled. As she pressed his face to her own, he felt the touch of moisture and realized she had been crying.

"What happened?"

"You wandered from camp. We were very fortunate to find you."

His eyes were beginning to heal. He knew Jeinan must have cast a spell to help the process along. The burning in his skin was fading too. Jeinan gasped as she fought back tears. She rubbed some kind of cream on the exposed parts of his face and arms.

Da'ad kept expecting her to say something, but she was too choked up to speak. After several minutes, she whispered, "Please, Thoren, don't ever do this again. I could not bear it if we were to lose you."

Da'ad found himself wanting to speak. He gradually sat up. She stood to assist him, but stopped short of an embrace. "Forgive me. I forget myself sometimes. I know that you are a Paladin and have sworn off love, but I have not, and I cannot help how I feel. Please take care of yourself. We've much left to do, and I need you with us."

A new swell of tears formed in her eyes as she turned away.

She felt ashamed and would not look him in the face. "I love you," she whispered. "I know you've done nothing to encourage my feelings. The fault is entirely my own, but I cannot help how I feel." She attempted to pull away, but he stopped her and wrapped his arm gently around her shoulder. She rested her head on his shoulder and continued crying for several minutes.

A conflict was brewing in Da'ad's heart. He felt trapped by his feelings for Sela, yet he knew he would be lying if he told himself that he had no feelings for Jeinan. It was a conflict that would not be resolved on this night though. He gently patted her on the shoulder. "It's been a long day. Perhaps we both need a little rest." With that, he took his leave of her and returned to his tent.

—⚬⚬⚬—

He spoke with Phineus over breakfast. "Tell me, when I was outside of camp, how did they find me?"

"That's an interesting question. I was sleeping when I could have sworn I heard a woman's voice ask me to check on you. I thought it was my imagination, but I decided I'd better look. When you weren't there, I asked the sergeant if he'd seen you. He said no and thought it unusual that you would have left the tent. I was about to shrug it off when the voice returned. Only this time, the sergeant heard it too. He found footprints headed out of camp and informed Lieutenant Bek, who took a team after you."

Da'ad touched his hand to his heart and whispered to himself, "Thank you, Sela." He looked up at Phineus. "When I was out in that sand, I truly believe that I saw Sela again."

"Are you certain?"

"I was then. I would have done almost anything to be with her. Funny thing, though. When I felt the life slipping from me as we were traversing a plane of light, I couldn't help but to fight it. I wanted more than anything to go with her, but I couldn't."

The old sage scratched his beard. "It is not unheard of for the dead to visit this realm. Perhaps she did return."

Da'ad shrugged. "But for what purpose? She told me that she returned as a protector, but why?"

Da'ad paused. "I do recall something else she said. Look to the sun for guidance. She repeated it to be certain I heard."

"What does it mean?"

"I'm not certain. I hoped you might have an idea."

"Perhaps it will make some sense later."

"You think I might have just dreamed it all?"

"Dreams are a powerful mode of communication."

"They can also be just dreams."

"Be patient, my friend. We'll learn in time, one way or the other. For my part, I can't help but think some outer worldly force had a hand in this. I know of no other way to explain how both the sergeant and I heard a voice."

"I would love to think Sela was with me again, but I can't."

"Can't or won't?"

"How's that?"

"You're afraid. You fear being wrong and so won't dare to hope."

"That doesn't make sense."

"Ah, but it does. You were hurt badly when she died, and you still miss her?"

"Yes."

"And how would you feel if she were back and you lost her again? I mean, if you believed she had returned and then it wasn't so? Thoren, someone called to me. Whatever evil was at work here, something very real has spared you."

Da'ad looked down thoughtfully. "Perhaps I've misjudged you. Your insights are clearer than my own. Losing Sela was the worst time of my life. I nearly lost myself to madness when she died."

"Courage, my friend. No one would want to go through that twice."

<hr />

Days later, the group reached the White River Valley, which bordered the desert to the east. The river valley was quite a contrast with the dry, salty sand of the desert. It was filled with rich soil and trees. To the distant southwest, it touched on the Great Fruited Forest. The tops of the mountains were barely visible along the southern horizon. The massive White River ran through the center of the valley. There was a small lake not far to the west with two tiny streams flowing into it, one of them from the river.

The group spotted a house near the lake. It was weathered and unpainted but very lived in. The porch was partially blocked by a small boat. The front door appeared to be loose and leaned to one side. The hinges were in poor shape and not fully fastened to the frame. The wood suffered from severe rot in places, though the frame appeared to be sound and the roof looked new.

Several holes in the walls allowed light into the house, though no one believed this was intentional. Da'ad motioned for Leatis and Riada to follow him to the door. There was a fishing pole resting nearby. A small clothesline stretched from a tree to the building's corner. Da'ad knocked loudly, causing the door to open slightly. It was quickly pulled back into place by gravity.

"I'm coming!" a man's voice called out.

The voice was cracked and unrefined but not old. It was neither friendly nor hostile. After a short time, a dirty, little man opened the door and smiled. He looked as though he had not seen a bath in years. The stench was strong and offensive, but Da'ad did his best not to show it.

"What can I do for you?" the man asked with a heavy drawl.

"We'd like to borrow your fishing pole. We can pay you."

"What would I do with money? There ain't nowhere to spend it 'round here."

"Perhaps a trade then?"

"What are you offerin'?"

Da'ad showed him a few odd items. He seemed pleased and motioned to the pole next to the door. "Thank you. I'll return it when we are finished."

"Keep it. I've got another one in the house."

Da'ad thanked him again and handed the pole to Riada, who passed it to Leatis. The elf replaced its rusted hook and made a few adjustments before returning it to Riada. "Who's the best fisherman in camp?" Da'ad inquired.

"I am a fair fisherman," Leatis volunteered.

Riada quickly chided, "I grew up fishing."

"Good, then I'll let you go to the lake for fish."

In the hour or two that he spent at the lake, Riada caught several sizable fish. Many of the others took time to wade or bathe in the cool water. They took nearly the whole day off to reacquaint themselves with daylight travel. The next morning, they set out to cross the river.

It was far too wide and deep to wade. The nearest crossing was well out of the way, so they built their own. They began with a pair of wooden rafts, which they used to move rope and one of the heavier carts across the water. They next used logs and planks to construct a sturdy bridge. The rafts were converted for use in the bridge. When finished, their crossing was the sturdiest on the river.

The group set up camp a few miles away and waited until morning to do any serious travel. Fish were plentiful, and the group ate well. What they could not eat, they smoked and saved for later. In the evening, they sang songs around the fire and told stories. Jeinan even coaxed Da'ad into a dance.

After an embarrassing breakfast conversation with Phineus and Jeinan, Da'ad seemed pleased to escape back to his duties. He directed the group north toward a small town of only five homes, where they acquired supplies before turning east toward Verne.

They reached the Thorn Mountains a short while later, which more closely resembled large rolling hills than an actual mountain range. The group followed a trail along the banks of a small stream that weaved and meandered for miles. The trail was littered with wild berries, which the group ate liberally.

Only two days later, they crossed the mountains then stopped briefly at a small inn along the trade route. Due to brigand activity, the inn housed a sizable security force. It was frequented by merchants who gladly paid the higher price for a secure room. To the weary merchants, the Paladins were a welcomed sight. It meant that the roads would be clear of brigands for a brief spell.

While Da'ad and his team rested, his fate was once again being discussed in dark corners of the world. A deep voice inquired, "Did you stop them?"

"Da'ad wandered into the desert as planned. Though I've yet to confirm his death I am confident that he will bother us no more."

"I want confirmation. Have your spies in Thornguard send word the moment they hear anything."

"Yes, Master."

THE PIRATE CITY

D a'ad decided to camp outside the city rather than risk unwanted attention within. Most of the ground around Verne was soft and moist, making it difficult to set up tents.

After some effort, they located a sufficient site on a large stone overhang above a stream. The rocky surface was curved, enabling the water to run away from the tents. The site was less than ideal but better than the mud.

When morning came, Da'ad called everyone together for a quick meeting. "Verne is a lawless region inhabited largely by thieves and pirates. The city has a token governor, but I caution you not to expect much help from him. Government is merely a competing criminal enterprise, and the governor, the head of the state-sponsored crime ring. The law is little more than an excuse for the governor to eliminate his enemies.

"Most of you will remain with the camp for the time being. Those who enter the city are to remain together in assigned groups. No one is to wander off without my permission. Talk to no one unless I authorize it. That includes street vendors. They may be feeling you out as a potential target for some criminal venture. Be cautious, and prepare yourselves for all manner of immorality. The slave trade is very real here. Many of the pirates sell off captives from the ships they hijack.

"We are not here to save those people, unless it can be done without compromising our mission. This is a cruel and inhumane territory, and everyone must be aware of that, or you will be overwhelmed by it. If those of you who remain must contact me inside the city, you are to send no more than two people at a time. Those who enter should disguise themselves and show nothing of value except to bribe the guard. If they bar your entry, then return to Tabor for help."

After addressing the others, Da'ad turned to Jeinan. "Are you certain this is what you want? It may be safer for you to remain here."

"Remain and do what? Worry? I'd rather assume the risk and be timely informed. Besides, all things considered, I don't believe the risk is that high. Like it or not, you're going to need me in there, especially when we find the vaults."

"Very well. I can't say that I'm disappointed. Just be aware of the attention that a beautiful woman, such as yourself, will attract."

"This won't be the first time that I have had to defend myself against an immature male ego."

"Just do so quietly. We don't need a lot of attention. Remember, there is more at stake here than egos and wealth."

"No one is more aware of that than I."

Da'ad nodded then announced to the group the names of those he intended to take into the city. The list included Riada, Jeinan, one of the elvish scholars, and Phineus. Bek was left in charge of the camp.

A single guard patrolled the city gate, serving more as a tool for the controlling criminal organization than as a protector of the city. In fact, his primary duty was to ensure that no visitor left Verne with his purse intact. He performed this duty well.

Those who had regular business in Verne knew to bribe him. Those who would not pay for the privilege to enter were quickly detained and separated from their money. Officially, this was done under the guise of a tax. Individuals who protested too loudly often disappeared, some never to be seen again. The lucky ones were sold off at auction.

Having selected his small team, Da'ad proceeded to the gate, where he confidently held out a purse for the guard. The greedy brigand snatched it, making a quick inspection of its contents, smiled deviously, and motioned them past.

This intrigued Riada. "I expected he would barter for a greater fee."

Da'ad shook his head. "That's not how they operate. The controlling faction is well aware that these bribes fund its organization. If it pinches visitors too heavily, no one will visit. So those who offer a generous bribe are never harassed and may even find themselves under the governor's protection. If the bribe had been insufficient, we would have been met inside by a group of mercenaries and taxed."

Barely a few feet into the city, the team was propositioned by dozens of prostitutes hoping to earn a few extra coins and possibly a warm room for the night. Many of them were little more than walking skeletons.

Da'ad quickly chased them away, tossing a few spare coins into the crowd and shouting, "Now let us alone, ladies. We've no time for such trifles."

Across the street, the auction block was empty. A sign near the door indicated that it opened only twice a week. The streets were frequented by drunks, many of them sailors from the several pirate ships in port. They passed from bar to bar, spending their captured bounties on whiskey and prostitutes before returning to their ships. Da'ad noticed that several of the ships were damaged, possibly by cannon fire. Their crews were busily making repairs, hoping to get them seaworthy as quickly as possible.

A fight broke out across the street. One of the combatants was stabbed and his corpse tossed carelessly into the street. No one seemed very concerned by the murder. A few of the prostitutes casually went through the dead man's pockets. Twice a day a cart passed by, picking up the corpses and taking them to the water for a tradition burial at sea. Most of the bodies were weighted down with stones.

"Mustn't show too much compassion here. It's seen as a weakness," Da'ad cautioned.

Most of the buildings near the water were made of wood from old ships. Several were in ill repair. The air was salty, masking the scent of rot and decay.

The buildings farther inland were nicer, many of them made of brick or stone. The governor's mansion was by far the finest building in town and the only one with a manicured lawn. The lot was surrounded by a fine stone wall, a steel gate, and several uniformed guards. It stuck out like a shark in a pool of piranhas.

"They don't tolerate trespassers here. I suggest we stay away from the mansion for the time being. When the time is right, I'll arrange for a meeting with the governor."

"Are you sure that's wise?" Phineus asked.

Da'ad nodded. In addition to his usual confidence, there was a coldness about him. Riada and the other soldiers showed it too. It was as though they had turned off their emotions.

The city of Verne was divided into four quarters, known as bureaus. Each bureau was controlled by a separate criminal organization. These organizations kicked back a small percentage of their income to the governor, who occasionally mediated their disputes. He otherwise preferred to stay out of the bureaus' business. It was only when he perceived a threat to his own position that the governor acted to curb the bureau chiefs' growing ambitions.

There were no accurate maps depicting the current boundaries of the bureaus. By far the least of the bureaus was the southwest quadrant. It was said that in Verne only two kinds of people resided there: the dead and the dying. It was filled with the sick and diseased of the city. Though its bureau chief was by far the weakest, the others seldom trespassed on his territory.

The bureau's major source of revenue came from the governor, who paid to have the sick kept there. The southwestern chief was largely a henchman of the governor's and did not pay the tax as the other chiefs did. In fact, he resided near the governor's mansion and seldom set foot in the quarter.

The eastern shore was frequented by traders who came to deal in stolen goods. The northern portion of the shore housed the slave market. Captives were stored near the port until sold at auction. The area was frequented by goblins who paid pennies for those no one else wanted. Captives were encouraged to cooperate so as not to end up in a goblin stew.

Verne was built on the ruins of an ancient city. Many of the oldest buildings dated back thousands of years. Some of the original stone structures were still partially in use, and many served as the foundations for more recent buildings.

Da'ad searched for landmarks, comparing the structures with those on his map.

The elf scholar assisted. "The vaults could be anywhere beneath this city. The ruins are more than two thousand years old."

Da'ad studied the map. It showed the precise location of the vaults within the ancient city. With most of the ancient landmarks in disrepair or missing, he compared the map to the present layout of Verne.

Phineus determined several possible locations. "The possibilities are limited. I'd like to sit down inside and better compare the two maps."

"All right. I am a bit hungry."

Da'ad followed Phineus into the nearest establishment, an old pub. The sage continued to look over the maps while the others ate. "It appears that the vaults are in the vicinity of the governor's mansion."

Da'ad stood and walked from the table toward the door. He looked outside in the general direction of the mansion and paused for thought. After several seconds, he rejoined the others. "I think we need to take a closer look at the structures surrounding the mansion."

"What about the mansion itself?" Riada asked.

Jeinan walked to the door. "Its foundation is too new. It is possible we may need to look at some newer buildings, but the solid foundations will be ancient. The brick used in constructing the mansion is no more than a century old. The foundation we are seeking will be made of cut stone and must date back at least one thousand years."

"Very impressive knowledge of history, my lady. You are most correct. The vaults would have been constructed underground of stone, not brick," one of the elves agreed.

"I think it's time we get to work. Let's examine the block and see what we find."

They walked to the mansion's outer wall, where they quickly examined the surrounding buildings. Only two had stone foundations, one of which caught Da'ad's particular attention. The building appeared to be an ancient temple. Part of it had collapsed and been replaced with wood. The structure now housed a pub. In the front, Da'ad studied a large stone slab partially protruding from the ground. Its image was what caught his attention. The top of the slab was inscribed with a depiction of the sun rising over the horizon. The image was duplicated on a wooden carving above the door.

Da'ad reflected on Sela's warning. He turned to Phineus and pointed to the slab. "You don't suppose that could be the sun I was instructed to look to?"

"It may be. I think we should take a closer look."

He motioned to the sign above the door and said with a laugh, "Look. It's called the Sun."

Da'ad led the group inside, where trouble soon found them. Within seconds, he was challenged by an angry drunk, hoping to take out his pent-up aggression on an easy target. The man could not have chosen more poorly. Da'ad easily eluded his punches. Frustrated, the sailor removed a knife and lunged forward. Da'ad again eluded the blow then, using the hilt of his sword, knocked the man unconscious.

Other patrons quickly rustled through his pockets. Da'ad skirted around them and approached the bar. An obese barman looked up. "What'll you have?"

Da'ad pointed to a bottle behind the man, "I'll try that."

The colonel whispered something to Riada as the barman prepared the drink. Most of the bar's patrons recognized him as an outsider. Ordinarily, this would have been problematic, but given his appearance and following his brief encounter with the drunk, most kept their distance.

Still, there were some not yet convinced of his talents. A small group of brigands relaxing near the rear of the pub eventually built enough foolish courage to confront him. They approached with weapons drawn.

Riada moved his hand toward his sword, grasping the hilt, but remained in the background. Da'ad turned to face his would-be attackers with his sword in hand.

Phineus leaned toward Riada. "Aren't you going to help him?"

"He won't need it."

Da'ad slew three of his attackers in a matter of seconds. The final two lost their taste for combat and retreated through the open door.

The barman and two burly guards carried the others into the street. A waitress tossed a large bucket of water over the floor to wash away the blood. The bar gradually thinned out as patrons found various excuses to leave.

"When do you close?" Da'ad asked the nervous barman.

"What do you mean?"

"What time do you kick everyone out and lock the doors?"

"We never close our doors."

Da'ad tossed a small sack onto the counter. "Close them tonight."

"That's bad business."

Da'ad stared him down. "Close the doors tonight, or I will close them for you, and they will never reopen."

"I suppose we can say it is for maintenance. You spilled a fair amount of blood on our floors."

Da'ad nodded. "Good."

"Why do you want us to close anyway?"

"Don't ask too many questions. In a place like this, knowledge could be hazardous. My companions and I would like to be alone. Close down now and leave."

"What time will you be finished?"

"Come back at sunrise."

Reluctantly, the man secured his money and dismissed his staff. "It's all yours for the night. Please try not to break anything. It may not be much, but it's all I have."

When the barman left Da'ad ordered, "Watch the door. He might send for help, and we don't need any surprises." He turned to the others. "Fan out, and see if you can find any sign of a hidden chamber."

"The vaults won't be so easily found. There may be a hidden chamber, but the vaults themselves will be magically sealed," Jeinan advised.

She cast a revelation spell and motioned behind the bar. "Right here." We need to remove these stones."

"The hammer, quickly." One of the soldiers brought it forward and handed it to Da'ad. The colonel smashed through the stones, revealing a hidden stairwell. Jeinan cast a spell to light the area then led the way down the stairs into an old cellar. There were several kegs lying around and a few loose stones, but nothing that would hint at a hidden treasure trove.

"The vaults are here," Jeinan declared.

"Are you certain?" Da'ad asked.

"Yes. There is magic in this place. I can feel it."

"The question is, how do we get to them?" Phineus asked.

"That won't be very difficult. The real concern is what to do when we find them."

"Let's take it one step at a time. Get us inside, and we'll worry about the next step when we get there," Da'ad stated.

Jeinan whispered something under her breath. Within moments, light began shining between the cracks in the stone. The wall gradually opened, revealing a lengthy passage.

Da'ad glanced at Phineus. "Go upstairs and have Riada fetch the others. Tell him we'll wait until his return to make our next move. Have him hurry back. I'll join you in a moment."

Jeinan examined the passage. "It is made of stone and obviously very old, but in good repair. It should be structurally sound."

"Let's get back to the pub. It makes me nervous losing our lookout."

Da'ad had a soldier take up position at the door and then took a seat and waited. It was nearly an hour before Riada reported back. "I left two guards and the cooks in camp."

"That's all right. We shouldn't need them. Have everyone else line up near the stairs and wait. I want you to remain here. I'll take Phineus, Jeinan, Leatis, and the other elves downstairs. When I'm ready, I'll send someone up for you."

With Da'ad in the lead, the group moved back to the cellar. Jeinan sealed the wall behind them. Many of the stones were loose, though there was little risk of collapse. The architecture gradually improved as the group traveled farther beneath the city. The rough stone and wooden beams eventually turned to polished marble pillars. The pillars supported several massive archways holding up the vast ceiling of a large room or chamber. The interior closely resembled a cathedral. There was a great stone statue near the far end guarding two locked metal gates. The rooms behind the gates were dark.

"I cannot light those rooms until the gates are opened."

The gates appeared to be made of gold and were locked with no visible keyhole. Phineus used the wizard's text to translate an inscription above the doorway. When he finished, Jeinan requested, "Read that again."

Phineus did so. "What language are these characters?"

One of the elves examined the inscription. "It's the dead language of the centaurs, my lady."

"Can you read it in its original tongue?"

"I can."

"Good, then do so."

As the elf finished, the group heard several clicking sounds within the gate. Da'ad gave it a light push. Leatis opened the second gate.

Jeinan called out, "Wait!"

She carefully inspected the stone guardian. "What is the centaur word for reveal?"

"Vetral."

Jeinan shouted it out loudly and then stepped back. A small box appeared beneath the statue. Inside, she removed a key and handed it to Da'ad. "There is a second gate just inside. Use this key to unlock it, and then give it to Leatis and let him do the same for the other vault. The vaults should light up automatically when they are unlocked."

As Da'ad entered the first chamber, he marveled at the wealth inside.

Phineus followed a few steps behind. "The wealth of the centaurs. No wonder Lothar wanted it so badly."

Jeinan stepped forward. "No wonder Reglis went to such lengths to keep it from him. Imagine what wealth like this could do in the hands of a tyrant."

"Wealth like this tends to create tyranny in any heart. The centaurs paid dearly for their prosperity even before Lothar destroyed them," Da'ad cautioned.

One of the elves stepped forward. "It is true the centaurs weakened themselves in civil war during the centuries before Lothar, which was undoubtedly a major reason for their quick demise."

Conversation soon gave way to the overwhelming awe of the treasure. No one said much for several minutes. No one in the group had ever seen so much wealth in a single place. It was difficult to fully comprehend what they were seeing. The vastness of the vault and its treasure was staggering.

"Could it have been best to have left this place undisturbed?"

"Don't fear success, Thoren."

"Success I can handle. It is temptation I fear."

"Why is that? Do you think you will conquer the world with this?"

"It isn't the world I want. Men have murdered one another for a mere fraction of what we are seeing, and yet all the wealth of this world could never provide me with what I desire."

"What do you desire, Thoren?"

"Peace of mind."

Jeinan smiled. "Peace? Here you are with the world at your fingertips, and all you wish for is peace of mind. I think Reglis meant for you to find this place. Any lesser man could never be trusted with it."

Moments later, Leatis approached. "The other vault is filled with much the same. It has a large collection of books inside from what I imagine was once Reglis's personal library." Mention of the library caught the attention of both Phineus and Jeinan, who simultaneously excused themselves to make an inspection.

The vaults included numerous magical objects ranging from weapons and armor to the simplest-looking household items. Jeinan instantly recognized many of the pieces from her studies of Lunorian history. After a brief excursion to look over the library, she began cataloging the collection.

The question now was how to safely remove the contents to Tabor. Da'ad ordered Leatis and the elvish scouts to remain with the treasure until he could think of a way of removing it undetected.

Satisfied that the treasure was secure, he returned upstairs to speak with Bek. "I want you to go downstairs and retrieve enough of the gold to buy this establishment, but only just enough for the purchase, no more. As soon as you have the deed, I want you to track down a barrel maker or brewer."

"What do I tell the barman if he asks me why I want this place?"

"Tell him you've decided to invest in ale and need a place to sell it. Our cover for getting the treasure out will be that we are shipping ale to the elves. We'll need to start emptying these kegs as soon as you get back."

"What is a place like this worth?"

"Just take what seems reasonable to you. If you have to, you can promise him more, but keep it sane. If you overpay, people may start asking questions."

Bek nodded and then left with two others.

Meanwhile, Da'ad approached Riada. "When Bek returns, I want you to set up the bar outside and offer discounted ale to the locals. See if you can't empty some of these kegs."

"I can start emptying them now if you like."

Da'ad shook his head. "No. I need you sober."

He walked to the corner table and waited nearly forty minutes for Bek to return. "I found the owner. He seems willing to sell but wants double what I offered. I told him that I would need to speak with you."

Da'ad was pleased.

"This may be fortunate. Take me to him. I think we can negotiate a price that will serve both our interests."

"If we can't?"

221

Da'ad paused. "We can't allow him to retake the premises. I will have to force him to sign over the deed. Let us hope it doesn't come to that."

"I hope not, though from my encounter with him, I think it an unlikely scenario. He is nearly as much a coward as he is a miser. It shouldn't be too difficult to twist his arm."

"Stop downstairs and retrieve another bag of gold, but keep it out of sight."

With the gold in hand, they left to meet with the pub owner. He was a portly man who seemed eager to do business. "Have you considered my terms?"

"We have, and I think we can negotiate a price."

The owner shook his head. "You have my price. If you want the building, then you will pay what I ask."

Da'ad disagreed. "The building isn't worth what you ask. I've already offered more than it's worth, and I'm willing to go higher, but not that high."

"Then go away. I'm not interested in selling for less than I've asked. When you're ready to do business, I'll be right here."

"I wonder why you ask so much."

"Because you came to me. I'm not eager to sell, nor am I desperate. You could have any building in town for what you offered, and yet you came to me? Why?"

"It was the first place we saw that seemed suitable. Perhaps you are right. Maybe another place would suit us better."

He turned to leave, reaching the door before the owner called out, "Wait!"

Da'ad turned around. After a brief silence, he asked, "Yes?"

"Perhaps I was a bit hasty. How much are you willing to pay?"

Da'ad set out his terms and explained, "I will require the name of a good brewer to supply me with ale. Is there one in town?"

"There is."

"My needs will be great. Do you think he can meet them?"

"Perhaps. I cannot speak for him, but if the price is right, I think he could supply you with as many as one hundred kegs a week. That's what they produce now."

"You mean to tell me that you went through one hundred kegs a week at that pub?"

"Not the pub alone. They produce for just about everyone in town."

"I don't think I can use that much in a week. I wouldn't want to upset the local establishments."

"Very wise. They do like to drink here, and the bureau chieftains own many of the bars. They don't like it when anyone cuts into their business."

"I might be able use three dozen kegs a week. How is the supply of hops in town?"

"We've more than we can use. Grow some ourselves and then usually get a few shipments in."

"Good. I think things are going to work out nicely. When can you introduce me to the brewer?"

"How's tomorrow morning? You can pay me the agreed price, and then I'll take you to him."

"I'll see you outside the pub in the morning."

The owner agreed and then walked the men to the door. "Three dozen kegs a week isn't going to clear that basement very quickly," Bek observed.

Da'ad agreed. "No, but if we request any more, we are begging for trouble. I think three dozen kegs a week will be just fine until we can get word to the elves to send more barrels. Once Archibald's ships arrive in port with a full complement of marines, I don't think we will have much to fear from the locals. We will, of course, need to build false bottoms into many of the barrels and hide the treasure within the ale, especially for our first shipment."

"You've really thought this through."

"Battles are often won or lost on the strength of one's strategy. I can't afford mistakes."

———— ∞ ————

They spent the night inside the pub. The pub's owner arrived midmorning. There was a small gathering outside of brigands and pirates curious to learn why the doors were closed.

Riada was nearly finished moving the bar outside, and many of the locals were already getting drunk on cheap liquor.

Da'ad proceeded into the basement where Jeinan joined him. "The wall is set to open any time you wish to enter. All you have to do is wait a few seconds."

"Will it open for anyone or just me?"

"Aside from yourself, it is set to open for Master Phineus, the elf scholars, and myself. I thought it best to limit access to this small group for the time being. The chances are that if any of the others need access, they will be able to find at least one of us."

"Good thinking." They walked to the vaults, where they continued their conversation. "We'll need to bribe the governor. No point having anyone snooping around. If the governor believes we are shipping ale to the elves at a profit, he will be more than happy to protect the shipments for a share of that profit," Da'ad explained.

"Lieutenant Bek mentioned that you planned to use the barrels as a cover, but we won't be able to ship things very quickly. We don't have nearly enough kegs for storage."

"I need to go upstairs and meet with the pub's owner. He's supposed to introduce me to the local brewer. We should be able to acquire at least three dozen barrels a week, possibly more. That will see us through our first shipment. I expect that the elves will be able to provide us with what we need after that. Once Archibald's marines are in town, the locals shouldn't be any trouble."

"You best be getting back. The pub's owner must be growing wary."

"You're probably right. We'll discuss the contents of these vaults in more detail later."

"Good. Perhaps by then I'll have something to report."

Da'ad hurried upstairs, where Bek greeted him with a mild shout. "He's outside!"

"Very well. Lead the way."

The pub owner was eager to get paid. He was pacing the ground in front of Riada when Da'ad exited. "You have the money?"

Da'ad turned to Bek. "Go ahead and get the purse."

Bek returned momentarily. Da'ad turned the purse over to the barman.

"And now, I imagine you'll be wanting to visit the brewery."

Da'ad nodded then followed barman for several blocks to a midsized warehouse. He thanked his escort then examined the building before entering.

"Where's the owner? I wish to speak with him."

The owner was a tall, muscular man who, in many ways, resembled a human brick. He smelled of ale. Da'ad at first thought him drunk but quickly realized otherwise. The smell was emanating from his clothing, which was soaked in the beverage.

"You're the owner?"

"Yeah. What's it to you?"

"I'm hoping to acquire several dozen kegs of ale a week for the next few months. I just purchased a pub in town and was told that you are the local supplier."

"We do supply most of the ale in town, but several dozen kegs a week is a hefty order. I'll have to look into it and see what we can do."

"We are rather eager to send a shipment south to Tabor, so anything you can do to expedite the matter will be appreciated." Da'ad tossed a small purse on the desk and said, "I'll be at the Sun Pub," then left.

When he returned to the pub, Bek was waiting for him. "When do you expect to make the arrangements for more ale?"

"I just left the brewer. He needs to look into our request. I'd like you to accompany me in the morning to look at ships."

"Ships?" Bek asked, somewhat puzzled.

"Yes. We'll need to contract with one of the local ship's captains to deliver the first load to Tabor."

"I suppose we will. Have you eaten?"

"Not yet, but I have other things to take care of first."

"Do you mind if I eat then?"

"Be my guest. I'll be in the basement."

Bek excused himself as Da'ad returned downstairs.

Jeinan was busily inventorying the second vault. Many of the items stored there had powerful magical properties, and she did her best to document them all.

"Any sign of Zarg's amulet yet?"

She shook her head. "Not yet, but I've only just begun. I still have thousands of items to sift through."

After his conversation with Jeinan, Da'ad returned upstairs for some needed rest. He slept on a mat near the far wall. The night was quiet except for a fight somewhere near the waterfront.

Riada and his relief continued selling liquor outside well into the evening. The empty kegs were quickly carried below and filled with items from the vaults and then stored in the basement.

The next morning Da'ad took Phineus and Bek with him to the docks. They conversed with several captains and their mates. All boasted of their boats, though Da'ad thought it unlikely any of the ships would perform as billed. He reexamined each ship meticulously, finding only three worthy of further inquiry. Most of the boats were captured merchant vessels converted for piracy. Their holds were plenty large enough to accommodate Da'ad's needs, but they were sorely wanting in other areas.

Some of the ships suffered from wood rot. Leaky hulls were not uncommon, though few leaked so badly as to be dangerous.

The ships varied considerably in their upkeep. The more experienced crews tended to take better care of their boats.

Da'ad did not make any final decisions, opting instead to return to the pub and think on the matter. Work at the pub was coming along nicely. Riada was making a small profit selling ale to the locals. The brewer left a message that he could meet most of their request, with the first shipment to arrive on the morrow. All and all, Da'ad was pleased with the progress.

Though business was good, his success was not well received everywhere. Many reacted with jealousy to the added competition. They filed numerous complaints with the local bureau chief, hoping to have the new venture shut down in its infancy.

The chief was aware of Da'ad's reputation with the sword and hoped to avoid a conflict. He visited in person with two large thugs. They hovered clumsily near the doorway. Neither impressed much intellectually. Da'ad almost laughed at the sight of them.

The bureau chief seemed nervous.

"May I help you?" Da'ad asked.

"Yes. I'm looking for the new owner of this establishment."

"I am he. What can I do for you?"

"I've received numerous complaints from other proprietors that your operations are undermining their business."

"Isn't that the nature of a successful enterprise?"

"Indeed, it is, but they pay me to look after their interests."

"I see. And you want me to pay too?"

"It would make matters easier."

Da'ad tossed him a sack of coins. "Don't let it be said that Thoren Da'ad doesn't pay his taxes. Now, unless you have other business, I'm a very busy man."

"No, I have no other business. Thank you, Mr. Da'ad, and good luck to you."

Da'ad watched as his visitors left. He then turned to Riada. "Keep your eyes and ears open. I smell trouble."

"Yes, sir."

Da'ad wandered downstairs, where he informed Jeinan of their visitor.

"You think he means trouble?"

Da'ad shook his head. "I doubt it. He seemed pleased to avoid a conflict, but the forces that sent him aren't likely to content themselves with his visit."

"What do you think they'll do?"

"I expect, if we're lucky, we'll hear from the governor soon."

"Do you think it will be a problem?"

"Not if we play our cards right. It may even turn into a bit of good fortune. Still, I don't want to take any unnecessary risks. We have to keep this operation looking like a legitimate business."

"We've kept everything downstairs. If you're worried, we can move it all back into the inner chamber."

"That would make me feel little better."

"Good. Then I'll speak with Leatis and have the elves begin moving everything immediately."

Da'ad returned upstairs where he secluded himself in the corner again. He remained there for some time before eating a small meal and retiring to bed.

───

It did not take the governor long to get involved. He sent one of his lieutenants following breakfast the next day. The man was tall and well dressed. He stood smartly in the doorway for several seconds. "Where is Thoren Da'ad?" Da'ad stood but took his time reaching to the door. The governor's representative offered a hand. "Mr. Da'ad, I presume?"

"I am. Who is asking?"

"I am Volke, the governor's personal envoy. The governor has heard that you are selling ale to the elves. Is this true?"

"It is."

"The governor would like to propose a partnership."

"And what does he bring to this partnership?"

"Much. He will ensure that shipping arrangements are made and that your cargo makes it safely to its destination. There will be no taxes to the dock captain, nor will there be any need for inspections or impoundment of your merchandise. You may come and go with it as you please. However, for his services, the governor requires half of the profits from this venture."

"One-third, and I don't pay until I receive payment from the client. The elves never pay in advance. If the shipments don't reach Tabor, neither of us will get paid."

"I believe we can do business. I shall take your proposal to the governor at once."

Da'ad watched with a look of satisfaction. The prospect of a partnership pleased him. He motioned toward Phineus and said, "I think we may have just caught a break."

"How so?"

"The governor wants to partner with us. This will make it much easier to get everything to Tabor."

"I hope you're right, though I must admit, I'm not certain I understand."

Da'ad left Phineus to think about matters and hurried downstairs to speak with Jeinan. "Making any progress?" he asked.

"It's slow but steady. I've heard of many of these items but never dreamed I would see them in person."

"Any sign of the amulet?"

"Not yet, but I'm barely a quarter of the way into the contents of this vault. When I'm finished here, there is still the other one."

"I thought the other vault contained only gold and jewels."

"It certainly appears that way, but then an amulet is jewelry. I've not seen anything to indicate that the other vault contains no items with magical properties. In fact, this vault is strangely missing many pieces of jewelry. It is known that Reglis possessed several such items, some having great power. Since they don't appear to be here, they very likely are there."

Da'ad looked down at the floor in thought. "I'd like you to have a look at that vault before deciding what items to place in the first shipment. I'll trust your discretion, but I want to be certain that it is an informed judgment."

"Of course. May I ask, when do you expect to send the first shipment?"

"I'm not certain, but I imagine you have several days at least to continue your work. The governor sent a representative today. I think he will want to see us soon. His representative proposed a partnership."

"A partnership will provide certain protections, unless you think it a trick."

"I don't. He has no reason to suspect our true business and would be a fool to turn on us before we ship the goods. He cannot be certain that Archibald would still honor the deal. The governor may not be the brightest individual, but nothing that I've seen indicates he is willing to assume that kind of a risk. I think this will work to our advantage so long as we provide him with rational payments, representing one-third of our fictional earnings from the sale of ale and have Archibald sign several false receipts for the shipment."

"I'm inclined to think the risks are greater if the partnership fails. As long as the governor believes that our business is legitimate, he will work hard to protect his investment. He might even provide us with a ship."

"That was part of his offer, I believe. I'll be upstairs for a while if you need me."

Da'ad remained there for the rest of the afternoon. He was engaged in a conversation with several of the soldiers when the pub door opened and the governor's advisor entered, followed by a rather large balding man. The man smiled quite insincerely as he entered the room.

A minute or two went by before Leatis approached. "Sir, you are wanted at the door."

"Who is it?"

"I don't know, but he looks important."

Da'ad noticed the rather large bald man still standing near the door when Volke was standing behind him and pointed as Da'ad entered.

The man laughed loudly and offered his hand. "I am the governor of Verne. I've come to meet my new partner now that I have a fifty-percent stake in your venture."

"One-third!" Da'ad corrected. "And you have to accept it first."

The governor laughed a bit less heartily than before. "Ah, yes, I forgot. My aide did tell me the amount was somewhat less than I requested. I'll tell you what. How much are you expecting in profits from this venture?"

"We make four tokens a keg."

The governor considered the matter. "And how many kegs are you going to send south?"

"As many as we can get our hands on. Right now, that's about three dozen a week. It should take us almost a month to fill a ship with that. Of course, if you're impatient, we can send several smaller shipments and subtract the added cost from your share."

The governor laughed. "That won't be necessary. I think I will accept your one-third offer, and then I'll speak with the brewer and see what we can do about speeding things up. Have you selected a ship?"

"No. I've narrowed it to three, but I haven't had time to make a final decision."

"Don't bother. I'll have my captain meet you near the docks tomorrow. Be there by ten."

"That's very kind of you, but how much extra is that going to cost me? This is a business, and when it ceases to be profitable, then there is no point in proceeding."

"You are too suspicious, Mr. Da'ad. The goods will ship for free. All I ask is that you fill the hull before you leave and pay my fee to the captain before the cargo is unloaded."

"Agreed, except that I will pay half at the dock before we unload and the rest when everything is accounted for on the pier."

"This building looks a bit worn. How long has it been since you've had a good, home-cooked meal?"

"I guess that depends on what you consider home-cooked to mean."

"I think I'm really going to enjoy our work together." The governor turned and exited, disappearing into the street.

Riada approached Da'ad. "So what do you make of that?"

"I don't know. He has the appearance of insincerity about him, is certainly arrogant, almost too friendly, and yet there is something likable there too." Several of the others laughed. "Do you trust him?" Phineus asked.

"Yes and no."

"What do you mean by that?"

"I trust him to be dishonest when dishonesty suits him. Right now, he has no incentive to betray us, and so he won't. Trust is not always an assessment of integrity. It can be a prediction of deception. If the deception and treachery are predictable, then we can trust in them the same as if an honest man had told us the truth."

"That's only true if you can get into the liar's head."

"I already have."

Besides, when all else fails, I still have this." Da'ad flashed his ring.

"You were taking quite a risk by refusing him the fifty percent."

Da'ad shook his head. "Not at all. In business, it is always best not to appear too willing. If I were quick to jump at his offer, then he might have sought an excuse to take sixty or more. We are not dealing with an honest man, and he has no interest in our financial survival except to the extent that it serves his own. If we seem too eager for his help, you can believe that he will charge us for it and then accuse us of hiding profits from him."

"You've seen what's downstairs. We can certainly afford to pay."

"To pay, perhaps, but not to raise suspicions. We don't need anyone snooping around here."

Da'ad apologized and then walked to his mat.

The next morning, he ate a light breakfast and hurried to the docks. He paced back and forth for nearly thirty minutes before a scrawny, old seadog caught his attention. The man was not much to look at. His beard was white and partly matted. He walked with an obvious limp. His voice was high and raspy, very painful to the ears.

"Aye, be ye Thoren Da'ad, mate?"

"I am."

The man laughed with a loud cackle that resonated of insanity. "Arrr, the governor sent me ta find ya."

"The governor sent you?"

"That he did. Come. I've sometin ta show ya." The pirate motioned for Da'ad to follow. As they walked, he asked, "Have ye heard of the famed boat Fanciful?"

"I can't say that I have."

"Then ye be missing much round here. The Fanciful only be the greatest ship in these ports. And I be her captain. Felk is the name." He extended his weathered hand and smiled.

Da'ad hesitated, mostly out of surprise, then took the hand cautiously. "Perhaps you should show me your boat."

"It be round the bend. There be plenty of time ta see her. A proper introduction were needed first. Now we be ready fer seein' the boat." He motioned to a large ship, still partially hidden behind two others. "There she be."

Da'ad walked past the other ships until the Fanciful was in full view. To his surprise, the boat seemed quite adequate.

"This is your boat?"

"That it be."

"Then how come I didn't see it here the other day?"

"We just put in to port last night. Care ta come aboard?"

"All right, show me your boat."

Da'ad examined the ship carefully. It was clearly the cleanest and fanciest in the harbor and one of the largest.

"The governor contracts with us to carry shipments fer 'im from time ta time. He met me last night ta see if we could help you git ta Tabor."

"Very well, but our cargo isn't ready yet."

"We be tied up here fer a few weeks. Have yer cargo ready by month's end."

"It depends on our supplier. If we can't get the supply of ale we need, we won't be ready to depart for Tabor."

"The governor assured me ye'd be ready on time."

"Under present contracts, we will only have half the barrels necessary to fill this ship's hold."

"That be the governor's concern. He be paying me to take yer shipments, and take them I will."

Da'ad continued to look over the ship. "She be a grand boat, aye?"

"She will be more than accommodating. We'll have what cargo we can ready in three weeks. My men and I will be traveling with you."

"Will ye be needin' a ride back then?"

"No. We'll make arrangements with the elves for our return."

As Da'ad prepared to leave, Felk stopped him. "Not so fast. The governor left ye a message." The old pirate handed him an envelope and wished him luck. Inside was a dinner invitation. The signature at the bottom was illegible, but it was clear he was to dine with the governor.

On his return, Da'ad immediately spoke with Riada. "I met our captain. Wait till you see him."

"How is the boat?"

"The boat will be just fine. In fact, I doubt we'll find anything better." Da'ad paused a moment. "I also recieved this." He handed Riada the dinner invitation.

"I want you to accompany me tonight."

"Me? May I ask why?"

"Because I trust you. Still, if you would rather not, I'll have a word with Bek."

"Heaven knows I can use a good meal right now."

"Good. Then meet me here an hour before supper."

It was near lunchtime, and most of the group was gathering around the bar.

Da'ad watched as Jeinan returned from the vaults and joined him at his table.

"Do you have plans for tonight?"

"Only to inventory the vaults. Why do you ask?"

"I've received an invitation to dine with the governor. He said I could bring two companions. You interested?"

"Of course."

"Good. Be certain you are ready an hour before supper."

Following lunch, Jeinan returned to the basement.

Da'ad was reading when a tall, slender woman entered wearing a uniform.

"May I help you?"

"The governor is ready for you. Follow me, please."

"You're early. I'll need to get my people."

"Then do so quickly. I will wait here."

Da'ad called for Riada. "Go fetch Jeinan. The governor is waiting for us."

"Already? It's more than two hours early."

"Go fetch her, please."

"Yes, sir."

Riada reemerged alone. "She is on her way."

"Good. As soon as she gets here, our escort is ready." Jeinan arrived a moment later.

She exited the pub next to Da'ad and listened as he spoke. "Is it just me, or is there something strange about that woman's face?"

"It isn't just you. She was probably purchased at the slave market. Who knows what corner of the land she once called home."

A short time later, they reached the gate to the governor's manor. The guards detained them briefly until the young woman announced herself.

"The governor is expecting these people. Let them pass." Both guards instantly stepped aside.

"Follow me, please."

Jeinan removed her cloak, attracting an unusual amount of attention.

The group was quickly led into a large waiting room.

"Please be seated. Someone will be with you soon." Da'ad watched as their escort disappeared out the door.

The waiting room was filled with fine art and decorative wooden furniture. The chairs were well cushioned and quite comfortable. A fancy crystal chandelier hung from the vaulted ceiling. The walls were lined with small oil lanterns. To the west was a life-sized portrait of the governor. A very large hanging mirror covered the east wall.

Riada and Jeinan quickly sat down. Da'ad preferred to stand and paced slowly for several minutes while Jeinan admired the room's decor. Following her remarks, Riada wondered aloud, "Makes one curious how such goods found their way into Verne."

"Probably taken from the many ships the pirates have attacked over the years," Da'ad speculated.

"Perhaps some, but most of this work was probably commissioned by the governor or his predecessors. The portrait, for example, could not have come from a ship, and these are not the kinds of pieces one would take on an extended voyage," Jeinan corrected.

Da'ad bowed his head. "Of course, you are correct. I wasn't thinking."

Moments later, their escort returned and motioned for them to follow. "This way please."

She led them into a fine dining room, one of several in the manor. The room was spacious and offered a nontraditional seating arrangement of pillows and soft mats. There was a raised stage along the north side containing a few small instruments. It was separated from the rest of the room by two large curtains tied in the open position. Two heavy suits of armor were positioned to either side of the entryway. They were primarily decorative and seemed ill suited for actual combat. A fire burned in a small fireplace along the west wall.

There was no one waiting for them in the room. The guide motioned to the floor. "Make yourselves comfortable. The governor will join you shortly."

Da'ad took a seat between Jeinan and Riada. They conversed for several minutes before the governor arrived, accompanied by two large guards and an attractive young woman. The woman was wearing a fancy black gown, perfectly accented by her long, dark hair and hazel eyes. Like Jeinan, she also seemed out of place in Verne. She took a seat to the right of the governor, who was very attentive to her needs.

As soon as she was seated, the governor turned his attention to Da'ad. "Welcome, my friends. Let us begin with a toast. To a profitable venture and a long partnership."

The governor was all smiles. Da'ad had suspected that his excess flattery was merely a bad acting job. After the toast, he wondered if his host might actually be as shallow as he appeared. He thought it odd that such a man could survive long in a city like Verne then quickly shrugged off the notion, believing the governor was merely keeping up appearances. The thought crossed his mind that underneath the façade was a shrewd, possibly ruthless, man, well prepared to defend his political position.

The group was privileged to sample several fine appetizers. Whatever else it was, the meal was certainly not rushed. In fact, the main dish did not arrive for more than an hour. Conversation was dominated early by the governor. He told of his excitement for the new partnership and inquired, "Have you met Felk yet?"

"Yes, I had that pleasure early this morning. In fact, he was the one who presented me with your invitation."

"Yes, so he did. He may not look like much, but he is a capable captain, I assure you. One of the best in the city."

"It doesn't hurt that he has the best ship in town."

The governor laughed. "No, it certainly does not. Felk captured that ship a few years back. He's a very cunning pirate."

Riada sat up a bit. "Don't you worry that he might be too cunning?"

The governor shook his head. "No. For all of Felk's faults, he has always been true and loyal. He'll fight like the devil, if provoked, but he has never gone back on his word. Felk swore to me that he would deliver you and your cargo safely, and so he will."

"That's comforting. Even so, I think you should know, my men and I are experienced fighters and very capable of sabotaging our cargo if we're betrayed."

The governor looked at Da'ad sternly. "There will be no betrayal. I want to be paid, just as you do. After all, what use are several hundred kegs of ale when I already have more than enough for my needs? By the way, I spoke with the brewer. He is going to double his production for the next few weeks. He assures me that you can have up to one hundred kegs a week. I trust that you can afford the increase?"

"We can, though it may make it difficult for us to afford much else for a time."

"Good, then I expect you'll be shipping out at the end of the month."

"I think, under the circumstances, that is likely."

The governor glanced at Jeinan and then back toward Da'ad. "My compliments on your choice of women." He turned back to Jeinan. "Pray tell, what is your name, dear?"

Jeinan did her best not to make eye contact as she reluctantly gave a false name. She was well aware of the governor's attention and did nothing to encourage it.

"She is a great beauty." He boastfully turned to the woman at his left. "Keirtra here is quite a catch as well. She has magical abilities, you know."

"Really?" Jeinan remarked halfheartedly.

"Yes, it is true. Would you care to see a demonstration?"

The woman seemed mildly embarrassed and attempted to play down the boast. "Kemrick is too kind. I am merely an amateur. My abilities are very limited."

"Nonsense, my dear. Let them see your talents and judge for themselves." He looked squarely at Da'ad. "Would you care to see?"

Da'ad was unsure how to respond. He took a sip of wine and then chanced a glance toward Jeinan, who seemed more than a little curious about the claim. She gave him a slight nod.

He chanced a second glance at the young woman. "I wouldn't want to impose."

"Nonsense. It's no imposition," the governor boasted.

"Very well. I suppose a short demonstration won't hurt."

The governor laughed. "A short demonstration? My friends, we've all the time in the world. Let us not be hasty." He nodded to the young woman. "Go ahead, my dear."

"Are you certain you want me to do this?"

"Yes, yes. Go ahead. You ought to enjoy this, Mr. Da'ad."

The young woman smiled, almost as though she found the situation amusing. She bowed to the governor and exited near the back of the stage.

Several musicians entered and picked up their instruments. They played a few warm-up notes and then sat silently for a time. The woman reappeared wearing a golden dancing costume. After a few seconds, the music began, and she started to dance.

Da'ad was about to politely compliment her skills when the governor proclaimed, "You haven't seen anything yet. Watch this."

As he nodded, the young woman uttered a strange phrase. Almost instantly, her legs began to change color. They grew scales and gradually fused together into the long tail of a serpent. The transformation did little to interrupt her dance.

Surprised by this, Da'ad turned toward Jeinan, who was now watching the woman's activities very intently. The dancer smiled seductively and shed the skirt from around her waist, exposing the full serpent's tail that used to be her legs.

The governor cheered as Da'ad squirmed within his seat, not sure how to interpret the situation. Just as he began to settle himself, the dancer uttered something else.

Within moments, two large lumps formed beneath her arms. They pulsated in and out several times until they took the shape of small hands protruding outward, gradually growing larger. They eventually formed a new pair of arms, virtually identical to the first.

The dance continued uninterrupted for several minutes until she moved from the stage to the floor and began stroking her four hands enticingly across the governor's face, wrapping him lightly in the coils of her serpentine body. After only a minute off stage, she returned to the platform and concluded the dance. As soon as the music stopped, she disappeared into the back, reemerging several minutes later once again in her black dress and completely restored to her usual form.

As the governor boasted of the woman's talents, Da'ad stared at Jeinan, attempting to gage her thoughts. The presence of magic in the city was something he clearly had not expected.

Riada obligingly complimented the dancer on her performance. This led to an extended conversation between the governor and himself. Da'ad was appreciative of the mild break and took a moment to whisper something to Jeinan, who smiled faintly but said nothing.

As his conversation with Riada concluded, the governor asked, "Now, wasn't that glorious?"

He looked toward Da'ad and waited for a response. Da'ad nodded quietly, unsure what else to do. Riada was quick with another compliment and soon rekindled his previous conversation.

The dancer was mildly embarrassed by all of the attention and yet seemed to be enjoying it. Jeinan offered a few brief compliments, which eventually spun off into a separate conversation regarding the woman's magical talents. Da'ad was pleased to be the odd man out and remained silent in the face of both conversations.

After a few minutes, the entrées arrived, which came as a welcome relief to Da'ad, who was exhausted at the prospect of discussing the strange dance any longer. As the food was slowly distributed by the governor's staff, Da'ad enjoyed another sip of wine.

Riada's conversation with the governor quickly shifted to the meal. The governor boasted of his chef for ten minutes. Da'ad had to admit the food was good. Still, it pained him to do so. Riada felt no such guilt, readily complimenting everything he sampled. The steady flow of compliments delighted the governor.

"Forgive me, but where did you say you studied magic?" Jeinan asked the dancer.

"I didn't. I learned most of it from my aunt."

"Was she from Lunora?"

"No, she never once mentioned Lunora, but she did tell me she grew up in the west on one of the Dragon Islands. She used to entertain dignitaries for a living. When I was old enough, she taught me a few small tricks. I inherited most of her books when she died."

"Would you mind much if I had a look at your books sometime?"

"I'm sorry, but the spells in those books are a closely guarded secret. My aunt left them to me with the strictest instructions not to share them with anyone outside of the family."

"I understand. I was just curious to learn of their origin, but as you say, that is part of your family secret, and I wouldn't wish to intrude."

"Do you practice magic? I might be able to show you the books for a moment if you would be willing to teach me a thing or two about your own magic."

Jeinan shook her head. "I'm afraid that I have very little to offer one with your talents. Still, it would be nice to know the origins of those books."

"You're a scholar then?" the governor asked.

"Somewhat, but mostly I'm just curious. The origins of myths, spells, and traditions have long fascinated me."

"Are you a wizard?" he inquired.

Jeinan shook her head. "My knowledge of magic is limited."

The governor laughed. "Don't feel too badly. We can't all have such marvelous talents."

Da'ad said relatively little for the remainder of the meal. Jeinan continued her conversation with the dancer, and Riada entertained the governor with a series of half-true tales, mostly aimed at averting suspicion.

At the conclusion of the meal, the governor stood and thanked his guests. "This has been most fascinating. You must come and visit more often. I'll inform the guards to admit you on the first and third of each week."

"You are most gracious."

The governor smiled. "I like to take care of my partners, though I must admit, I've enjoyed this evening more than most. I do expect that you will bring the lady again."

He turned to Jeinan with a bow and lightly kissed her on the hand. Satisfied that he made a good business decision, the governor walked them to the front door.

Little was said during the walk. When they reached pub, Riada moved to the bar. Jeinan requested that Da'ad accompany her to a secluded table near the far wall. There was an awkward silence as they both looked to say something but were at a loss where to begin.

Da'ad spoke first. "The dancer we met today. She claimed to be an amateur, though I was under the impression that type of magic was well beyond the level of an ordinary apprentice."

"It is. Still, she clearly thinks herself an amateur and in most respects is probably right. Her abilities appear to be heavily specialized for entertainment and little else. She is not a significant threat to us."

Da'ad took a deep breath and then exhaled slowly. "Are you certain?"

"There are only a handful of wizards outside of Lunora whose powers we need fear. I am confident she is not one of them."

"How do you know that?"

"She told me several things that clearly showed a lack of knowledge of basic magic. She has a rather limited understanding of magic as it applies off stage. If she was lying, then she was most convincing about it."

Da'ad shook his head. "No. She was not lying."

"Then she is no master wizard. Transfiguration is a difficult skill to master. Still, even though I'm not particularly fond of it, I think it is safe to say that my skills in that area are probably on a par with her own. I am a master wizard of Lunora and one of the best in that city. If it comes to a fight, she will not outduel me. Da'ad picked up a bottle and asked, "Care to share a drink?"

Jeinan agreed and moved her cup toward him.

He poured the wine, filling her cup first. "To success."

"To friends."

Da'ad smiled. "To friends then."

With a look of satisfaction, he touched the cup to his lips.

"What's next?"

Da'ad shrugged. "We found the vaults and the necromancers are gone."

"But you don't believe we're finished?"

"No. I don't."

"Why is that?"

"Someone hired the necromancers and sent that wraith after us. Until we learn who, I mean to keep up my guard."

Jeinan bowed her head. "A wise precaution. Any idea who might want to stop us?"

"I had thought it could be the dancer, but evidently not."

"I would sooner suspect the governor. The dancer is too obvious and not nearly skilled enough."

Da'ad stretched his shoulders a bit prompting Jeinan to lean forward.

"You seem tense."

"I ought to be. I'm in charge. If anything goes wrong—"

"I think we can afford a brief celebration, Thoren."

Da'ad raised his cup. "I suppose."

———

Elsewhere, a cloaked woman was leaning over her reflection dish.

"Thoren Da'ad lives. He was recently sighted in Verne. I fear he will be more difficult to kill than we expected. Perhaps we should consider a new course."

A deep voice resonated from the dish. "Yes. Tell your spies in Verne to keep their distance. We will go after his reputation. Are your agents in Thornguard prepared?"

"They await your orders, Great One. Da'ad will either die at the hands of his friends or be banished forever."